Indian Nation

Austin West

First Edition

Published by

Indian Nation

Austin West

© Austin West, 1999

All rights reserved. No part of this publication may be reproduced in any form or by any means without the written permission of the publisher. Published in the United States by Marketing Directions, Inc. All inquiries and suggestions for future editions of *Indian Nation* should be addressed to Marketing Directions, Inc, P. O. Box 715, Avon, CT, 06001-0715

ISBN 1-880218-36-4
Library of Congress Catalog Card Number: 99-70335

Chapter 1
INDIAN NATION

Hundreds of years ago, greed such as the white man had, was not known in Indian culture.

Condo Cherokee thought of this as he dealt out cards indifferently to gambling-addicted white men at the blackjack table. It was in the open plains that the Indians were masters of the earth. Indians would ride together with a common interest.

They hunted for a common purpose; so that they and their families could eat. The hunt was a simple enough ritual. The braves would surround the herd and kill one buffalo. This single animal would feed their families, clothe their bodies, and bring pride and courage to the tribe.

The white man came and the buffalo were now target practice for gun slingers. The Indian would go out to the plain to hunt, but would turn back because thousands of buffaloes were being butchered and left to rot. The tribe and its values were hunted closed to extinction.

* * * *

Civilization advanced in the form of white settlers putting down roots in state after state. Where once there lay the open plains stretching out as far as the eye could see, now there towns and settlements filled mostly with European immigrants.

And gradually, over the course of time the Indians were forced from their tribal lands and forced to live in squalor and filth and poverty.

Condo had read his Indian history, and knew of great chiefs like the Shawnee chief, Tecumseh who lived near the Ohio River. He knew that Tecumseh believed that all Indian land belonged to all Indian people, and that no one had a right to sell any of it.

Tecumseh also preached the philosophy that in order to protect their lands against white invaders, Indians would have to fight them as one nation instead of many. Tecumseh and his brother traveled the land all over Indian territory to spread this message of Indian pride and unity.

He also knew that when the Indians were promised safety if they moved elsewhere, as soon as they did they were forced to give up their lands.

2   Austin West

Condo felt that whatever side of politics you came down on, you couldn't help but be impressed by some of the tales of Indian struggles with whites, such as the tale of Wounded Knee. The attack on Wounded Knee drew the attention of the entire world. The Oglala Lakota had taken over the town where a group of Sioux had been massacred in 1890.

* * * * *

Basically, the Indians wanted the government to honor the Fort Laramie Treaty of 1868. Members of the American Indian Movement joined them. This did not escape the notice of federal marshals, the FBI and local police. A full-scale assault was launched on the people. Other Indians who tried to bring food were arrested.

After seventy-one days, the United States agreed to negotiate. 120 people in total were arrested. Charges against them were later dismissed because the government had lied under oath, tampered with evidence, used illegal wiretaps, and committed several other illegal acts. The government then decided that even though the treaty was valid, it could still take Indian land.

The issue of Indians and their land was always a contentious one. In 1988, the Senate Select Committee on Indian Affairs spent a year investigating abuses in federal Indian programs. The committee discovered corruption, fraud, and mismanagement in the Bureau of Indian Affairs, which oversees such programs. In fact, in 1989, several Indian leaders testified before Congress about these problems.

He had read where there was an audit conducted which showed that the government had mismanaged an Indian trust fund. The Bureau of Indian Affairs fund managed over $1.7 billion for 200 Indian nations and nearly one million individual people.

Some $17 million could not be accounted for because of sloppy bookkeeping. The audit report said that the money could have been stolen. And another $19 million was lost because of bad investments and poor management.

Condo felt after reading this, that it was just another example of the kind of negligence and exploitation of Indian people that the Senate was investigating.

Eventually, the Senate recommended that Indian nations should be given more control over their land and money. In the summer of 1990, the Department of the Interior started a project to try out this idea. Six nations were given more control over how to budget and spend their share of federal funds for Bureau of Indian Affairs programs.

Condo knew, for example, that the whole issue of treaty provisions was a double-edged sword. While there were tribes who genuinely had treaty rights to certain lands, there were other unscrupulous tribes who were claiming their rights where no treaties existed.

* * * * *

The Bureau of Indian Affairs was run by white men, primarily. And in many cases, they opposed some of the additional compensation the Indian tribes were looking for. There was one case where one tribe from North Dakota asked Congress for $178 million. They wanted to use the money for work projects, alcohol treatment, and other programs that Condo thought were good.

But the Bureau went against the extra compensation because they said the tribes had received enough compensation already.

Then were the acts of civil disobedience that Indians did to try and bring attention to them and their treaty problems. Condo read about a tribe in Vermont called the Abenaki, who deliberately tried to get arrested and prosecuted for fishing and hunting without licenses. They claimed that they were the original inhabitants of Vermont, but the federal government refused to recognize them as a tribe.

They wanted their cases to go to court so that they would have a legal ruling. Finally, the state agreed to prosecute. A year later, a state judge ruled that the Abenaki did not need licenses. He said that they were on land before Vermont ever became a state, and that they had never given up their rights.

Then there was the case of the Seneca Indians in Salamanca, NY. A few years ago, they began renegotiating the town's lease. Salamanca is the only town in the United States built on land leased from an Indian nation.

In the 1800s, it was illegally established on Seneca land. Eventually, the Senecas wound up asking for $800,000 a year, plus $60 million to make up for the low prices of the last century.

Condo could only shake his head at such things. The history of his people was filled with such bitterness and treachery from white men that it didn't matter what the compensation was. It was never enough.

It was always the same. The Indian was stereotyped as a savage, sub-human creature with absolutely no rights. As a result of this view, in 1871 the U.S. government made Indians wards of the state. That meant they were no longer able t make any decisions about themselves. The government would decide where they would live and what jobs they could do. Indians were stripped of all rights.

* * * * *

In the intervening years, unemployment, illiteracy and alcoholism plagued the tribes. Drug use was common and some tribes even raised marijuana plants which they sold. Some of the men managed to get low-level construction jobs, but for most, poverty and hunger were a way of life.

Where once, braves spread a blanket on the ground and gambled with crude symbols of the time that reflected the wilderness, now there were roulette wheels, black jack tables, slot machines - and money. More money than the Red Man ever dreamed about. More money than all their tribal ancestors would ever know.

In 1988, Congress passed the Indian Gaming Regulatory Act. It gave Indians a foothold where none existed before. The Act protected the sovereignty over gaming on Indian lands, tied into the first interactions with tribal entities.

All the proper, dignified Congressmen, men who spoke in measured tones and read through the thousands of documents on gambling prepared by competent assistants - these men were giving the Indian something better than trading moonshine and blankets:

Roulette wheels, baccarat tables and dice tables, that's what.

In addition to promoting "tribal economic development," the government was thoughtful enough to add a ruling that because the lands were sovereign, the federal government could never audit their books.

The tables had indeed been turned. The hunted Indian was now the hunter and their prey came in the form of men addicted to gambling. To the scent and thrill of the casino where small fortunes were made and lost in the course of hours. White men, black men, it didn't matter. They sat sweating through their clothes, patiently waiting for the day that they would beat the house. More often than not - that day never came.

Condo Cherokee thought about this as he dealt the cards; eyes alert to all the whirrings of machines and voice levels throughout the casino. Condo had often been able to head off trouble before it started by having the uncanny ability to focus his hearing.

He would cock his head to one side and listen... listen. There it was: Table 14. It was then a matter of sauntering casually over and placing his hand on the troublemaker's shoulder. A look into Condo's eyes usually took the steam out of the most determined person.

His imposing physique didn't hurt, either. Condo was a chiseled six foot two. Had the culture been different, he could easily have been a star football player, for he had the quickness, strength and agility demanded.

He had been raised by strict Indian parents that believed in all the old Indian ethics. Condo prided himself on his heritage. Whenever he could get his hands on educational books, he read about his history.

And so he knew what being an Indian really stood for, namely, ethics, wisdom and pride. When Condo thought of pride, he thought of work. The two were intertwined; you did not separate them. In his mind, he would picture the whole tribe watching him. This comforted Condo for he knew that he was a hard worker and he would never let his tribe down.

As Condo stood at the table, his hands moved rhythmically and fluidly with a steadied practice. His thoughts, though, continued to drift off into his past.

* * * * *

He is thinking of the time when his ancestors roamed this country. When all Indians had pride, not because they were wealthy but because they lived their lives to be proud. The Indians lived by a strict code that punished, among other things unfaithfulness in marriage severely. This was looked upon among the Indians as a great crime.

By tribal law, a husband could punish a wife who had been unfaithful, even to the point of death. There would be no sanctions against the husband. Conversely, if the husband was unfaithful to his wife, he would find himself outside the tribe.

The code was strict, and everyone knew the rules. Indeed, Condo could count on one hand the number of husbands that had been unfaithful to their wives. It was as if there was an invisible boundary which all knew about - yet no one crossed.

It was a tight-knit community and crime was virtually non-existent. If anything, crime was something that plagued the white man's community. Relationships with neighbors and friends were valued, with people always willing to lend a hand.

Condo felt very strongly about his people losing money, particularly their hard-earned life savings. He knew all too well that when a person loses their life savings, the temptation was to turn to crime, robbery, drugs or other illicit activities. Condo considered himself to be a man of ethics and would not tolerate something like this happening.

Condo was a blackjack dealer. On a typical afternoon, you had a bunch of stragglers that just floated over to the tables. Some very odd combinations happened when people started to play cards.

Now the basic premise of the game was that everybody plays against the dealer. All the players simply put their bets on the table. Chips were used for money. Then the players receive two cards dealt face up. The rule of the house was that they were not supposed to touch the cards.

Now the dealer (in this case, Condo) would get two cards, however only one is showing. The other card is called the "hole" card and that was dealt face down.

The regular cards counted for their number but the Jacks, Queens and Kings counted for 10. An ace could either be a 1 or an 11.

The object of blackjack was to beat the dealer without going over 21. Positioning was very important in the game as well. It usually went like this:

The player who sat to the dealer's left was in the "first base" position.

The player who sat to the dealer's right was in the "third base" position.

The dealer deals from the left and the deal goes around the table with all the players being offered extra cards. Now if any player's hand goes over 21, he basically "craps out", that is his hand is worthless and he loses his bet. The dealer then collects the chips.

Now after this happens, the dealer shows everyone what the hole card is. One of the advantages of being the dealer (indeed there are many) is that he or she has the advantage of going last. However that is pretty much it as far as that goes. The dealer has no discretion, say, in taking cards.

Now, in certain casinos, the rules say that a dealer must draw a card if he has total of 16 or less and they must stand on 17 or more if they have that.

The way a player wins is if the dealer goes over 21 and a player still has a bet on the table. In that case—he wins.

Some dealers, like Condo, tend to be sympathetic to beginning players who come in, sit down, and basically have no idea what they are doing.

For example some will use basic types of strategies that they feel work for them well. They will watch and observe the movements of the game very closely and win in that manner.

While he was ruminating about all of this, one of the players at his table, a young, muscular guy, impatiently started tapping his feet. He angrily scowled at this Indian dealer who wasn't keeping his mind on the blackjack game, especially since he had a king and ten showing.

As he impatiently waited for Condo's attention to shift back to the game, the young guy felt confident because he knew that the goddamned redskin would have to take a hit because he has a ten and a four showing.

Condo turned over his cards.

A smile curled around the corner of his mouth as he saw the 7. Condo reached out to collect the money the player had lost. 10 $100 chips were scooped up - a bad turn of luck.

The young guy stood up so suddenly that his body shook the table. The veins in his arms stood out like ropes as he angrily hissed through clenched teeth: "You really scalped me you fucking redskin."

All eyes at the table turned from the young guy towards Condo, as they waited for his reaction to this slur at him.

Condo stood across from the guy and felt a moment of blind, hot rage sweep across his body. Rage at the hundreds of years of ignorance that produced assholes like this standing before him, rage at all the injustice that the Indian had to endure on a day to day basis.

And just as quickly as this feeling swept across him - it passed, and Condo felt in control again.

He lowered his eyes, shuffled the cards again crisply - then looked up expectantly at the guy, ready to resume play.

The guy stormed across the floor of the casino, cursing and mumbling to himself all the way.

Condo could only wonder at what the Indian pride had sunk to, taking money from poor bastards that had a gambling problem and could not afford to lose the money. He sighed to himself and wished once again that the day would come when Indians had pride.

"Hey, dealer." A short, compact fire hydrant of a man was leaning over the table gesturing to him. "Stop dreaming about your squaw. You owe me fifty bucks."

This time, Condo was not so cool. "Deal your own damn cards," Condo threw the remaining cards at the annoying player and took off.

* * * *

Chapter 2
THE PRIDE OF CONDO

Condo stepped outside and walked over to his truck. It was almost time for the start of the tribunal council meeting. He wouldn't have to contemplate what the topic for discussion would be: The deal that Vito Leone had forced on him and his tribe: A 70-30 split, with the bulk of the money going straight back to the mob.

Yes, he knew that some of his people were prospering from all the money from the casinos. Living conditions were better, and there was a sense of community now that had been lacking.

But Condo knew that the inequity of the split was like a noose around the neck of the tribe. Vito could force huge concessions from him freely and at will. Condo had to laugh when he read all these news stories from reporters who were eager to get the real story on Indian gambling.

The reporters, like everyone else in the country were convinced that the Indian Gaming Act had cleared the way for Native Americans to finally prosper. Condo had a little story he could tell them:

Years ago, when the Indian fair trade act was being voted on, a short, compact man resplendent in a dark pin-striped suit sat there every day. Same seat, every day. Looking at him, you might mistake him for a local businessman who had wandered in, intrigued by the goings-on. And then there was that red silk handkerchief.

But his eyes warned you away. They were the serpent eyes of a killer. The man's name was Brasti, and he was a head assassin to one of the chief Mafiosi, Vito Leone.

If the assembled congressmen voting on the most important piece of Indian legislation to come down the pike in decades knew who he was - they were keeping up a good front.

All the congressman knew why Brasti was present and to a man they were frightened about what would happen to them and their families if this legislation was voted down. If it was, Brasti had his ways of finding out who voted against it; that much they knew for sure.

They also knew that one by one terrible accidents would happen in their families, maybe not this year, but Brasti would never forget. There were many ways: A letter bomb. Or an explosive timed to go off on a simple drive to the grocery store. Or a child that never made it home from school.... Yes, Brasti's presence assured the mob of victory.

Condo, of course, had no way of knowing that the man he had thrown the cards at earlier was none other than Gino Gambino... Leone's hit man. Hit man #2 might have been a better reference; Condo was aware of the intense rivalry between Brasti and Gino Gambino.

After Condo stormed away from the table, Gino sat there, furious. How dare anyone storm away on him? Didn't they know who he was? Gino decided to run upstairs to see his boss, Vito.

* * * * *

Vito Leone is a silent, handsome man in his forties. In an earlier era, he would have resembled the movie actor, George Raft. Vito was partial to double-breasted Armani suits that gave his lean figure an imposing air. He prided himself on being able to say something only once and that was enough; his orders were carried out. Either that - or someone was carried out.

Vito looked upon the people that worked for him as his family. They were like kids that you had to straighten out sometimes. That's just the way things were.

He put his feet up on the desk and shook his head. It was at this time of day that he liked to stretch out and catch 40 winks. He could do that because he was the boss. If there was any crap going on outside, his secretary Ginger would take care of it. (He would have liked Ginger to take care of him—but that could wait.) Just a little cat nap, that was all he needed. . .

"Jackomo, FERMARE GIOCARE DIRETTAMENTE!!"

Jackomo froze in mid-toss just as he was about to hurl the rubber ball against the side of the building. His mother, Giancarla, was craning her neck out the window looking for her boy. She didn't have far to look.

The town of Carneseca was a sleepy little village. For centuries, fishing had kept it alive, but even that was being threatened now that the new order was in power. "Il Duce" had marched through Italy and now controlled the country with his iron will and military reign of terror.

The war had imposed much hardship on the little villages that made up Italy. Rationing had been strictly enforced, and villagers were constantly instructed that they must sacrifice for the war effort. Certain types of food and clothes were scarce and there were weeks when families could never really count on much of either, so everyone learned to hoard supplies.

A curfew had been in effect for some time now and the soldiers policed the streets enforcing it. There were whispers about the Italian jails and what went on there. No one really wanted to find out if the rumors were true, that much was certain.

Giancarla Massi didn't know much about politics, in fact couldn't tell you very much about Benito Mussolini. At this moment the only thing she knew was that a scruffy 12-yr. old boy was loose somewhere in the streets of Carneseca and if he didn't get his skinny little behind in here quick, she'd warm it for him good. Even though times were hard in the country, children were still permitted to play in the afternoon—but never past dark.

Jackomo turned to his playmates, Antonio and Marco, and shrugged that primordial roll of the shoulders that all little boys learn when their mother is hollering for them. It meant the fun was over—but only for now.

He took the ball and caromed it off the stoop and sent it flying high in the air. As the ball sailed down and Marco reached over to catch it, Jackomo flung up his arm and ran off down the cobblestone streets, his cheap canvas sneakers scuffling the stones.

All the old Italian women hanging out of the windows looked on approvingly as young Jackomo ran home to his mother. Such a good boy he was. Now if only their boys were h-a-l-f as good. And so the chorus started up: "Santino!" "Marco!" "Tommasino!"

Jackomo ran up the rickety stairs out of breath and sat down at the kitchen table. A steaming pot of cavatelli awaited him on the stove. Giancarla said, without even lifting her head from the pot, "Jackomo, wash your hands!" "Yes, mama," the boy said, dashing away to use the tiny sink next to her.

Giancarla always made it a habit to speak English around the house with Jackomo. Not that she knew it that well herself. Indeed her command of the language was somewhat stilted. She had picked up bits and pieces over the years mainly from libraries she had visited. She had in turn passed it on to Jackomo as best she could.

* * * * *

He was a quick learner, particularly when he would point with his little finger at a word from one of the books she brought home. He struggled over some of the words, true, but eventually he learned some basic sentence structure.

The way Giancarla looked at it was that this war was not going to last forever. Sooner or later, it would end and then Giancarla's dream of sending Jackomo to America could be realized! America, the land of the free and the home of the brave! Home to Yankee Doodle Dandy and ice cream and fireworks and big houses and, well, much more than Giancarla could even dream. But dreams were all she had right now until the day when she planted her son on the ship for Ellis Island.

Giancarla brought her head out of the clouds and gazed affectionately at her boy. He sat back down attentively at the table with his plate, waiting for his mother to serve him up dinner.

Giancarla had a dilemma. She wanted to wait for her husband Gino a little while longer so that the family could all eat together, but she knew her little boy was starving. Maybe just a little bit for now, she thought. To hold him over until his father gets home.

Gino worked as a cobbler, not far from their home. His days were spent repairing the shoes of common working people. It was his experience that most people in the village had only two pairs of shoes, one they wore to work and one they wore to church on Sundays. Gino spent a lot of time waiting for those shoes to wear out, that was for sure! But he supplemented his income with expert belt craftsmanship.

His belts were something to see. Intricately carved and handsomely decorated, they were worn by their patrons with pride. Gino knew that most people could never afford these belts if he priced them too high. So he set his prices at what he thought were a very reasonable level. He found that he got more business this way.

Giancarla had often wondered if Jackomo would follow his father into the business. Gino had never pressed it and neither had she. Probably because both of them harbored other dreams for Jackomo. What good did it do if the next generation simply followed what their father did? Nothing.

She had often tried to figure out what Jackomo was gifted at. She thought she caught glimpses of it here and there, from little telltale signs she saw in his schooling. But it was very difficult.

Suddenly she heard movement outside in the hallway. Gino had indeed come home early. He walked in the door and hung the small striped hat he always wore on the hook behind it. He held out his arms to Jackomo but the child just sat there and said, "Hi, Pop." Then lowered his head again and resumed eating.

Gino sighed. Ah, his boy was growing so big, it wasn't like the old days when Jackomo would come running to him and he would hoist him into the air. Nowadays, the child probably figured he was too old for that. So he tended to shy away from open displays of affection toward his parents.

Giancarla noticed it too. Jackomo wasn't her sweet little angel anymore, now he was just another brooding 12-year old who wanted to be with his friends all the time. It's a stage, she thought to herself.

Gino sat down and motioned to Jackomo to lay his spoon down. The child obeyed, and Gino said grace. Giancarla went back to the stove and ladled out a huge dish of cavatelli for Gino, because she knew he was starved. She was relieved that Gino was not one of those husbands who stopped off at the local bar after work to unwind. He came directly home to his family.

She was still an attractive woman, with dark hair and a figure that although coarsened through the years by hard labor was still pleasing to Gino. She loved it when he came up behind her at night as she stroked her hair and put his arms around her and caressed her tightly. They made love with regularity when she was in her "cycle." Still good after all these years.

Gino sat down with a worried look on his face. "What is it, Gino?" asked Giancarla.

"Some soldiers come around today," Gino said as he ran a hand through his hair. His English was not as good as his wife's. He had never had time to learn it like she had. "They ask questions. No good neither."

Giancarla felt her throat constrict. Oh, God, if this was about what I think it is...

"Is it about... Jackomo?" she asked with hesitation in her voice.

"Yes," he said simply. And sighed a long sigh.

"What do they want?" she asked.

Gino pushed back from the table. He hesitated as his eyes swept back and forth between his wife and his son. "The soldiers want to know how old he is. They ... they need help carryin' guns."

"Well, tell them he's too young, Gino!" Giancarla wailed. She rushed over to protect her son with her arms. Jackomo felt himself being squeezed.

"Si, I try, Giancarla, but the soldiers, they say come back with birth ..." He struggled to complete his sentence.

"Certificate, Gino?" said Giancarla.

"Si," said Gino.

"But he is our only child, Gino," Giancarla pleaded with her husband. "My little fanciullo."

"Yes," Gino said as he hung his head in his hands. "Maybe tomorrow, soldiers, uh, not take."

Giancarla was pacing now. She had heard on the radio that only boys 15 and older were being drafted for military duty. When she said this to Gino, he merely shook his head.

"But Mussolini, he... he lose war, so he take everybody," Gino said, practically pleading with his wife to stay calm. "Come, sit, eat," he said to her as he guided her to her chair. "We see tomorrow."

Jackomo sat there not saying a word, an apprehensive look on his young face.

* * * * *

The next day, the soldiers came knocking on Gino's shop door in the afternoon. They got right to business. One of them simply walked in, set his gun down by the front door and reached over the counter for the birth certificate.

Gino sighed inwardly for he knew that he was handing over his son's fate. But there was nothing he could do. If he did not cooperate, they could very easily come to the house and take Jackomo by force.

The soldier looked at the birth certificate, grunted affirmatively to himself and nudged his partner, who did the same. He handed it back, reached into his pocket for a pad with a long list of names on it, and his pencil. He licked the pencil, and wrote down Jackomo's name, then put a big checkmark next to the name.

He snapped the pad closed and put it back in his uniform. He motioned to the other private and without a word they both shouldered their guns and left the shop.

Gino stood there and felt the need to weep.

* * * * *

In the next few weeks, Jackomo's life changed radically. Although he was deemed to be too young to be a soldier, he was thought to be old enough to haul arms to the front line. Although Giancarla thought seriously of spiriting him out in the middle of the night, Gino talked her out of it. "He not shoot gun," he said to her in his halting English. "Safer what he doing."

That was small consolation to a mother who was about to lose her 12-year old son to the army.

Three weeks to the day after Gino gave the soldiers Jackomo's birth certificate in his shop, Jackomo found himself sitting in an army barracks with a number of young boys his age. Soldiers passed by them and looked at them curiously. They were there for one purpose and one purpose only: to haul arms to the front where desperate soldiers were trying to hold off onslaughts from enemy forces.

At this time, Italy was in the last stages of the war. They had lost the battle on all fronts and now were in the process of defending their homeland. They had used all their modern weaponry and were now reduced to using primitive techniques that had not changed much since World War I.

It was explained to Jackomo and the other boys that they would ride along in the horse-drawn wagons that carried shells and extra guns to the soldiers who were on the front lines. The reason the boys were needed is that some of the terrain was so treacherous that the horses would go no further, and would stop in their tracks.

At night, Jackomo and the other boys stayed in the army barracks alongside soldiers who had seen all the horrors of war. They didn't dare speak to them for fear that the guards would beat them. But from what little they did hear, it scared the hell out of them.

Jackomo cried and cried the first few nights he was away from his family. He was given no clue as to how long they would be needed. They were given drab olive green clothes to wear, with heavy boots and work gloves that swallowed up their hands.

It usually took four boys to man the wagon full of arms as they guided it to the soldiers who were encamped. The old trailers that they carried the arms in were wooden and creaky. Jackomo was a strong boy for his age, which is one of the reasons he was selected. But even he was not strong enough to guide the trailer if it veered off course.

Which is exactly what happened two months after he was there and caused the death of one boy.

Jackomo and the boys were guiding the trailer down a steep hill one day when it started to rain. The wetness of the slope caused them to slip and slide and they hung on for dear life so that the munitions would not go spilling over the sides. Between the guards yelling at them and their terror of being crushed to death, the boys were having a miserable time of it.

Just as they were almost at the bottom of the hill, one of the boys lost his footing and in the process, lost his grip on the arm of the trailer. This in turn caused a chain reaction and the other boys lost their grip as the trailer sagged. It went cascading down the hill, hit a deep boulder imbedded in the side of the hill - and split wide open.

The impact from this caused all the mortar shells and guns to spill out like crazy in all directions. And one of the boys had the bad luck to be in the path of a 100-lb. mortar shell as it came bouncing down the hill and pinned the boy down, the impact of the blow snuffing the life out of him.

Jackomo had been lucky enough to be at the back of the trailer when the accident happened. He was shaken up slightly but mostly stood and watched in horror as the guards and soldiers and other boys streamed down the hill to help the fatally wounded boy. But even in his dazed state, Jackmomo noticed something else:

No one was watching him.

In that split second, Jackomo knew that he could make a break for it. Which is precisely what he did.

He slopped his way back up the hill in the rain to the road and looked around wildly. He had no idea where he was, the only thing he knew was that this was the chance to gain his freedom.

He started walking quickly at first so as not to draw any attention to himself, and once he was at a fork in the road, he looked around, saw no one observing his movements, and took off running down the road. He didn't know where Palermo was exactly-but he'd find it somehow.

* * * * *

Jackmomo walked for three days and three nights. Once he got his bearings, he found that he remembered the roads that they travelled from the barracks and thus was able to re-trace his steps. He didn't dare stop and ask anyone for directions for fear they would turn him in.

He was tired and hungry but he managed to get lucky one day and spot a baker who was out in the back of his store dumping some stale bread into the garbage. Jackomo waited till he was gone and leaped on the can like a wild dog, tearing into the bread and ripping it off in hunks and stuffing it down his throat.

He found that if he kept his head down and scuffed along the street, hunched down, no one paid any attention to a scruffy little kid.

Finally, he reached the outskirts of Palermo and felt so glad to be back in his home village that he knelt down right beside the road and started to cry.

He got up and resisted the urge to break into a run, for he was near his mama and papa now. So close. Nothing could hurt him anymore!

He came to his street and was about to mount the stairs, when a thought occurred to him: What if the soldiers had reported him missing and they were looking for him? The thought unsettled Jackomo and he crept around to the back of the alley behind his mother's house. He huddled down behind some old pieces of lumber. Soon it would be dark and he would be able to call out to his mother.

When darkness fell, Jackomo took some gravel and threw it up at the window so that he could get his mother's attention. Once, twice, three times he threw. The gravel tinkled softly against the windowpane. Finally he saw his mother open the window and stick her head out.

"Who's there?" Giancarla called.

"Mama, pssttt, M-A-M-A, it's me, Jackomo, down here," Jackomo called out in a loud, urgent whisper.

"Oh, Jackomo, where are — "

"Sshhh, mama," Jackomo whispered. "Just open the door around the front."

She slammed the window and raced around to the front of the apartment. As she did this, Jackomo walked quickly away from the alley and toward the street. He came around to the front door and his mother let him in.

Once upstairs, she fell on her knees weeping and thanking God that he was alive and safe. She couldn't stop hugging him and saying his name. She got him out of his dirty clothes, filled the bathtub with warm water and left to him to scrub the dirt off himself while she ran to the kitchen to warm up some soup and bread that she had.

An hour later, he was fast asleep in his mother's arms after eating a huge bowl of soup. Jackomo had survived his terrible ordeal.

* * * * *

Both parents paced around the room like two nervous cats.

Gino and Giancarla now knew the grave consequences that Jackomo was facing. If it was found out that the boy had run home and in effect deserted his post, they might throw him in jail, they might throw the parents in jail - anything could happen. It didn't matter that Jackomo was just a young boy and not a soldier. The army would not tolerate this kind of behavior even from a civilian.

"Giancarla, we put Jackomo on boat, si?" said Gino in his halting English. He was clearly quite frantic and almost beside himself at the thought of his son's safety.

"Si, Gino, we will send him to America," said Giancarla, although her heart was breaking at the thought of it.

"But... but with who?" asked Gino, spreading his hands.

"I... I don't know, Gino," said Giancarla throwing her hands up helplessly. The truth was they only had very few distant relatives in the new country. Worse, Giancarla was not at all sure that they could take care of Jackomo.

For the next two days, Gino was a bundle of nerves as he waited to see if any soldiers would visit his little shop, asking questions. At night, he and Giancarla packed as many belongings for Jackomo as he could carry in anticipation of his departure on the ship.

Finally, the morning came when they would smuggle Jackomo on board the boat bound for America. They had taken the precaution of dressing up Jackomo in old rags so he would not arouse suspicion. The weather was cloudy and foggy in the morning; an advantage since they had to walk down to the docks.

They had secured passage for Jackomo on board one of the ships. It was all the savings they had. Gino had bribed one of the deckhands he knew to stow Jackomo safely away.

Finally, the moment came for Jackomo to leave. Giancarla clasped her son to her breast.

"Jackomo, oh my son, I love you so much," whispered Giancarla. Get to America safely. And when you get there at Ellis Island, take this letter to your Aunt Rose. The address is on there. She will help you."

Jackomo nodded and held on to his mother for as long as he could. Gino reached over and added a hug, his eyes misting over with tears for his son and the journey he had ahead of him.

Suddenly the crew member poked his head out the door of the cabin. He motioned to Gino, "Gino, now, now."

He looked right then left and hustled Jackomo inside the cabin.

* * * *

The next few days at sea were calm. Until the day before they were scheduled to land at Ellis Island. That day a terrible storm rose up out of the sea, grasping the boat in its huge grasp like an angry fist. Most of the passengers on board the ship got seasick.

Jackomo was no exception. The breakfast he had eaten came right back up as he lurched around from side to side in his tiny bunk bed, feeling miserable and longing for his home. Eventually the storm subsided and the sun came out over the ocean again.

As the boat steamed toward Ellis Island and the Statue of Liberty in the harbor, all the passengers ran to the side of the boat, shouting excitedly. Jackomo found himself waving at the statue like crazy and then caught himself—there was no one to wave to. Oh, well, he thought. He would soon see his Aunt Rose.

* * * * *

A few hours later, Jackomo was walking around the strange streets of the biggest city he had ever seen. He just kind of stumbled along. The last food he had eaten was on the boat and he was hungry. He went in search of a bakery figuring that he would get lucky again and find a baker who was throwing out loaves of stale bread.

Sure enough, as soon as he started walking along Delancey Street, he could smell the aroma of fresh-baked bread. It made his mouth water. He found the bakery and walked around towards the alley.

He found he was'nt the only one hungry.

Scrounging through the garbage can was another young boy, around Jackomo's age. He looked up with a startled expression on his face and then put his finger to his mouth to motion for silence. His mouth was stuffed with bread. Looking around, he broke off a huge piece and quickly gave it to Jackomo.

When they got done chewing and swallowing, the young boy held out his hand.

"My name is Antonio. What's yours?"

"Jackomo. How... how long have you been here," he asked as he looked the boy over.

The boy shrugged. "Couple weeks. It's easy to get food if you know how. But don't let the police catch you. Little kid like you - they toss you in the slammer!"

Jackomo was confused. "What is slammer?" he asked.

"Jail, stupid!" Antonio said impatiently.

"Oh," Jackomo said quietly.

"So you looking for work, hey?" Antonio asked Jackomo.

"Yes, I... I need to eat, so I work for food," Jackomo said. "You know places to work?" he asked, his eyes pleading with Antonio.

Antonio thought briefly of running a con on this naive kid. Then looked at him and thought, hey, he's a paisan. I can't do this to this kid. 'Cause then I'd be doing what everybody else is doing to me.

So with a sigh, he said, "Jackomo, first thing you know is, it's tough for kids like us. Jobs, they don't hire kids like us."

He looked up and saw Jackomo's crestfallen face, and said, "Allright, look, I know a storefront we can sleep in tonight. Tomorrow I take you around with me while I look. And I'll say, look you take both of us or not at all!"

Jackomo felt better because he had made a friend already in this new land.

* * * * *

The next day, true to his word, Antonio and Jackomo hit the streets and walked from shop to shop. Antonio told him to remember not to loiter, lest they meet up with an overzealous police officer who might be tempted to ask them for their I.D.

They walked from shop to shop and talked nicely at first to the owners— then as the day wore on, a bit of desperation crept into their voices. Around midday, they did the bread trick again. Jackomo wondered how long they would have to eat bread, but Antonio pointed out that they could live on bread a lot longer than meat that was half-rotten.

Finally they knocked on their last door for the day. With a weariness so heavy they could hardly life their small arms, they knocked and stood back to receive yet another rejection from an owner.

"OK, what do you kids want?" came the weary reply behind a plume of cigar smoke as they looked up at a tall man who suddenly loomed in the doorway.

"Well, mister, we were wondering if you had any use for manual laborers," Antonio said bravely, sticking his chest out. "My name is Antonio, and —"

That was as far as he got. "Forget it, kid," said the man impatiently. He turned to go back inside. Antonio and Jackomo turned on their heels and started to walk away.

"Hey, wait a minute."

They both turned back around.

"You, you're a little taller, ain't you?" he said to Jackomo.

Both boys looked at each other.

"I could maybe use you," the man said, pointing to Jackomo.

Jackomo watched Antonio's face fall and his shoulders visibly start to droop. I can't do this, thought Jackomo.

"C'mon kid, follow me," said the man as he headed back in the door.

"No, we work together — or not at all!"

The man turned back to see Jackomo standing there with his thin chest poked out and his jaw thrust at the man "C'mon kid, follow me," said the man as he started to head back in the door.

"No, we work together — or not at all!"

The man turned back to see Jackomo standing there with his thin chest poked out and his jaw thrust at the man. He started to laugh.

"Well, you're quite the little hothead, hey punk?" said the man, although he was smiling as he said it.

Jackomo wavered a little bit, but held his ground. "Antonio is my friend. So he needs work, too, mister." he said in a voice a little more uncertain this time. It came out almost pleading.

The tall man shrugged. "What the hell, I can always use two little guineas. C'mon." He walked back inside.

When Jackomo followed him he and Antonio walked down a long hallway towards what was presumably the door to the basement at the end. It was. Although what Jackomo saw caused him to open his eyes wide.

Apparently the basement was a factory of some kind. There were men working beside what looked to be mini-blast furnaces. And also machines that shaped the hot liquid into what would eventually be machine parts. As they came down the conveyor belt, a worker sprayed cold air on the parts until they cooled sufficiently for them to be crated up.

But what amazed Jackomo was the water...

For the men were standing knee-deep in water. Cold water. Both Antonio and Jackomo reflexively took a step backward when they saw the water.

But the man pushed them forward. "Oh don't be scared. We, uh, have a little flood here every once in awhile. Nothing serious." he chuckled. He went to the wall and grabbed two pairs of men's waders and some heavy gloves. He came back and tossed them to the boys. "Here, you'll need these. After you get dressed, I'll have my foreman show you what you do."

He noticed the look of apprehension in their eyes. "OK, look, my name is Mr. Smith. We manufacture machine parts here. The army pays me a damn good price to keep this factory moving. You get me, kid?"

Four pairs of eyes nervously nodded.

"Your jobs are gonna be to move the machine parts over to the crates so that the men can lift them up and put them in the crates. I'm gonna pay each of you $5 a day. We start work at dawn and end when it gets dark."

Jackomo thought, wow, this is more money than I've ever seen in my life! Mama would be so proud!

The man looked at his watch. "OK, it's noon. I can still work you half a day. So get changed and get going."

A heavy ox of a man stepped over beside Mr. Smith. He looked at the boys with hooded eyes. Mr. Smith hooked a thumb at him. "This here is Mr. Malone. He's the foreman. This one's name is Jackomo and the other kid's name is whatchamacallit? Antonio, yeah, that's it. They'll be helping Sam down there lift the machinery up."

Mr. Malone shifted the toothpick from one side of his mouth to the other. "Allright, guys, let's go. See me when you're ready," he said in a bored, flat, disinterested voice.

Both Jackomo and Antonio dressed quickly and then went down to see Mr. Malone who was standing waiting impatiently already.

"OK, this is what you do," he said, demonstrating. "As the machine parts come down the line you grab 'em and hoist 'em on to the conveyor belt up there. See?" He pointed to a belt that ran slightly at an uphill angle. Perched beside it were men who were unloading the parts into huge wooden crates which would then be driven away by a forklift.

"You got any questions?" said Mr. Malone in a voice that didn't invite any questions.

Antonio piped up: "Um, doesn't the work stop when there's this much water?" He sloshed around in the water.

"Stop?" said Mr. Malone in an incredulous voice. "Whaddya kidding, sonny? No, it doesn't stop. You want to work, or don't you?"

"Yes, sir," both boys piped up in unison.

* * * *

A week later, Jackomo and Antonio were both exhausted. They worked like animals all day long, lugging machine parts. Mr. Malone only let them take a break to go to the bathroom and to eat.

Bathroom breaks meant pissing in some filthy hole in the back, and lunch consisted of a quick 10-minute break to shove a few pieces of sausage and bread (more bread!) into their mouths before hustling back to work.

One day, Antonio happened to slip and drop a piece of machinery into the wetness below him. Mr. Malone came over screaming at him. "You're fired!" he yelled at poor little Antonio. "Get out," he roared. Then he whirled around and pointed a finger at Jackomo. "And don't YOU get any ideas, kid. Back to work!" he ordered Jackomo.

Jackomo watched Antonio wearily begin to take off his wading boots and gloves. There were tears in the boy's eyes. Jackomo put his arm out and gripped Antonio's shoulder. "Don't worry," he whispered. "I'll get your pay for you!"

Antonio squeezed Jackomo's shoulder back. "I wait for you at the place, ok, Jackomo?" Jackomo nodded.

Antonio picked up his coat and climbed the long stairs as men gave him sympathetic looks. They had all liked the kid even though he had been there just a short time. Many times they came up and ruffled his hair when the boss wasn't looking. But they couldn't help him now. Antonio had to go.

Jackomo stood there in his wading boots and looked up at the ceiling filled with metal piping. The veins in his young arms swelled and he thought for a long moment.

Mr. Malone noticed him standing there. "Hey, you, get back to work."

But Jackomo didn't hear him. He was already on his way up the stairs toward Mr. Smith's office.

He paused outside of Mr. Smith's office. At that moment Mr. Smith was on the phone, grinning into the receiver. "Yeah, sure, baby, I'll be over later. OK, keep it warm—" When he saw Jackomo the grin went off his face as if slapped off. "I'll talk to you later," he said curtly and hung up.

"Yeah, what do you want?" he said to Jackomo. "And this had better be good, walking off the job like that. Does Mr. Malone know—"

"I'd like pay, please," Jackomo said, cutting him off.

"You would, huh, you little fucking guinea," Mr. Smith said as he got up from the chair and came around to the front.

He took out a $10 bill and waved it in front of Jackomo's face. "I'm not gonna pay a guinea like you, especially when you walk off the job like that. No, you little bastard, you forfeit your pay today to me. And that goes for your little guinea friend as well." Mr. Smith walked back behind the desk and sat down. "Now scram."

Jackomo felt a burst of energy come over him. He reached over and snatched the $10 bill from Mr. Smith's hand. He then hightailed it out the door as Mr. Smith started to say, "Hey, you litte bastard, come back here!"

Jackomo started running wildly down the hallway. He looked over his shoulder and sure enough the guards were after him. He looked right, then left, and finally spotted an open window.

Jackomo looked around frantically, measured his leap and jumped. He fell through the air and landed with a sharp grunt. He rose shakily from the ground and ran off.

* * * *

Vito woke with a start. Wow, he had really been dreaming of his grandfather.

At the moment that these thoughts are running through Vito's mind, Gino stopped at Vito's secretary's desk.

"Can I see him, Ginger?" said Gino, out of breath.

"All, right, Gino," sighed Ginger. With a swivel of her fine shapely body, she knocked on Vito's door lightly and gets the ok.

Normally, Gino's eyes would have followed those delicious curves from top to bottom. No time for that today, though. Today was about revenge, he thought as he narrowed his eyes and smoothed his lapels before marching into Vito's office.

"What can I help you with, my friend?" Vito asked cautiously, half-knowing what the answer was.

"An Indian dealer on table seven just insulted me," said Gino in an excited tone. "These Indians need to learn to give some respect to the family that is really running this joint," Gino said in an excited tone. "I want your permission to drop him. Un Morto..."

So, it was just as he had suspected, Vito thought. Gino is good, he reflected, but he has to be kept in line. Too much impulsive, rash behavior like this is bad for business. So, Vito did what he normally did in these situations and that was to explain the facts of life to Gino.

"Gino, we are making too much money to be upset with the Indians right now," Vito patiently explained. "When the American Government smartens up and starts to crack down on this money laundering, then we won't need these Indians." Gino looked at him expectantly. "You've got my permission to drop this savage - un morto."

"But," Vito cautioned sternly. "Until then the only thing I want to see you drop in this casino is the dirty money, so it can be cleaned."

This was not an idle concern to Vito. Indeed, he spent about half his waking hours thinking of how to keep himself and the family out of the casino spotlight. No, it would not do for the federal authorities to suddenly develop a keen interest in this casino.

The men who kept the books for Vito gave him weekly reports. Reports that were read and shredded after a xerox copy was stored in a safe that only Vito had the combination to. At least eight hundred million dollars a year.

His bookkeeper had devised an elaborate scheme designed to keep the money floating in bogus businesses and also being loaned out to scores of people at a very reasonable interest payback rate: 200%. Payable immediately. Either that, or risk a visit from Brasti...

Of course if Brasti was busy, Vito could always use Gino. Although after today's little episode he was beginning to wonder if Gino's noggin was on tight.

For that matter, Vito had questions about the sanity of several members of his crew. As un capo he had the responsibility of ultimately settling any petty grudges or beefs about territory or personalities. The world which he inhabited was a world with its own set of rules. There was no court to take grievances to, n no jury to mete out monetary settlements if you felt your "employee's" rights were being violated. He was judge, jury and executioner as far as that was concerned.

* * * * *

The men who worked for him were guys from neighborhoods very much like the one that Vito had grown up in. Blue-collar neighborhoods with a singular, rough code of ethics. Vito's own father had been a longshoreman, a man who lived by his physical strength and toughness. As well as a certain affinity for the bottle which kept his temper always at the ready.

But his father couldn't control his drinking or his temper and one day in a fit of rage over some petty overtime dispute, his old man took a swing at the dock foreman. Connected to, with a right hand that would have done Sugar Ray Robinson proud. Only thing was, it cost him his job. The foreman's jaw may have been sore, but Carmine Leone was out of work.

Vito swore that would never happen to him. He took off as soon as he got out of high school. (Mercifully, his mother had made sure he at least got that much out of the higher education system). He drifted into a series of odd jobs. He also made his presence known to local law enforcement, through a couple of stolen cars and petty thefts.

However, Vito was always smart to never settle anything with violence. Somehow he knew that once that cycle started, it followed you around. It was like a disease that got in you that you couldn't shake.

No, Vito was tough enough. He had one move which, when done right, took the fight out of any guy. Whenever someone started jawing at him, he would stare back silently at his tormentor, letting the guy get closer and closer into his face.

It was then that Vito would suddenly grab a meaty fistful of the guy's shirt or jacket, straighten his arm so that his elbow was jammed into the guy's stomach, and in one movement twist him down so that his face was an inch away from the ground, and whisper menacingly: "Allright, scumbag, what's it gonna be?"

There wasn't a lot of guys who pushed it any further.

Vito had seven daughters and one son. They were all his pride and joy. It had been hard during the early years for him and his wife. Of course, in many respects Vito was pretty old-fashioned when it came to raising kids. That is— his wife stayed home and did it.

As long as Vito put bread on the table, he didn't worry too much about the way his kids were turning out. Not that he didn't care, but he let his wife handle that department. If there was ever any disciplining to be done, believe me, she could take care of it. The only person his wife couldn't boss around was him. Vito had seen to that early on in their marriage.

He'd never forgotten the incident. It was when they were first married.

* * * * *

He and Sophia were riding in a car with her mother and her sister, Vito and Sophia in the back seat, the sister driving. Somehow they got lost, and Vito started to make a suggestion, when all of a sudden Sophia raised her voice: "SSHHUSSHH, Vito! Can't you see my sister's trying to concentrate? What are you trying to do. Be quiet!!"

Vito put one hand on his sister-in-law's shoulder, squeezed slightly and said, "Vickie, stop the car. Now."

Vickie stopped the car, and turned back to eye Vito warily. She had warned Sophia about this greaseball.

Vito looked straight at Sophia and said in a low voice filled with threat: "Sophia, don't you ever, EVER talk to me like that again in front of your family." He leaned forward until Sophia's eyes started to widen. "I'm gonna pretend I didn't hear that, ok?" he said more softly this time. "Vickie—move it." He sat back with his bullet-like eyes still on his wife.

It was the last time Sophia spoke like that to him...

For the most part, their marriage had been good. Of course, with seven kids, that didn't leave a whole hell of a lot of time for Sophia to do much else. So early on, Vito had been forced to seek, ahem, pleasures from other women who could tend to his physical needs. If Sophia knew that many other women had felt Vito's manhood, she didn't let on. Which was the way he liked it.

No, Sophia had done all right by him and he by her. The kids grew up healthy and never having to worry about food or clothing or shelter. Questions about Daddy's business went largely unanswered as sort of questions that kids didn't need to ask.

Vito was'nt there for many school plays or athletic events. Things like that. For that he let Sophia take charge. No, Vito was too busy taking care of business in the early days to attend to things like that.

Naturally, his daughters gravitated towards the old man, and Vito liked that. He spoiled them rotten with all these little gifts that would mysteriously turn up under his daughters' pillows and in their rooms. Sometimes a few of the girls would go to school and reach into her pocket and low and behold, out would come the most beautiful bracelet a girl could want.

Vito didn't spoil his son in quite the same manner. For Carlo, Vito had larger plans, plans that involved getting involved in the family business someday.

But for his girls, nothing was too good.

When the girls got a little older, Vito was confronted with the spectre of dating. Always a problem. Even for a father who did what he did for a living. Since the girls were staggered in age apart by about 2 years or so, it seemed like he always had a fresh problem because one was always coming on the heels of the other.

There was, of course, the incident with Angela that changed her life and everyone's life around her, most of all her father's...

* * * *

Looking back, Vito had never seen it coming. His daughter had started dating this boy, Michael. Good kid, Vito thought. They were about the same age that he and Sophia were when they started dating. So Vito didn't think there was anything unusual about it.

The kid was a mechanic, a good one as it turned out. He had taken Vito's Cadillac and tuned it to perfection. Vito felt the kid was a little awed around him, but he always treated Michael with respect. Michael even talked about joining Vito's crew, but Vito didn't want any part of that. No, whoever married his daughter was going to remain clean and out of the business.

Vito had been against his daughter staying out so late, but Sophia talked him out of that. "Listen, he's a good kid, let them stay out a little later. Remember when we used to stay out late, honey?" she said with a smile.

Vito grunted. "Yeah, and I remember your old man used to practically chase me with a shotgun. That's what I remember."

So he compromised and let the kid stay out past midnight. Little did he know that his natural insomnia would cause him to bump into his daughter quite unexpectedly one night after midnight when she did indeed come in after midnight herself.

He had gone downstairs to rummage through the refrigerator, hoping to get some milk or something to soothe his stomach. Sophia was an excellent cook, but her cooking sometimes did him in.

When Angela came in, he heard her stumble. That was what gave him his first inclination to go over to her.

"Angela, are you all right?" he said as he saw her in the darkened hallway.

He watched her turn around, and then saw the ripped skirt. Even from the dim hallway he could make out the faint bruises on her face.

He put the knuckles of his right hand to his mouth. Bastard!

He went quickly over to her. Even from a two feet away, he could smell the faint odor of booze on her.

"Angela, are you all right?" he said with alarm. It was clear that Angela was not all right. She was still slipping slightly and she wasn't doing too well standing.

It was when he went to touch her that she screamed...

Vito withdrew his hands as if a snake had bitten them. Something happened to my little girl, he thought. Something bad.

"NO, NO, don't touch me anymore, ALLRIGHT!!!" Angela cried out, half in hysterics.

Vito saw Sophia on the stairs. She had come flying down as soon as Angela started going into hysterics.

He saw the look of concern on her face.

She went over and finally persuaded Angela to come into the living room. Vito snapped on the lights and instinctively Angela put her eyes to her face as if blinded. "Turn out the light, PLEASE!!" she pleaded.

Vito and Sophia looked in horror at their daughter.

Not only were her clothes a mess and her face bruised, but her nails were completely broken. Vito found that strange because Angela had always been so obsessive about her nails.

Vito started to launch into a tirade asking her where she'd been—but Sophia shushed him. This time, he let her.

Sophia brushed back a strand of hair from Angela's face. She said quietly:

"Angelina, what happened, sweetie? I know something went wrong on your date. Your father and I can see it. For God's sake, tell us so we can do something!"

Angela fidgeted around at first. Her eyes went warily to her father's face. She knew her father and she knew his volcanic temper. She knew that if she told them what had happened between her and Michael that her dad would want to kill Michael. And Angela didn't want to see that happen.

Because she wanted to do it herself...

The time passed and both parties grew silent. Angela felt as if time was suddenly frozen and her thoughts just seemed to drift up and away. The evening had started out so promising. Michael had come to pick her up and he didn't seem in an unusually bad mood or anything. He tended to be moody sometimes, but tonight had not seemed to be one of those nights.

They had gone to a favorite bar of his for a few drinks before dinner. Angela was not a big drinker, she tended towards mostly girl drinks like daiquiris and things like that. But Michael liked to pour them down, especially after a bad day.

She didn't know what she said to set him off. It could have been something, anything that was said in passing. An innocent remark that had somehow caused him to go into orbit. Maybe it had been when they were at the motel.

One of the problems it seemed being Vito Leone's daughter was that they couldn't even kiss goodnight on the porch without being spied upon. And no guy wanted to have someone like Vito breathing down his neck. That was like a death sentence.

What her dad did not know, Angela thought, was that this was supposed to be the night that she gave herself to Michael. "Gave it up" was the parlance for it.

The reason, as far as Angela was concerned was that Michael was sexy as hell. And he had started to grow dissatisfied with being teased so much and wanted the real thing. Too many nights in the back seat of a car would do that to you as he told Angela.

And so Angela had thought really long and hard about everything. And because she didn't want to take a chance on losing him to another girl, and because, well, yes she TOO was getting turned on—Angela Leone had decided to give up her virginity to Michael Stipiconti.

They had picked a little out-of-the way motel where they figured no one would see them, and where they could get into minimum trouble.

Angela had'nt figured on rape.

She sat there, fuzzily trying to piece together the details of exactly what had happened. It was tough because after Michael had stopped hitting her—she had blacked out momentarily. Long enough to lose her memory for what had occurred.

Michael had insisted that they stop at a liquor store so he could get a bottle for the room. She hadn't really been crazy about him doing that, but said nothing. He went inside the store, picked up a bottle of vodka and brought it back out to the car. He gestured towards her, but she smiled wanly and said no thanks. He shrugged and took a healthy swig. Then he got going.

The motel they had picked was not exactly the Hilton. A threadbare room with just sort of a coverlet on the bed. Angela bent down to sniff it. Well, at least the bed was clean.

As soon as she took her coat off, Michael had fairly jumped on her. She tried to be light-hearted about it but he wasn't in the mood for any of that. Before she knew it, he had surrounded her and was ripping at her clothes!

She could remember wanting to scream, but he clamped his big, sweaty hand across her mouth and whispered in her ear: "You try and scream, you bitch, and I'll beat the shit out of you. Understand me?" Angela understood. She didn't try it again.

But when he started in again, she put up a fierce struggle, until he began to beat her around the face to get her to stop. And then suddenly, he was in her, hard as molten steel, ripping through her vagina, shredding layers of skin and tissue, his blood-engorged rape tool battering her into submission. Mercifully he finally came and sank inside her.

She remembered that he got up, and watched him stagger around the room. Stopped to pick up the bottle and downed another long swig of vodka. She remembered that he knelt down beside her and said, "If you ever tell your old man about this, I'll find you and kill you."

She clutched the pillow and wanted to die. . .

But she didn't die. Michael threw her clothes at her then got dressed himself. Swaying tipsily towards the car, he opened the door for her, took a long look at her and started the drive back to Vito's house.

She wouldn't look at him in the car. The few times he tried to talk to her were met with stony silence. He dropped her off and watched her go inside.

Angela thought about all this and couldn't quite see herself having an old heart-to-heart with her dad about this...

Vito broke into her thoughts. Trying to control his legendary temper, he asked her, "Angela, look, did this little bastard—I mean did Michael touch you at all? Tell me the truth, Angela, 'cause I got ways of finding out. Just tell your pop the truth." The way his eyes bored into Angela's made her afraid.

"We, uh, got into a little fight, dad, and well, Michael kind of well, lost his temper," Angela said in a suddenly very small voice.

"Lost his—what? Sophia, will you listen to this fuc—I mean, will you listen to this stuff?" Vito said, now suddenly exasperated at Angela's refusal to level with him. He got a brainstorm. "C'mon, Angela. Sophia, I'm taking her to the doctor. That's it, I've made up my mind. Get her coat and let's go, ok? I'll get the car out."

Sophia started to put up a protest but then nodded her head. She knew it was the right thing to do.

* * * * *

The doctor came out of the examining room. Vito thought it was curious that his smock was still completely white this late in the day.

He came over to where Vito and Sophia sat. As he approached, they both got to their feet at the same time, the same worried look on their faces.

Vito took three giant steps towards the doctor, effectively stopping the man in his tracks. "How's my little girl, doc?" Vito asked, his face flushed and worried—yet still managing to contain a menace that made the doctor want to be very careful about the words that he chose.

He cleared his throat and spoke in his best authoritative beds manner. "Your daughter has suffered rather severe trauma. She is resting comfortably now, but there has been trauma to her face and body and the swelling needs time to go down. In addition—."

Vito cut in on him. "I KNOW that, doc. I've seen my girl, remember? What I want to know is-." He took a deep breath, looked back over his shoulder at his wife, then lowered his voice. "What I want to know is—was my daughter, you know—was she raped?" Vito's eyes pleaded with the doctor to tell him the truth.

The doctor hesitated before answering. He thought to himself that it was never easy to tell parents. He knew who this man was, knew the rumors about him. Yet at that moment, Vito Leone was no mob tough guy; rather he was just another anguished father wanting to protect his daughter.

"I've done some preliminary vaginal swabs and sent them to the lab. But at this time, yes, there was severe trauma to the vaginal area and some indication of tearing. Was your daughter a virgin, Mr. Leone?" the doctor said.

Vito grabbed a fistful of the doctor's spock in his meaty hand. "Hey, doc, watch your mouth when you talk about my daughter. That ain't none of your concern—just do your job!" he said heatedly.

Sophia came over and pried Vito's hand away from the doctor's spotless smock. "Vito, what do you think you're doing! Doctor, er, Sanford here is only trying to help us. There you go again, losing your temper. Think of Angela, will you?" she implored Vito, disgust tingeing her voice.

The doctor had lost all color in his face and just hoped that Vito wouldn't smack him. Upon being released from Vito's iron grip, he tried to compose himself, and said in a shaky voice: "Yes, Mr. Leone, I can say categorically, your daughter was—sexually molested. Yes, it does appear that Angela was, in fact, raped. I'm very sorry. Now, if you'll excuse me, I have other patients to see. You can see her for a few moments if you like. But she's a little sedated so she won't be that lucid. She needs to stay the night here for observation. I'll check in on her later." With that, the doctor beat a hasty retreat before Vito could try something again.

Vito and Sophia went into the semi-darkened room and saw Angela laying there. In the half-light, she looked just like an angel, a completely innocent little girl. Vito put the evil thoughts he was thinking to the back of his mind for the moment. Right now, he had to concentrate on re-assuring his little girl that everything would be all right.

Sophia started to cry as she saw her daughter's face rise and fall slightly with each breath. She tried to compose herself.

Vito whispered: "Angie, honey, it's us. Can you hear me?"

Angela stirred. She had been half-dozing. Instinctively, she whispered, "Oh, God, daddy, I'm so ashamed."

Vito touched her hair and made a vow: When I get ahold of that kid, he'll wish he was dead. 'Cause I'm gonna put a big-time hurtin' on that boy.

* * * * *

Vito faced the three guys who made up part of his crew. "I'm looking for a scumbag," he said plainly. "His name is Michael Stipiconti. I've got a personal beef to settle with him. Now, what I'm going to tell you is in the strictest confidence. If I ever find out that word of this has leaked to my enemies, there's going to be one less guinea standing here in this room. Do we understand each other?" Vito didn't have to ask twice.

"This little scumbag raped my daughter. OK? She was underage and a virgin and he took advantage of that. And he's going to pay like he never knew how. OK?"

"Now, I got some information about where this kid hangs out. It's the weekend, so I know he ain't gonna be going into work till Monday. So that leaves tonight.

I want you guys to fan out and check out some of the clubs. Go to Manny's and go to Club Riviera. I got a pretty good idea you'll find him there. He's just barely drinkin' age so they let him in. And when we find him, I want him taken out quietly. No rough stuff yet, till I say so. Got it?"

The boys nodded. They got it.

* * * * *

The music blared at Club Riviera. Actually, that was a rather grandiose name for a small, neighborhood club. In reality, it had a bar and a small stage where a house rock band played low-key, good-time rock and roll to the mostly white, clean-cut audience.

Which is why Michael Stipiconti stood out. Although he was young himself, he dressed differently than the other kids, in black leather jacket and tight black jeans and scuffed motorcycle boots. (He had, quite conveniently left this part of his wardrobe home when he took out Angela).

But it was more than the clothes that made him stand out. He had a touch of the hood in him. Nothing murderous you understand. Just something in the way he talked and looked at the other patrons. And the way he tossed back his shots of Jack Daniels and smoked his unfiltered Luckies. (He had also, quite conveniently, left those vices at home when he took out Angela).

Michael sat there, fidgeting and highly nervous. He sat next to his running buddy, Glen Wallace. Glen looked the same as Michael, just a little shorter and squatter. The pockets of his black leather jacket were well-spread from continually thrusting his hands into them. He tried to get some conversation out of Michael.

"So what gives, Mike?" Glen asked apprehensively. "How was that date the other night with that chick Angela?"

Michael shifted around in his seat. "Uh, it was allright," he said, his mind racing as he tried to decide how much he should tell Glen. He decided he couldn't hold it in any more.

"Actually, man, things got out of control," Michael said in a low voice. You never knew if there were spies in this place.

Glen gave him a funny look. "Uh, whaddya mean, 'out of control,'?" "There's like all kinds of outta control, you know Mike. What kind of outta control are you talking about anyway?" Glen had a feeling he didn't want to know the answer.

"Well, things got out of hand sexually—know what I mean?"

Glen stopped him cold. "Wait a minute. You mean to tell me, you're dating Vito Leone's daughter and things got out of hand?" Glen stared at him in disbelief. "Mike, not for nothing but I think you need your head examined. Do you have any idea what Vito would do to you if he found out? Wait a minute, what exactly are you tellin' me? Was this thing between youse, what's the word—consensual?"

Michael shifted his glance. "Uh, not exactly. I'd been um, kind of drinking and I popped her cherry, you know?"

Glen groaned. "Oh, my God, Michael. Now you have really done it." He leaned closer to him and whispered: "Are you tellin' me you raped her? Is that what you're sayin', Michael? Is it?" Glen's eyes on Michael were hard.

Michael nodded and said in a small voice, "Yeah."

Glen groaned again. "What the hell were you thinking, dude? Do you have any idea how much trouble you're in? Yeah, I guess you do. You know, I don't think this is like the best place for you to be hanging out. C'mon, let's go." With that, Glen got up to leave and so did Michael.

As they did, Glen felt a meaty palm on top of his shoulder. And then heard a voice low to his ear: "Hey, what's your hurry, bud? Stay awhile." The hand exerted such force on Glen's shoulder that he didn't budge. Just sat there meekly looking up into Carmine's eyes. His partner stood next to him saying nothing.

Michael had the same visitor exerting pressure on him. Underneath that giant paw, he looked like a scared little kid.

Carmine released his grip. "Now, which one of you is Michael Stipiconti?"

Michael meekly nodded. "I am," he said in a very small voice. "And this is my friend, Glen."

Carmine fixed his eyes on Michael. Without taking them off him, he spoke to Glen. "Take off, ace. And remember, you didn't see us, this never happened. Got it?" He then turned to fix his steely glare at Glen who withered.

"Sure. I mean, yes sir," Glen said as he looked helplessly at Michael for one more second, before picking up his leather jacket and bolting. He didn't have to be told twice.

Carmine then leaned back down to Michael's ear and said, "OK, twinkletoes, now let's move it out nice and easy. We don't want to create any kind of scene here. Just smile real nice and easy at all the boys and girls here. I'll be right behind you. Let's go." With a small hard nudge, Carmine got Michael going.

Michael hoped to get the bartender's attention, but one look backward at Carmine made him forget about that idea. He sighed deeply, put his jacket on and went out towards the exit.

* * * * *

Once upstairs on the street, the three of them were joined by two other sides of beef who closed ranks with Carmine. Nobody talked. They just motioned the driver of the limousine to come down the street. When it did, they threw Michael none too gently in the back seat and took off.

Approximately 15 minutes later, Michael was sitting in a chair opposite Vito Leone. If he had any kind of weapon he would have used it on himself. He knew Vito's reputation and he didn't think he was going to survive this one.

Vito had sat there looking at him silently for several minutes, as if regarding something unpleasant that he had discovered he had stepped on the street. Finally, he spoke.

"What is it goes through someone like your's mind, scumbag?" Vito said slowly and deliberately. "I mean, I'm curious. When you started going out with my daughter, didn't you think about what the consequences might be? You didn't think I'd find out about something like this?"

Michael coughed nervously. "Mr. Leone, you gotta understand, I never meant to hurt your daughter. Things just got a little outta hand," he finished up lamely.

"A LITTLE OUTTA HAND?" Vito roared. "THAT's WHAT YOU CALL ATTACKING AND RAPING MY DAUGHTER, YOU ASSHOLE? Carmine reached over and tried to steady his boss by lightly grabbing his arm. Vito shook him off. Then sat down again and kept glaring at Michael.

Michael didn't know what to do. He had never been in a jam like this before. If only there was something he could say to Vito to smooth things over. But it was obvious Vito was intent on killing him. The only question was when.

Michael sat there numbly taking it all in, trying vainly to recall why he had done what he had done. He had been drinking that much had already been established. But was it the booze that set him off? No, it wasn't that. It was more like Anglea had been trying to be a cock-tease, flirting with him, bringing him so close to the brink every time and then pulling back. Bitch. If only she had spread her legs sooner, none of this would have happened. A man has needs, Michael kept telling himself. Why did this have to be Vito Leone's daughter though?

Carmine looked over at Michael's sad, pathetic face sitting there just waiting for it to be over. "Whaddya wanna do with him, boss?" he said, salivating at the thought of sticking it to Michael. He hadn't liked this little snotnose since he first set eyes on him.

Vito looked over at him with hooded eyes. "We're going to take a little trip down to the river. And Carmine, make sure you bring the little black bag. Let's go." With that, he pushed his bulk out of the chair and waited for one of his boys to get his coat.

Michael sat there sweating. The little black bag? What the fuck was that?

He was soon to find out...

* * * * *

Thirty minutes later the limousine pulled up beneath a deserted pier. Michael looked around for signs of life but he could see nothing. All he saw was a light fog coming in off the river. For a moment, he thought that it looked like a scene out of an old Peter Lorey black and white movie.

Then he suddenly snapped to and remembered that this was no movie. This was the real deal, and he was the main star of this particular movie. The one written and directed by Vito Leone.

He sat hunched in between Carmine and Tommy in the front seat. There was no way he could budge an inch even if he wanted to. He idly wondered where Angela was right now. And for that matter, where was Glen? Where were all his supposed "friends." A lot of good it was doing him right now to have those friends. With people like that, who needed enemies?

Michael wondered how they would do it. Would it be a simple bullet behind the ear, or a garotte, like they did in "The Godfather." He had no idea. All he knew was that whatever it was gonna be, he wished they would get it over with quick. This waiting was the hard part.

At that moment, Vito was having similar thoughts. Jesus, he had been so wrong about this kid. At first, his instincts were such that he thought, hey, the kid's OK, nothing to worry about. In a way, Vito almost felt that the reason he was going to whack Michael was first because of what he did to Angela, but second because he had been so wrong about him to begin with. And Vito didn't like that for a second!

Michael noticed that the car was angled in such a way as to shine the streetlight directly on the hood of the car. The rest of the car was dark, but you could see quite clearly on the hood. He thought that was pretty strange. If you were going to knock someone off—why would you want to have the hood of the car lit up like a movie screen?

He was soon to find that out also...

Vito walked down a little ways with Carmine and Tommy leading Michael by the arms. Now they were down by the river with just enough light to make each other out. Michael thought that Vito looked more like a shadow than anything else. They were now a good 500 feet from the car.

"The reason I wanted to walk down here is because I want to tell you in graphic detail what it is I'm gonna do to you. See, I want you to think about it for awhile. Now after I tell you, I am gonna go back to the limo and have a little snooze because I'm a little tired.

So, scumbag, you're gonna have time to think about things. But just in case you try to run, Carmine and Tommy will have guns trained on you. So they'll be right near you, there's no where to go."

Michael started to sweat with anticipation. He knew it was gonna be bad.

Vito reached over and grabbed a handful of Michael's cheek and shook it. "You know what the Arabs do if you're caught stealing a loaf of bread? They cut off your hand. Sounds kinda bad, huh?" Vito said with menace in his voice.

Michael blanched at the word "cut."

"I'm gonna apply what the Arabs do to thieves into your situation here. The way I figure it, you won't have any need of your dick anymore after today. So I'm gonna cut it off."

Michael gulped air inward and immediately buckled at the knees. Carmine and Tommy held him up.

Vito leaned over Michael and cracked his face hard. "What's the matter, tough guy? You were so big and tough when you were raping my daughter, what's the matter now?"

With that, Vito stood up and yawned. He said to Carmine and Tommy over his shoulder. "I'm goin' back to the limo. Watch that turd, you got me?"

Michael stood there contemplating his awful fate while Carmine and Tommy stood there nonchalantly, their hands resting on their guns.

He started to walk a little further down toward the river, but heard Tommy grunt, "Hey, douchebag, stand still."

Michael wondered if you could live without your dick. He had heard that it was possible to bleed to death. Oh, God, this couldn't be happening to him!

He began to think about making a break for it. Where he was standing now all he had to do was distract Carmine and Tommy for just the flash of a second and then take a dive into the water. He needed something to distract the two goons with. But what?

He looked up at the sky and saw pigeons and birds flying overhead. Suddenly he had it. He waited for a moment until they were directly overhead.

All of a sudden, he let out a yelp. "Oh, shit," he said. "Some pigeon took a crap on my head. Goddammit." He began to hop up and down like a madman just for effect.

Carmine and Tommy nudged each other and took turns laughing. "Hey, look at that dumb shit. Can you believe that? Some bird takes a dump on his head." They continued to crack up, looking at the dumb cluck standing there looking stupid.

Suddenly, in the flash of an instant, Michael was sprinting towards the river while Carmine and Tommy realized what had happened and took off after him, shouting and cursing at him.

Although the night was dark, Michael was able to swim out a little ways towards the middle of the river. It wasn't very deep and he couldn't really go that far. All around him he heard the sounds of "ping" "ping" as the guns went off. Carmine and Tommy were shooting at him!

He looked around and tried to clear his head and focus on where he was. It was very confusing. He felt like he was treading water, not really going anywhere.

Eventually, Carmine and Tommy began to tire of this. They yelled out to him, "Hey, scumbag, you can either come in to shore or stay out there and freeze to death or drown. It's your choice." They walked a little further along the way and then just plunked themselves down on the ground waiting for Michael to come back in.

*   *   *   *   *

Stuck out there in the water in the dark, Michael suddenly felt stupid. Stupid for trying to think he could get away, and stupid for doing what he did in the first place to get into this mess. Some choice he had: He could stay out in the water and freeze to death, or swim in to shore and get whacked by these two goombahs. Michael felt miserable.

To top it all off, Vito had awoken from his nap and was feeling grumpy. When he saw what was happening, he hit the roof. Here were his two lieutenants waiting for some jerkoff to come in from the water where he shouldn't have been in the first place!

Vito bellowed out: "Will you two get that guy? What the hell is he doing out there? Do I have to do everything around here? Wade in there and get that guy!!"

Dutifully, Carmine and Tommy waded up their trousers and went in after Michael who sat there like a wet huddled mess. He came without hardly any resistance at all. Both of them wondered what the hell he was doing out there in the first place.

They dragged him over to Vito who smacked him in the face. "What the hell is going on here? What the hell were you thinking, kid?" Vito bellowed.

Vito then took matters into his own hands. He half-pulled, half-dragged Michael over to the hood of the car. Carmine and Tommy trotted a foot away. When he got him over to the shiny part of the car, he said to them, "Strip him down then sit him up."

Carmine and Tommy both began ripping off Michael's clothes. He started to scream but Tommy punched him in the mouth. The screams then came out as a dull whimper.

They then propped him up and wrenched his legs so that his legs were spread wide on the hood of the car.

Vito said: "Yank that thing out where I can see it."

Carmine reached down to Michael's dick and pulled it erect. He held onto it and as he did made a sarcastic kissy-kissy sound and winked at Tommy who laughed himself. They both shut up then as Vito came toward them.

Vito had removed a short stiletto from the black bag by this time. In his eyes were murder and vengeance...

He looked once at Michael and said, "This is for my daughter." With that he took a short downward stroke and cut off Michael's dick in one motion. That's how sharp the stiletto was.

As the organ came away in his hand, Vito looked at it for one long moment then stuffed it into Tommy's hand. "Here," he said. "We're going to use this as postage when we mail this fucker down the river."

By this time, Michael had passed out from the pain, re-awakened, took one look at himself, then passed out again.

They dragged him down to the river, took an industrial strength building nail gun and fixed his dick on to his arm. With one driving motion, they drilled the organ into the man's arm. Immediately, blood spurted from the open wound. Michael murmured and moaned to himself but he was clearly out of it.

Carmine and Tommy then dragged Michael out about 500 yards and dumped him face down in the river. Floating that way for a minute he was washed out to the middle in a matter of minutes.

They all watched him for a moment, sneered as a collective group and walked grimly back to the limousine.

* * * *

This was precisely what was on his mind today. The fact that he had guys who would push it further. A whole lot further. This guy Gino was just the tip of the iceberg. Lately Vito had been getting reports on all sorts of strange shit happening out there. There had been an incident that had happened a few weeks ago when Vito was in his office late at night...

"So, Tom, the uh, arrangement that we discussed will go through without any problems, I assume?" Vito was talking to Thomas ("Easy Tommy") Esposito, a local politician with whom Vito had frequent dealings.

"Sure, Mr. Leone, the property in question is still certainly available to any bids you might care to put on it." Esosito said as he leaned back in his chair. He was referring to a couple of acres of prime property that (surprise) were adjacent to the casino property. Other local entrepreneurs had bid on the property, but Esposito had been instrumental in shutting them out. Not without howls of protest and cries of favoritism of course.

Esposito was well aware that it did a local politician's career good to keep on the right side of Vito Leone. In this case, the right side meant appropriating any requests he had for certain zoning restrictions to, ahem, go his way.

In return for this, Esposito was the recipient of regular Fed Ex packages which came through the mail, all perfectly legal, all of which contained a small green brick-type parcel... Cold, hard, coin of the realm, all of which went into a bank account, far, far away in another land...

"I'm assuming that the compensation issue will be taken care of?" Esposito asked carefully, not wanting to come right out and ask Vito directly about the bribe money.

"Sure, sure, Tom, that will be no problem. I'll make sure that accounting has the proper paperwork, you know? Anyway, I'll talk to you soon, OK?"

"Fine, Mr. Leone. Best to the wife and family."

"Thanks, Tom."

Both men hung up.

Vito looked at the black receiver for a minute. In these days of electronic sweeps and routine office bugging, no one could afford to be too careful. Any conversations he had with Easy Tommy were strictly on the up and up.

He was just getting back on the phone to call his lovely wife, Sophia to tell her he would be home in a little while for a late supper, when Sal knocked on his door and came in slightly out of breath. For Sal, that was pretty unusual. Sal was so low-key and emotionless, Vito sometimes wondered if the guy had a pulse.

Sal got right to the point. "Boss, we got a big problem down at one of the loading docks."

Vito's ears perked up. The loading docks were always trouble. Part of the problem was that he couldn't monitor them as well as he could the workings of the casino. True they were only a few miles away, but he had to rely on reports from his foremen down there. Straight-up guys all of them, but they were definitely out of Vito's direct reach. He didn't like that.

He sat back with an inward groan in his leather chair which creaked under the weight of his rock-hard bulk. "So let me have it. What's the damage?"

"It's Angelo and Mikey. They mixed it up with some local Indians down there who came around looking for trouble."

"Mixed it up like how?"

"Uh, like broken heads, that's how."

Vito fixed Sal with eyes carved out of the coldest hardest granite imaginable. He leaned forward, the chair creaking very, very deliberately.

"People die from broken heads, Sallie."

Sal swallowed hard as he forced this next sentence out in a whisper: "Thhaaaat's what happened, boss."

KA-POW! Vito's hand slammed directly down on the desk with a huge crash. "Goddammit, Sal, I told you I didn't want this to happen."

"Boss, I didn't do anything!" Sal felt a cold chill go down his spine. He was getting the blame for a couple of assholes who got out of hand—and he wasn't even there!

Vito cut him off. "Yeah, you weren't there. But Sal, it gets outta hand like this—well that reflects on you, my friend. Because these strombolis, they're supposed to fear you just like they do me. Let's go see the damage."

* * * * *

The headlights of Vito's limousine cut through the damp chill and fog. Gravel crunched under the wheels as the heavy car eased down the small entrance road that led to the huge loading dock complex. Just off to the side were a group of men who stood in a semi-circle. The lights of a small delivery truck illuminated the scene.

As Vito and Sal approached the men silently, the circle opened up and a small, wiry man named Hansen darted forward. He was the dock foreman, responsible for all the freight that went through. The trucks were part of Vito's lifeline and Hansen could be counted on to keep things running smoothly. (It helped of course that Sal provided him with two whores every once in a while that serviced Mr. Hansen's needs in a way that Mrs. Hansen could never dream of).

Tonight just wasn't Hansen's night, though.

He half-fell to the ground, regained his balance and stumbled again. He was trembling so hard he could barely get his words out. "Muh... Muh... Mr. Llleeoonnee, I dunno what happened here. One minutes, these two Indian guys came up to the office to inquire about loading jobs, the next thing I know, they jumped on me, then all of a sudden there's punches being thrown, and Angelo and Mikey start wailing on these two schmucks..."

As these last words left his mouth, his head jerked toward the two assailants reflexively who were suddenly staring very hard at Hansen, and his eyes widened as he tried frantically to shove the words back in his mouth. "No, no, no, I mean, they didn't hit them that hard—"

Vito cut him off with a ruthless wave of his hand. "Forget it, you asshole. I already know who did it." He took a few steps over and stared down at the body of the man in the glare of the truck's headlights. Angelo and Mikey had done a whale of a job on him. Judging by the looks of him, it looked as if he had caught the crack of a tire iron in the skull. The impact must have been enough to cause him to lose consciousness quickly and bleed to death. The guy's skull looked like it had been butchered. Christ, what a mess, Vito thought.

Angelo and Mikey were standing off to the side now, their hand stuffed in the pockets of their leather jackets, their faces etched with that peculiar, defiant, wise-guy crease across it. These two hard-ons aren't about to cop to anything, Vito thought.

"Let's take a walk shall we?" Vito said, motioning for Sal to follow, as he headed toward the central loading area. It wasn't an invitation.

All four men walked the short distance inside the bay, where they stood in front of a row of trucks all neatly parked together.

Vito waited until they were out of sight of the rest of the crew. Suddenly his right hand lashed out and cuffed Angelo first, then Mikey, across the chops. His pinky ring drew blood and both men reacted sharply as their heads snapped back. Any flash of anger was quickly extinguished, and the look of pain on their faces turned way to two sullen expressions beneath hooded eyes.

Vito pointed his finger in Angelo's face. "Now start talking to me you little coglione. How in the name of Christ did this redskin get dead?"

Mikey spoke up. "Well, boss, the first thing is they went to Hansen to apply for general loading dock jobs. But before they could even get the paperwork filled out, Hansen told 'em 'Look, you're wasting your time.' They didn't want to believe there wasn't any work."

"So then one of the dudes stiff-arms Hansen, you know?" Angelo chimed in, suddenly growing some courage. "Well, we hear the commotion going on and we run out to where Hansen is. He's like half on the ground and this guy is standing over him threatening him—."

Vito waved his hand impatiently. "Wait a minute. You're telling me these two stronzos were crazy enough to come to a loading dock filled with white guys and start shoving around the dock foreman?" Both Vito and Sal exchanged glances.

"Yeah, boss," both men sounded in unison.

"Allright, so what happened then?" Vito asked.

Right away when I shoved the guy away from Hansen, I could tell he was drunk," said Mikey. "You know, like I could smell it. Well as soon as we pulled him off Hansen, the dude takes a swing at Angelo and he bops him one."

"What about the other guy?" Vito asked, his face impatient for answers.

"The other dude hung back a little bit," Mikey said excitedly. "He gave Angelo a shove, but it was nothin'. No, the bigger guy was causing all the damage."

"And that's when you hit him with the tire iron?" Vito said.

Mikey hesitated. "Well, I ran over with it in my hand, and yeah, I grazed him with it."

"Grazed him?" Vito said incredulously. "You cracked his skull open!"

Both men seemed to shrink into the folds of their leather jackets.

"What happened to the other guy?" Vito asked.

Angelo piped up: "He, uh, took off, boss."

Vito gave a long, weary sigh. "We're gonna dispose of this body, and we're gonna do it quickly."

* * * * *

Condo parked his truck outside the building where the meeting of the Full Breed Supremacist Group was being held and walked inside through the dusty hallway into a cafeteria.

The group was a radical fringe of the tribes. The police had linked them to some pipe bombings and random other acts of violence. Condo was on uneasy terms with them, but he had to hash some things out.

As he made his entrance inside the dusty hallway, all the men fell silent. Bodies sat up straight, cigarettes were extinguished and styrofoam coffee cups scraped the plastic tablecloth on the table. Slowly, the meeting came to order. Condo cleared his throat. "You all know me. And you all know I'm a man of my word. So when I say I'm tired of kissing up to the mob henchmen - believe it." He pounded the table for emphasis. "We do all the work and these men take all the money." As he spoke, he eyed a sinewy man with black, greasy hair who stood in the corner, quietly observing.

Donald T. Hatchett emerged from the shadows and thrust his hands in the pockets of his Levis's. All eyes turned to watch him as he gazed over at Condo. As head of the tribes' radical Full Breed Supremacist group, Hatchett's silence spoke just as ominously as some of his words. To say Donald T. Hatchett made people nervous was like saying Donald Trump had a few bucks to his name.

He was the sort of man who made people instinctively want to keep their distance; the threat of imminent violence hung contained in his sinewy arms and muscular legs. He weighed in at a trim 175 pounds and although he showed the beginning of a paunch, most of it was all muscle. Prisons having weight rooms and all.

Don didn't agree with the council on issues of the way they should keep the tribes values the way they were before the casinos. Plain and simple, Hatchett had no use for the the white man. To his way of thinking, they had been responsible for much of the trouble in his life.

He used to watch old movies and feel his face curl with rage when he saw cowboys always slaughtering his people, raping the squaws and burning down their villages. How come the Indians always got the short end of the stick? John Wayne's picture on his dartboard had quite a few holes in it from his Blackjack hunting knife.

He stood a few feet away from Condo and then spoke. "Condo, I'm on your side. I don't want these greaseballs running our land any more than anyone here. We gave the land to the foreigners, the English and the French centuries ago."

He turned and faced the rest of the group. "Listen to me. We got the money and the political power to take this country back. Do you hear me? We as Indians never surrendered and it is time we take steps to take this country back!" He stood back and wiped his lips with the back of his hand, a nervous gesture. He then leaned forward again.

"I want all statues of Colonial Captains who killed our people to take over our land removed. I want all pro teams with Indian names to change their names. We can force these things now that we have political power because of all the money we donate to the parties. We will make the white man pay for what they did to us, but first we have to take our land away from Vito and the mob."

"O.K., Don? Just how are you going to do that," Condo asked. Hatchett took a deep breath. "I've got it all planned out. My plan is to first assassinate all the mob leaders and take our tribe back over. After we get control of all Vito Leone's holdings in New England, we then take back Chicago, Nevada, and all the territories in between."

A few murmured yeahs! broke out in the crowd, but several of the men sat there. Low nervous laughter swept around the room. At the sound of it, Hatchett glared out at the men and the laughter quickly turned to nervous coughing.

Condo, however, stared back at Hatchett in disbelief. He had long known about his penchant for crazy statements like this but this was the first time he had heard it up close.

"Assassinate Vito? That's your answer?" Condo said incredulously. "Don, let's rethink this. You're talking about taking out guys who are heavily guarded, who have so much power it isn't even funny. No, we need to take back what belongs to us - but not through killing."

Don stared hard and thoughtfully at Condo for a long second. Over the years they had managed to stay out of each other's way. But Condo represented the type of Indian that whites liked to deal with. Malleable, easy to handle. Oh, he might protest once in a while, but generally, Condo Cherokee played it straight down the line.

He smiled to himself because he knew Condo would lose it one day. Well, here it was, you chump. He walks into a meeting of the Full Breed Supremacist Group and challenges my authority. Perfect, Hatchett thought. Fucking perfect!

Hatchett would be buried in steaming tar before he'd let some do-gooder chump like Condo Cherokee tell him how to do his business.

He walked the few feet over to Condo and measured him for a moment. This was going to be dealt with and quickly. "Condo, I'm only going to say this once. Don't, and I repeat don't ever show your face at one of my meetings again." He leaned in close for emphasis and said slowly and with full menace: "Your slut girlfriend is a half-breed and the Full Breed Group doesn't like your type. You got it?" He stepped back.

Two men whom Condo knew casually sauntered over, one on either side of him. So, this is how he wants to play it, thought Condo. He shrugged his shoulders and walked out.

* * * * *

Condo drove home deep in thought. He felt like his life was crashing down around his ears. He had become the mob's boy, no doubt about it. There were no room for two partners in the casinos. Native Americans were as foreign a concept to the mob as any group.

Hatchett represented the side of the Indian that, historically, people associated with them. Condo knew that any attempt on the life of Vito or any other Mafia chieftan would be retaliated against - and quickly.

Condo believed that a certain amount of violence was to be expected, considering their business. If push came to shove, he was prepared to defend himself but only under attack. What Hatchett was talking about was an out and out hit. It was out of the question.

But how else to get the tribe back?

* * * * *

Chapter 3
SERENITY

Tonya's stood over the palenta on the stove and thought about her day. She worked for the tribe in the casino at the gift shop. As such she was required to look and dress a certain way. A tall, slender girl with flowing blonde hair, Tonya was aware she was good-looking. She was also aware of the men that lingered in the aisle whenever she walked by.

The attention made her uneasy, but she rationalized that these were only men and their looks meant nothing.

She paused, and for a moment drifted back into the mists of her past.

Tonya Smith had started life from the get-go two lengths behind as they say. Her mother's name was Poca Daisy, and when she barely twenty, she had been brutally raped and impregnated by an Indian who left her alone to raise her daughter.

The scum who did this to Poca Daisy was a drug addict and it was because of this that his tribe decided to adopt her as their own. And so it was that Tonya started life as a half-breed in an Indian tribe.

The incident had scarred her mother badly for life, Tonya knew. However, a wonderful thing had happened that helped make up for some of the scars that Poca felt.

Tonya remembered it very vividly. Poca's case had been in the papers and one day, Tonya was sitting at home when the phone rang.

"Hello," said Tonya.

"I'm looking for a Poca Daisy Smith. Is this her residence?" asked a man's voice. He seemed very business-like and Tonya did not think he was just calling up to offer to sell her something.

"This is Poca Daisy's residence. Who is this?" Tonya asked.

"My name is Bill Carlton. I am an assistant to Tom Crawford, the chairman of Computer Network. Perhaps you've heard of us?" the man said.

Heard of Tom Crawford? Of course, who hadn't.

"Yes, my mother and I are familiar with your company. Oh, by the way, my name is Tonya. I am Poca Daisy's daughter." Tonya said as almost an afterthought.

"Nice to meet you, er, Tonya. Now then, is Mrs. Smith at home?" Mr.

Carlton asked.

"Well, she is, but she's resting. I'm confused. What is the purpose of this call?" Tonya asked, a little confused.

"As you may or may not know, Ms. Smith, the chairman of Microsoft is very involved in many philanthropic affairs. And as you can also imagine, many, many people request various funding from Mr. Crawford for business projects they are involved in. He also receives many requests for funding from people who have been suffering with an illness." Mr. Carlton said all this in a kind of detached, dry business-like voice. Almost disembodied. It was spooky.

"So what does that have to do with my mom and me, Mr. Carlton?" asked Tonya.

"Ms. Smith, Mr. Crawford read about the terrible things that happened to your mother. First of all he would like you to know how profoundly sorry he is that she had to endure those things," Mr. Carlton said in a voice that was a little softer now.

"Ms. Smith, what I am proposing is this: Mr. Crawford would like to meet your mother—and you, personally. He would like to fly you out here on his private jet. At that time he would like to present your mother with something as, shall we say, a token of his concern for what happened.

"What is that, Mr. Carlton?" Tonya asked.

"I'd... uh, rather not say over this line, Ms. Smith. That is something best left to Mr. Crawford himself," Mr. Carlton said in his best smoothly professional manner.

"Could you and you mother make arrangements to leave soon, Ms. Smith?" Mr. Carlton asked. "Mr. Crawford is very anxious to meet your mother."

"Sure, we could be on the next plane tomorrow. Just give us time to make reservations, and then—" Tonya said in a rush now.

Mr. Carlton laughed. "No, no, Ms. Smith, remember I said Mr. Crawford was sending his private jet for you. Plan on leaving around noon tomorrow. I'll have a limo driver pick you up at your home and take you to the airport where Mr. Crawford's jet will be waiting."

"Thank you, Mr. Carlton, that will be wonderful," Tonya said. She hung up the phone.

* * * *

When Poca Daisy awoke from her nap, Tonya brought her into the kitchen and sat her down. All the bruises had faded pretty much from the terrible ordeal that she was put through. But Tonya knew that Poca would still suffer terrible nightmares from her experience. Maybe this news from Tom Crawford would help cheer her up.

"Mom, I have some terrific news to tell you," Tonya said as soon as her mother had a cup of tea in front of her. "What is it, Tonya?" asked Poca

"Well, out of the blue today, this... this man who said he works for Tom Crawford—you know, the chairman of Microsoft—called and said that Mr. Crawford had read about what had happened to you and he really wanted to help. So, he asked if we would be interested in flying out to the West Coast and meeting Mr. Crawford in person. And he also said that Mr. Crawford would be presenting you with something. We're going to be picked up tomorrow by limo and brought to the airport where we'll fly back in Mr. Crawford's private jet. Isn't it exciting, Mom?" Tonya said, barely controlling her excitement.

Poca's face had alternated between confusion and excitement. Now it was back to confusion.

"Oh, Tonya, I don't know if I could face Mr. Crawford like this. I mean, he's a very busy and important man."

"Now, Mom, Mr. Crawford sent his personal emissary to see us. He's expecting us to meet him at his office. We can' turn him down," Tonya said with an anxious voice. She did not want her mother to get discouraged about going to see Tom Crawford. Tonya felt the same way that Tom Crawford was a very powerful man—but he was only human!

Poca continued to sigh. Tonya thought that perhaps she was just tired. It was understandable considering what she had been through. Still, they had to plan for their trip.

"Mom, I'm going to pack some clothes for you and I want you to get a good night's sleep," said Tonya. "We have a big trip ahead of us tomorrow, and I want you to be ready. OK?"

Poca nodded a bit timidly. Her mother's spirit would come back, Tonya just knew it.

* * * *

The next day, right on time, the big limousine came at noon and picked up Tonya and Poca Daisy. Both of them were awed to be sitting in anything so luxurious. They sped to the airport where Tom Crawford's private plane was sitting, fueled up and ready to go.

Once on board, they strapped themselves in and marvelled at the marble and sleek, dark, wood-paneling that filled the plane. As soon as they were up for about 20 minutes, a very pretty flight attendant came around and asked them if they wanted anything to eat or drink. Poca prudently took a cup of tea. At first, Tonya was tempted to ask for a glass of champagne, but after a look at her mother, settled for a Diet Coke instead.

For lunch they feasted on Peking Duck served with wild rice and a tasty dessert. Tonya had never eaten so much rich food in her life. She thought: I can get used to this!

But of course she knew that the purpose of the trip was for Poca to meet Tom Crawford and let him present her with a gift. What that might be, Tonya still had no idea.

The trip took no time at all, it seemed, and the next thing they knew they were landing at the airport. Once again, a big limo picked them up and delivered them to Microsoft Headquarters in Redmond. As they sped along, Tonya thought it looked like such pretty country. She idly wondered if she should tell Condo about this in case he wanted to re-settle out here. Then she chuckled inwardly to herself: Condo would never want to move out here, he was too satisfied with where he lived now.

The trip in the car took about 20 minutes and the next thing they knew they were walking through the corridors of upper management of Microsoft. About the only thing that Tonya knew about the company was that there name sure was on a lot of computers in the United States.

Poca had dressed for the occasion in a nice print dress. Tonya chose a black business suit that she hoped would be appropriate. They were ushered into Tom Crawford's private office and sat in the anteroom while her secretary smiled at them and went in to announce their presence.

What struck Tonya about the offices right away were their simplicity. There were workers dressed very casually, many in jeans and shirts who walked easily back and forth between various cubicles. An air of informality hung over the place.

Finally, it was time for the meeting. The secretary came back out and motioned for them to come inside as she held the door open.

Tonya and Poca walked into a medium-sized office that also had an air of informality about it. Tom Crawford was on the phone and he motioned them to sit down in two chairs in front of him. Tonya noticed that there were two young men seated to his right who were very quietly working on a couple of computers. They looked up briefly, smiled, and then lowered their heads right back to work.

Tom Crawford stood up and smiled a broad smile. Tonya thought that he looked exactly like he did in his pictures. He was of medium height and had what could only be described as a kind of goofy, adolescent grin which gave his face a disarming look. His hair was tousled just like it was in the photographs and he wore thick glasses. There was even a hint of acne (could that be at his age?) on his face.   All in all Tonya realized she was looking face to face at the world's richest nerd. Fine with me, she thought!

"Ladies, thank you for coming on such short notice," said Crawford as he walked around his surprisingly small desk to greet them.

Poca rose and shook his outstretched hand. It was a surprisingly gentle handshake, she thought, but still firm.

"You must be Poca Daisy," said Crawford. "And you are Tonya. Welcome to Microsoft. Would you like the guided tour? No, wait, I think not," he said, answering his own question.

"No, I'll bet you're really curious to know what the leader of a computer company is doing asking you to come all this way, huh?" Crawford said in a very bemused tone of voice.

Tonya looked at her mother and said, "First of all, Mr. Crawford, my mother and I want to thank you for inviting us to come here. You can't imagine how much of a thrill it is to meet you!" (Tonya was laying it on a bit thick; she had never given a thought to Tom Crawford in her life.)

Poca chimed in: "Mr. Crawford I've heard so much about you. You've been so successful with this company and all."

"I take that as high praise, indeed, Poca," said Crawford with a twinkling grin.

He walked back behind the desk and motioned for them to sit. Then he put both arms on the desk in front of him and leaned slightly forward.

"Poca, when I read in the paper about what had happened to you, the first thing I thought was: What if that had been my mother? How would I have felt? What would have been my reaction? Now while I can't undo the terrible tragedy that happened, I am in a position to make things a little easier financially for you."

He leaned in closer so that both women could get the impact of his words.

"I would like you to have 100,000 shares of Microsoft stock. From one human being to another. The shares will be worth much money, money that you can use to help put your life back together. When you are no longer with us, it will be your decision as to how you wish to disperse those shares. Any arrangement will be acceptable, and I'll put that in writing for you if you like." Crawford leaned back in his chair and rested his his thumb and index finger against the side of his head.

Tonya and Poca both looked at each other in amazement. They were both thinking the same thing: How could this man just up and give them this fortune? And yet there it was, right on the table.

"Mr. Crawford, that's... a very... generous offer," Poca finally stammered out. "But how can we just take your money?"

Crawford leaned forward and smiled. "You're not taking my money, Poca, I'm giving the money to you in the form of shares," Crawford said gently. "Remember that the stock is always growing and that just because it's trading at a certain price today, well it could go sky-high tomorrow. So don't worry about it is what I'm saying,"

Crawford leaned forward and pressed a button. "Michael, could you come in here, please," he said.

A moment later, Mr. Carlton came into the room. He smiled at the two ladies. Under his arm, he carried a small manila folder.

Crawford gestured to Mr. Carlton and said, "Michael, here, will be the executor of this for me. Boy, that's a weird word, huh? Sounds almost like executioner!" He crinkled up his face in the puckish grin that you saw in so many pictures.

Mr. Carlton laughed and then turned slightly somber. He withdrew a formal looking document and handed it to Poca. "There you go, Poca, that is a stock certificate in the amount of 100,000 shares from Microsoft Corporation. You're now an official stockholder of our company. How does it feel?"

Poca was speechless. She stared at the handsome, handwritten caligraphy on the stock certificate and saw the numbers before her eyes. She was so overwhelmed she started to weep.

Tonya reached into her bag and pulled out a handkerchief. "It's ok, Mom," she said, a little embarrassed that her mother would cry in front of Crawford and Mr. Carlton.

Crawford reached forward across the desk and patted Poca on the shoulder. "I hope that this has been at least a partial help to you, Poca. I just know that your children and grandchildren will now have something they can depend on—financial security. I also know that nothing can relieve your suffering completely. But I have faith in you; you'll do fine," he said with another pat.

Tonya stood up. "Well, Mr. Crawford, we know you are an incredibly busy man. So we'll let you get back to work. Again, I just want to thank you for this. May God bless you," she said, extending her hand to shake his warmly.

Poca rose shakily to her feet and said, "Mr. Crawford, I'm speechless. I just know, though, that God has reserved a special place in heaven for you. Thank you again." She went around the desk and gave the surprised Crawford a hug and a kiss, which caused him to blush like a little boy.

Mr. Carlton led them out, for they had a plane to catch back home.

Poca lived a year longer...

* * * * *

She could remember the day of Poca's death so vividly, so clearly. The whiteness of the sheets in the hospital bed, the long black hands on the clock which read 10:20 pm as she breathed her last. Tonya closed her eyes tight and thought of her mother laying there, trying to speak through the pain of Hodgkin's disease, gasping for breath.

She lay in bed and called Tonya over. "Tonya you have been my reason for living and any time I would get depressed I would think of you and I would have a smile on my face."

"Mom, I love you, too," Tonya said, fighting back the tears.

"Tonya, I always asked God for strength but I was made weak so I could learn to appreciate everything I had. I prayed for wealth but I was made poor so I would be wise to appreciate the things that I had. I prayed for power, but was given serenity to understand what I was capable of controlling and what I could not control and to make the best of everything God had given me. I prayed for health and I was given a daughter to share a life with, my girl Tonya that has given me everything that I prayed for but I was given more and my prayers were answered."

"Tonya, you'll never have to worry about money again. The stocks that Mr. Crawford gave me last year, well, they're all yours now," Poca said, gasping a little for breath. She struggled on. "I hope you use them wisely. Use them to help raise your children. Raise them well, Tonya, I'm sure you'll be a fine mother."

Poca's eyes started to close and her grasp in Tonya's hand got weaker.

"Mom, don't die, you can't leave me like this." Tonya could no longer control the tears, and they ran freely down her face.

"Tonya, I love you, but it is time for me to go to heaven and look out for you." Tonya hugged her Mother one more time and then let go of her hand, watching it fall limply to the pillow...

* * * * *

Bzzzzzz... The timer on the stove buzzed its warning and Tonya snapped back to reality and reached over to shut it off. There wasn't a day that went by that Tonya didn't remember her Mother.

Tonya always had the greatest respect and pride for her mother, enduring the rape the way she did and still able to have the child. What was the line? God grant me the serenity to accept the things I cannot change versus the things I can change.

Tonya knew what she could change and what she could not. She knew that she loved Condo and was so grateful to be marrying him. However, there was, unavoidably, the issue of the money.

Tonya sat down with a mug of coffee near the window and watched the steam rise off the top of it. She hadn't broken the news to Condo yet about her inheritance. She was trying to pick just the right time and place. Unfortunately with all the crap that had been going on lately, she never knew what the right time and place was.

The money presented her with the one luxury in life that everyone lusted after: freedom of choice. When you knew that you could write your ticket for just about anything you wanted to do—well, life just got a whole lot more pleasant. The problem with that was that Poca would not have wanted Tonya to spend the money quite so carefree. Nor did Tonya have any intention of doing that.

The question remained: What best to do with the money? She would of course leave the bulk of it in a trust fund for her & Condo's children. But there was so much more that could be done with it. Things that would help the tribe a great deal. But what? Condo was so much more plugged into that side of things than she was. He would know. But he was just always so goddamned pre-occupied that she never knew.

On the other hand, she knew that she would be dealing with his pride. Pride that because she had inherited all this money now that somehow that was a slight against him. As in, "I-can-provide-for-my-family." Not that she held it against him, necessarily. There was still an old-fashioned side of Tonya that respected that.

But the death of Poca had made Tonya see that life was short. And that if you were presented with an opportunity, well, you had better grab it, because God knows when it would come back around again.

Her thoughts were interrupted by the tall, lean man who walked in the door and wordlessly took her in his arms.

As they entwined themselves in each others arms, Tonya rested herself on Condo's strong chest. They then kissed each other long and deep, and as Tonya stood back and lovingly appraised her man, she thought that they seemed to just melt into each other. With a sly smile, she led him into the bedroom.

She knew that Condo had been with other women. She was certainly not naive enough to know his attraction and allure.

Which is why she always tried to look her best for him. She knew it pleased him.

Sex, though, was another matter. For the fact was that Tonya was still a virgin. She often fantacized about her wedding day and making love to her husband. She had often wondered what it would be like with Condo.

It was not so much that she had vowed to stay pure; rather she reasoned with herself that she had plenty of time and she wanted sex to be the most wonderful experience of all. Of course, as Tonya well knew, there were certainly other ways to please a man and still retain the promise to herself. Condo had been an eager teacher and she had been quite the willing student!

He was patient with her for he knew they would have their time. Still, she worried about pleasing him. Sometimes late at night she would burrow against his chest, murmurring: "Is everything o.k? Am I doing it the right way." But he just laughed and reassured her in that way he had.

She led him over to the coverlet and kissed him again, running her hand slowly up his thigh pausing to stroke the bulge that was clearly starting to grow.

But Condo gently drew her hand away, brought it up to his mouth and kissed it. Not tonight. No, he was too keyed up right now. The incident with Hatchett had seen to that; he needed Tonya as an ally right now.

Condo walked out of the bedroom and plopped on the couch. Tonya came over to sit beside him. Condo got up again.

Tonya looked up and said, "Don't tell me - Don Hatchett."

Condo grunted and sat back down.

"Tell me what the creep said now," Tonya said wearily as she flopped back. She realized that she would have to wait awhile before talking about the money.

Condo let out his breath in one long exhalation, turned to face her and said quietly: "He said you were a half-breed slut and that I was to stay out of his meetings."

Tonya burned with a silent rage. "Well, as long as we're telling Don Hatchett stories, there's one that I didn't tell you about - because I didn't want to worry you."

Condo pressed forward. "Tell me, honey!"

"It was one day in the shop. I was getting set to close. You were out of town I think. Hatchett walked in and started talking me up. Which surprised me because I didn't really know him that well."

"Anyway, he started making these weird type of suggestions. Why don't you close early. Why don't we go have a drink? I tried to be as polite as I could - until he finally said, 'o.k., well I'll offer you $400 for the night - I've never been with a half-breed, I've heard they're good in bed.' I hit him in the face, Condo, but he just laughed and said good, I must like it rough."

Condo stared at her slowly as she said this and shook his head. It didn't surprise him, nothing about Hatchett surprised him.

The question was what to do about it. Condo knew it would'nt be long before he had a showdown with Hatchett. Because of this incident with Tonay, now Don Hatchett had made it personal.

Now he had made it very personal.

Tonya leaned over and brushed the hair off Condo's forehead. "Honey, I think we should talk about something important besides what's new in the life of Don Hatchett."

Condo gave a short laugh and said, "OK, you got my full attention. Let me have it."

Tonya got up and slowly took a deep breath. "Well, remember when my mother died? We, uh, took a little trip before that which I never told you about," she said with some hesitation, cringing at what his reaction would be.

"What kind of trip?" Condo said slowly.

Tonya thought: How do you tell someone that the world's richest man gave my mother 100,000 shares of one of the world's richest stocks? Hoo boy!

"We uh, went to see Tom Crawford, the chairman of Microsoft," Tonya said casually, as if this type of thing were an everyday occurrence.

Condo just stared. "Tom Crawford?" he said, dumbfounded. Tonya took another deep breath. "Mr. Crawford wanted to give my mother some, well, I guess you'd call it financial help in return for what happened to her." She said this in a way that she couldn't quite believe herself.

"And what exactly did Tom Crawford give your mother," Condo asked, his eyes narrowing. He couldn't wait for this.

"100,000 shares of Microsoft stock," said Tonya quietly. "And I've inherited it all."

Condo just sat there, staring.

Tonya sat there and watched him stare.

Condo got up and walked around the room, inhaling and exhaling. He sat down, looked at Tonya, started to get up again and then sat down.

"Condo, honey, I never DREAMED this would happen. I mean, you have to believe that. You do, don't you?" Tonya said pleadingly.

Condo nodded, but one half of his brain was still on that tremendous figure. How could such a thing happen? I mean, out of the blue, Tom Crawford calls and makes this tremendous offer?

Tonya cut to the chase. "Condo, I've been thinking what we could do with this money. There are so many things we could use. And you'll never have to work again, and we can travel, and—"

That was as far as she got before Condo cut her off. "Not work again?" he said abruptly. "Tonya, I am very happy for your mother's good fortune, and I'm glad that you inherited it, but it doesn't change our lifestyle. I'm much too proud of what I do to let money come between that. Surely you can see that?"

Tonya said very patiently: "Yes, honey, I know how you feel. But I can't help but think that, well, you could do so much with this money to help all the tribes and so forth. I mean, you DO want to do that don't you?"

* * * *

Condo was pacing back and forth, a knot of concentration on his forehead. He knew what Tonya was saying, and he knew that this good fortune could make their lives very comfortable but somehow he couldn't bring himself to say it.

It was true that Condo had a tremendous amount of pride. It was probably his upbringing but he had always been taught to never take anything that was not his and to work hard at whatever he did.

Now, here was his fiancee coming to him and saying, basically, hey buddy everything is allright. You don't have to worry anymore. Never have to pick up a deck of cards again, never have to take the insults of patrons as they sit there looking superior to the "fucking Indian" they have dealing the cards to them.

Condo knew that he wouldn't have minded quitting the casino, that was for sure. On the one hand he would'nt have minded being in a small business that he and he alone could run. That might be a possibility.

But what would he do? Condo had often asked himself that. I mean, it's not like he was suddenly going to be the CEO of some company. He had not the education or the training for that. So that was out. What it came down to was finding a business that would help his people. That was what he needed to do. But that was not easy, he knew that.

The other question he had was exactly how and when Tonya was going to get this money. He was not quitting the casino right away, that was for sure. Not until he was sure that the money was forthcoming.

Tonya, as if reading his thoughts, said: "Don't worry, Condo, the distribution of the sales of stock just has to be authorized and then we will take possession of it. If that's what you're worried about?"

Condo shook his head. "No, well, I guess I was thinking partially about that," he said slowly. "I was also thinking what it would be like to actually be able to quit the casino once and for all. Not to have to take anybody's crap anymore. You have no idea what they do to your pride their, Tonya!"

"Oh, I guess I have a fair idea, Condo," Tonya said sympatherically. "I see the way you come over here sometimes, so I can well imagine. But I agree. It would be smart for you to get out of there. The question is, what would you do?"

Condo nodded. "I've been thinking just that, Tonya."

Tonya came over to him as he sat brooding on the couch. "Does this mean that you're OK with the money then?" she asked in what she hoped was a very casual voice.

Condo looked at her and laughed. "We'll see, OK? I just don't want the money to come between us or to ruin our future together," he said seriously. "I know, I know," he said, raising his hand. "How could something as good as money ruin your life, right? Well, I've heard about it plenty. And I don't want that happening to us."

* * * *

Donald Hatchett stood and viewed the crowd of men that sat in the auditorium. It was a good turnout. He intended to remind everyone here that they must not forget how their ancestors lost this country to invadors. How they must never become weak. He knows where he has to start the transformation. It's with his own weak members of the tribe. Condo Cherokee, for example.

He reflected that the face-off that he had had with Cherokee the other day was a good thing. If anyone had doubted his force of will, his leadership capabilities - well, they had seen them on display against Cherokee, that phony bastard. Well, for now it was enough that he was banned from the meetings. He'd deal with Cherokee in his own way when the time came. For now, he had to convince his men that he was still fully in command.

The Full Breed Supremacist Group had been in existence since the late 1980s. Founded by one Henry L. Jackson, it had at first attracted your basic, young unemployed slightly alcoholic Indian. Jackson ran things like a paramilitary unit. He kicked out men who had a real problem with the bottle and insisted that all his men be disciplined.

At first the group had mainly stayed in the shadows, dogging the Mob through acts of sabotague and vandalism. Delivery trucks would mysteriously be smashed and have their tires slashed, things like that. But the Mob simply replaced the trucks and the pipeline was never stopped.

Enter one Donald T. Hatchett.

Hatchett had joined the group in the spring of 1991. A drifter by nature who had been by turns a construction worker, maintenance worker and truck driver, Hatchett had known first hand the slings and arrows of prejudice that young Indian men felt.

He had grown up basically without a father, who damn near drank himself to death. His mother did the best she could but conditions were tough for her. And so, when Hatchett was 18, he signed up for a hitch in the Marines. But the confines of military life chafed at him, until one day in a rage at having been denied a 3-day leave, he took a swing at his commanding officer.

Pvt. Hatchett was summarily court-martialed and shipped back home where he drifted in and out of odd jobs for the next several years. He was, in a word, a walking time bomb, and perfect for the Full Breed.

It didn't take Hatchett long to see that Henry Jackson's days were numbered. Jackson couldn't inspire the members and he didn't want to take the group a step beyond saboteuging trucks. That was a start, but Hatchett could think of many worse things to do to the Mob. Things that would make them sorry they had ever gotten into the casino business in the first place. And so in the next general election, Hatchett was voted in as their leader.

Henry Jackson just kind of vanished one day...

* * * * *

Hatchett walked slowly from the front of the room down the narrow rows of folding chairs, his boots making little scuffling sounds. Most of them had trouble with authority which made them perfect for Hatchett, with his subtle mind-twisting delivery. Once you talked to Don Hatchett for awhile, all the rhetoric started to make sense.

He had a way of appealing to a person's basic instincts and putting things in terms of a us-versus-them-stream-of consciousness diatribe that left you convinced, by God, Don Hatchett was one smart dude. A little radical maybe, but what the hell, the Indians needed someone like him.

Don Hatchett could basically make bullshit smell like a bed or roses...

He stopped his stroll and launched into this morning's sermon.

"Men, we have a problem on our hands. One that we've had for a long time. It comes in the form of Vito Leone and the mob. These people have muscled their way into our casinos and they intend to stay. Why wouldn't they? They control all the gambling, meaning the slots, blackjack, roulette, craps, baccarat. Everything. And what do we get? A lousy 70-30 split that's what."

"People like Condo Cherokee are content to work side by side with the Mob. They like him 'cause he's a 'good boy.'

In fact, there's a lot of our brothers who are like Condo. Guys who deal the cards, cook the food, park the cars, wait on wiseguys and their bitches, and shine their shoes in the bathroom."

"Well, I got a news flash for them. I ain't like those other guys. My philosophy: Someone steps on you, you step back on 'em twice as hard! I don't mean some work slowdown neither."

Hatchett paused for effect, so his words would have full impact, full meaning. He never wanted his men to forget them.

"The only way to deal with force is force back. I'm talking pipe-bombs, I'm talking extortion, I'm talking kidnapping. I'm talking EXTREME force."

"The way to deal with the Mob is to hit back at them, little by little, until their power over us loosens. Until they don't know which way is up. Until they're afraid to drive their car to the grocery store without looking in their rear view mirror. Until they're afraid for their wives and kids just like we are."

"Until, ultimately, they give back what is rightfully ours."

He let this last part sink in good, then turned and walked back up to his chair at the head of room and sat down. There was stunned silence for a long moment and then Butch Lightfoot stood up, cleared his throat and said: "Uh, Don, what you say is all well and good. Hey, I don't like the Mob's control over us anymore than anyone."

"But you know as well as I do that everything that gets said in this room is eventually going to get back to Chief Tonto. I mean, that's the way it's always gone down." Butch sad down, a little uncertain and nervous.

True, thought Hatchett, smiling inwardly to himself. But what Butch didn't know was that that old fart was not long for this earth.

Hatchett said very calmly: "Butch, you let me worry about Chief Tonto. Right now I want you all to understand that the days of slashing tires and smashing windows on trucks are over. We need to make our mark felt more strongly."

So, my friends, we're not simply going to smash up the trucks that carry the supplies to the casinos that the Mob uses, we're going to DESTROY those trucks with C-1 plastic explosives."

Hatchett turned and walked out, leaving the group to ponder this among themselves. This last statement ought to put to rest any lingering questions about his authority. He doesn't need the chief's permission on anything because very soon Chief Tonto will be out of commission, leaving him in total control of the entire group.

Then his plan will go into full force and Condo Cherokee won't have anything to say about it.

* * * *

Chapter 4
A Game Of Chance

Saturday night and the Mountainview casino in New England was packed. As you walked into the casino, you might think you'd walked onto the set of an old James Bond movie. Long expanses of thick red carpet gave the place a luxurious look. Slot machines lined all sides of the walls.

Further in were the roulette wheels, the craps tables and the blackjack tables. Further over in a secluded area separated from the main casino floor by a rope there was a fairly large area of the casino with long tables. This was the baccarat pit. Vito Leone made sure that there were plenty of shills at the table to keep interest in the game stimulated.

Most of the action though centered around the slot machines. They were the first thing you noticed when you walked in. Rows and rows of them. Spinning, bells ringing and coins falling constantly. The noise was constant and unrelenting.

The other area that was constantly moving was the blackjack tables. The game was played on a semi-circular table upon which there were seven positions marked by small rectangles or circles.

The casino attracted patrons of all ages and types.

They all had one thing in common, though. An almost insatiable need to gamble, sometimes for hours and hours on end. In the quest for the winning jackpot, food and rest were foresaken. Who needed those when there was the possibility to make a year's salary sitting right in front of you? So you gobbled a quick burger, downed a drink and plunged on.

It was amusing to see otherwise upstanding pillars of the community, nice little church-going old ladies here beseeching the gods of chance to please, just please be kind to them. Once you had the fever it was impossible to get rid of. Which is why the Mob knew a good thing when it saw it.

It was human nature to gamble. Oh, you could call it bingo or whatever else you wanted. But gambling was too much a part of American culture. Thoreau said that most men lead lives of quiet desperation.

Gambling was a way to convince yourself that you could beat the odds a bit. In a way, it was not so much about winning and losing in a house of chance like a casino, although there was that; rather gambling represented a way to beat the odds of life a bit.

A great percentage of patrons were average working stiffs. They didn't come with any great bankroll, probably just a few hundred that they had painstakingly set aside. The casino didn't comp them in any way, shape, manner or form. You held on to your meal pass, got your bus ticket stamped when you left, and that was that.

So the Mary Smiths and the Joe Blows of the world came and went. What kept them going was the belief (based on, who knew?) that they would have the next lucky pull and watch six months of paychecks roll out of the machine in a gusher.

When you got right down to it, the shrieking call of "jackpot!" for all to hear across the casino floor could be the most seductive sound of all...

But to get a sense of how a place like Mountainview came to be, it is necessary to have a partial knowledge of the casino industry. How the casinos are financed and who works there. Because Indian casinos certainly didn't spring up overnight.

Although casinos have been around for a long time, they didn't really start to catch on until the 1950s. Because casino financing has always been the key to getting one up and running.

In Nevada, for example, the history of casino financing was closely tied to what the public believed: namely that legality and organized crime were closely involved in the casino industry. For example, the early investment capital for a lot of the casinos was provided by families, individuals, or small groups of investors.

During the 1950s, Nevada had a terribly negative image particularly in southern Nevada where all the casinos were. But the profits were being raked in and it drew attention particularly among people of finance. Jimmy Hoffa, for example. Hoffa wanted in in the worst way. He used Teamsters pension funds to promote long-term loans to Nevada casinos.

Casino financing was also helped by adopting the widespread practice of equipment leasing. Most slot machines in casinos are leased. And it wasn't too long before conventional businesses got into the act. The Aetna Life Insurance Company got into bed with Caesars Palace for a long-term mortgage commitment to the tune of around $40 million.

Clearly, companies were seeing that since people liked to gamble so much, why not arrange the financing and have one big happy marriage? As long as everything was kept clean of course. And out of the hands of The Mob. Such was not always the case, however.

A sign that casino gambling was becoming more widespread and accepted than ever before, was the widespread use of what is known as "equity financing." In this case, publicly traded stock were issued as a source of financing for casinos. When New England casinos were in the planning stages, and John Andrews was anxious to get his hooks into the city, this was a hot issue.

But this cooled somewhat after a time. Financiers got cold feet and eventually, few new issues of casino stock were issued.

The bigger casinos can have anywhere from 500 to 3,000 hotel rooms, as a well as a broad variety of support facilities. But even though it may look like the casino wants to offer "all the comforts of home," the reality is one thing: the principal source of income, moolah, big green, buckaroos - is gaming revenue. And that means upwards of 60% of the total revenue. The rooms, food and beverages are pretty minor in comparison.

Because when you get right down to it, all the facilities of the hotel exist to serve the casino patron, either directly or indirectly. . .

The casino manager is the main honcho in the casino. He controls all the operations as well as the supervision of the various shift personnel. There are basically four areas that he supervises. One is the Slots. Under the slots category, you have the Slot Manager and all his assistants. Then there is the Keno Manager who is in charge of all shift supervisors and the writers and runners.

The Games Manager controls all the pit bosses for the tables, as well as the dealers, boxmen and stickmen. Finally, there is the Casino Host who spends almost all time meeting and greeting the high rollers and the not-so-high rollers that come through the doors nightly.

And since all that money that runs through there has to be accounted for somewhere, a casino has a very strict accounting organization. Now the people that are usually seen out front in the public areas are the pit clerks, change booth people and the dealers. As the money pours in from the betting, these people are responsible for making sure it gets taken care of right away.

The second level in this scheme are the cashiers in the cages, and those employees who issue casino credit or markers. The last group is one that is discreetly out of public view. They deal directly with the vault.

All casinos, when handling money, work on a very simple principle. That is, the more people that are involved in the processing and reporting of revenue - the greater the likelihood of fraud. In other words, theft with a capital T. This is why even though movies like "Casablanca" make it seem as if things run with such sophistication, in reality, there is a very tightly run, almost military precision to the way the loot is counted - and accounted for.

In fact, if a band of robbers decided they were bold enough to attempt a casino heist they might be surprised to learn that the money was'nt just laying around in one place. In point of fact it is laying around in a number of places.

Everything from Sports and Games to Keno, Bingo, Poker and Slots goes into the main cashier cage. From there it goes to the vault and from there it goes to the bank.

Which may explain why very few casinos have ever been robbed.

In many ways money accounting in casinos is like a football play where everyone laterals to each other. In the Casino Operations area, the dealers hand off to the pit clerks who hand off to the drop teams.

* * * *

Chapter 5
The Code Of Vito

Vito Leone certainly knew where the money went as he observed all the action from his office which had a two-way mirror. He had the latest in electronic equipment which meant video cameras that recorded every single dealer's actions.

It always amazed Vito that new dealers were so stupid. That is, they were trained for months and fully aware that they would be under constant surveillance. The smallest tic, hand gesture, cough, could be observed and magnified by security. Any attempt to steal would be cause for instant dismissal and prosecution.

Yet every year there were dealers who were brought before him for crimes ranging from petty theft of a few bucks here and there, to sophisticated larceny involving whole teams of people. He was amazed that people actually thought they could get away with stealing from him. The foolishness of people never ceased to amaze him. And each one was convinced that they had a foolproof method.

Take this kid Gary Matthews, for instance. He had developed an elaborate scheme that had an accomplice spill a drink all over the chips and in the confusion of mopping and cleaning up, substituted a counterfeit set of chips that were good enough to fool anybody.

Vito had to replay the tape several times to catch on to what Matthews was doing. He had him hauled in to face the music, and had held up the chips to the light.

"I've got to hand it to you, kid. These chips look real enough to fool the Gaming Commission." "Hey, Carmine," he said, gesturing to one of his lieutenants. "Didja ever see anything like this," he said tossing him one of the chips to examine.

Carmine took a close look. "I've never seen anything like this, boss."

At the sound of this joviality, Matthews allowed himself a slight smirk.

Big mistake.

Vito walked over to where Matthews was sitting and pulled up a chair next to him.

"Gary, I'm going to explain some things to you. Now, ordinarily when something like this happens, we would automatically hand you over to the authorities. So everything is on the up and up, you understand? But I'm going to make an exception in your case," Vito said in a kindly tone of voice.

Matthews looked at Vito with an expression that was somewhere between incredulity and gratitude. He was sure Vito would want to have his balls on a platter.

"No, first you're going to pay back the amount you stole - what five grand? We'll tack on the customary 20% which makes it a nice round number - $6,000. Take all the time you need just as long as I see it in two weeks."

Matthews started to protest and Vito cut him off with a wave of the hand. He leaned in close.

"After that - then I'm going to notify the cops about a thief who stole from me. Get him out."

That particular incident had gone pretty well. Dealers would always be suspect of cheating.

Patrons that cheated, though. That was another story. Take the incident that had happened the other day. Bad news, Vito thought. Really bad news, as he shook his head at the memory.

* * * * *

The day had begun fairly normally. He had spent most of it in his office looking over reports from his accountants to make sure his own men weren't cheating him. Vito had trained himself to be able to scan a report quickly. If something didn't look right, he quickly put through a call to one of the bean-counters. He knew he could trust them. A couple of unnaounced nighttime visits during dinnertime by a crew of very serious looking men in dark clothing took care of any idle thoughts of embezzling from Vito Leone.

Vito preferred not to have to resort to violence. His theory was that while violence was the great equalizer, yes, no doubt about that, it also should only be used as an absolute last resort. For it could come back to hurt you as well. That's why he felt the situation with Gary Matthews had worked out well - no fuss, no muss.

People who were convinced they were going to be hurt ran scared all the time. It affected their performance, ultimately their judgement might get shaky. Gangland violence in La Cosa Nostra was the stuff of epic legend. Vito much preferred the threat of implied violence.

He definitely had reservations about his men dealing in violence however. He knew that some of his crew thought that killing was the only way to solve the problem. Gino, for instance. A guy gives him a bad deal in a card game, and he wants permission to drop him? Now this was the kind of attitude that Vito didn't like. It was bad for business.

Just then there was a knock at his office door.

One of his pit bosses, Sal, knocked on the door. "Excuse me, Vito, there's something you might want to take a look at on Table 4."

"What is it?" Vito asked.

"Uh, it seems there's a creep, er, gentleman, at the table who is having quite a stroke of luck at blackjack," Sal said. "He's on his sixth winning game," he explained. "Too bad we're the ones who are losing money."

Vito walked over to the video camera and adjusted it to have a better look. Yes, he could see the guy Sal was speaking about, raking in his winnings. Vito believed in luck - up to a point. Could someone possibly win six straight games by cheating? And if he was, how the hell was he pulling it off?

"Let's go have a look," he said. Sal opened the door for him, and they walked downstairs.

Vito followed his man to table four and just when they arrived at the scene, there was a loud roar on cheers, another win for the second time. Sal motioned with a slight cock of his head for the signal to interrupt the guy's game, but Vito shook his head no. No, the first thing he wanted to do was get a good look at this guy's game.

A new dealer came in and proceeded to fill the shoe with brand-new cards, fresh out of the wrapper. The patrons ringing the table held a collective silence, as if they didn't want to break the spell of the winner.

The winning gentleman in question was feeling as if he couldn't miss. He had come to Mountainview with about a $1,000 which he figured to spread out evenly among dice and card games. Blackjack seemed to be his strong suit. He just stood there and waited for the cards to come to him.

He had practiced for this day - and now everything was unfolding very nicely, thank you very much.

The gambler looked at the cards he had been dealt. He placed them down flat. His hands then toyed with a tall stack of chips briefly, his fat fingers seeming to caress all his winnings.

While the other players were being dealt cards, he shivered as if cold. His hands went to slip on the jacket on the back of his chair.

Brought his hands back up the table and adjusted his cuffs.

That's it, thought Vito. It's in his sleeve.

The crowd, meanwhile, was intently watching the action. Everyone watched with breathless anticipation. This man was confident, you could see the sneer in his eyes, he wasn't bluffing, he was definitely going to win.

The guy bet very confidently with the cards he had. Once again the deal went around. This time the guy pushed out the remaining pile of chips towards the center of the table. With a small smile, he turned over an ace and a jack. He motioned to the table and scooped up his winnings.

Vito gave the guy a couple of minutes until the commotion died down. The last thing he wanted was for any rough stuff to happen in the middle of the casino on the busiest night of the week. No, no better to take this behind closed doors where he could have a little chat with the "lucky" gentleman.

This time, Vito gave Sal the go-ahead. Sal trailed the guy as he started to walk over to the cashier. He relieved the guy of his chips and set them down at the cashier's booth. waited until the commotion had died down a bit.

He escorted the guy around the side and up the stairs to Vito's office. He started to protest but Sal cut him off with a look.

When the guy saw Vito Leone sitting behind the desk, the color drained visibly from his face. Still, he attempted a little bit of a swagger as he sat down in the chair and waited for someone to speak.

He held his right arm perfectly still.

Vito had been sitting in profile, thinking about how he would approach this situation. He sighed inwardly. He wished he was home in bed with his fiery mistress, Maria. Instead, he had to deal with this bug.

"So, my friend, I see you have had some luck in my casino tonight," Vito said with a hint of amusement. "Tell me, do you play the game often?"

"No, Mr. Leone, I mean, ummm, yes, sometimes." The man was so nervous, he began to sweat.

"What's your name?"

"Catalano, Joe Catalano."

"Well, Mr. Catalano, for a guy who only plays the game sometimes, you sure do have a hell of a lot of luck," Vito said mildly. The leather chair creaked as Vito settled both feet on the floor and brought his manicured hands forward in a steeple gesture. "Or, is it skill? Eight straight wins - you tell me. Huh?"

Catalano just sat there, defiant, scared and sweating.

Vito knew a punk when he saw one. And sitting here in front of him was a world-class specimen. With a weary sigh, he motioned to Sal who walked over and turned on the video monitor and then the television to give it a larger picture.

Vito pushed a button on his remote and a familiar picture came to the screen. It was Joe Catalano in action. The camera focused in on some interesting body motions that his right arm was doing. Vito stopped the action, rewound it and enlarged the screen.

An extra card suddenly materialized out of Catalano's right sleeve.

Vito paused this scene and looked at Catalano expectantly.

"Now, Catalano, do you think I'm an ignorant man?" asked Vito. "Huh? Do you think that I am stupid?"

"No, Mr. Leone, no you're not stupid, no," Catalano said in a panic.

While he was interrogating Catalano, Vito had been casually slicing an orange into very careful, almost thoughtful slices on a plate in front of him. He took out a handkerchief, cleaned the blade of the gleaming switchblade, and shut it very deliberately.

"You're right, I'm not," he said with a silky sinister tone to his voice.

Vito tossed the knife over Catalano's shoulder to Sal who stood directly behind him.

Sal took a step forward and grasped the back of Catalano's shirt collar left hand, yanking it backward. With his right, he put the tip of the switchblade on the top of his collar and cut downwards in one long, forceful stroke. Both halves of Catalano's jacket and shirt fell away to either side. His arm instinctively went to grab at the short, metal one-armed bandit that was strapped to his right forearm as if to shield it from view.

Vito came around to the front of the desk in front of him and back-handed him hard across the mouth, drawing blood. He then turned to Sal and put his finger in his face. "Take him out of here right now. I don't want to see him or that arm again. When you're done I want a picture of that thing hangin' off his arm."

Vito turned back to Catalano who was sitting there cowering in the chair. "I'm not going to kill you. But I'm going to make sure you won't be able to use that arm again for awhile." He sat back down in his chair.

Sal lifted Catalano up and hustled him out.

* * * *

Sgt. Jack O'Brien shifted in his chair and looked out the window. Today was a quiet day around the station house. Not much going on. He supposed he liked that half and half. The first half would be the part of him that wanted the action and the second half would yearn for days when it was real quiet.

He and his men had managed to keep a lid on the Indian situation at the casino for awhile now. Once in awhile they would get a call to go out and settle some beef that someone had, but it was rare. Generally, things were pretty peaceable.

The only thing that bothered him were the clashes sometimes between the Mob goons and the Indians. That was a little more difficult to control. It was one thing to throw some drunken Indian in jail after he had gone on a bender and dented a few fenders.

However, it was quite another to go up against guys with automatic weapons. That he didn't care for. For a cop, guns made him nervous. He had seen too many accidents in his time to trust them. Usually people who thought they were so cocksure that they just did stupid things with firearms.

So when the Mob guys started reaching for their guns, O'Brien had to defuse the situation as quickly as possible. Usually he threatened them with jail, which they pretended to take seriously, but could tell they didn't.

O'Brien knew there was no love lost between the two groups. The Mob were basically mean bastards and racists when you got right down to it and tried to keep the Indians under their thumbs as much as possible. Maybe it was something that went back in their ancestry; O'Brien didn't know.

He had been a sergeant here for 10 years. He liked his job, it was quiet and he was able to raise his family here in relative peace and quiet. Which, when you got right down to it, was reason enough for living, he supposed.

He came from a family of cops, both his father and grandfather had been one. Of course, they came from a different era. An era in which you busted heads and asked questions afterward. An era in which the billy club and the night stick were your best friends. O'Brien could never understand that era.

It wasn't that he was afraid to use force. But using force and using violence were two different things entirely. Violence was when you sort of got off on things a bit. When you liked the way it felt to clobber a prisoner.

Force, on the other hand, was something that you used just to guide the prisoner, make them see the error of their ways. Yes, sometimes force had to imitate violence. But not very much, if O'Brien could help it.

So he maintained the balance in his district and was proud of the job he did. Nobody had many complaints. Nobody was trying to go after his badge. O'Brien knew that if he respected the badge and all it stood for, then he would get through his professional life just fine.

Today, though, was not going to be a good one...

It had started at around 11:30 in the morning when his patrolman, Mark

Mackovoy, called in with a report on a dead body that had washed ashore in the river.

Dead bodies were not usually something that you saw very much in O'Brien's district. When that happened, it sure had a way of getting your attention. O'Brien sat upright when Mackovoy came in and told him.

"Sarge, we got a floater that washed up," is basically the way that Mark said it to him. "Came in early this morning and we haven't been able to i.d. the body yet."

"Look bad?" said O'Brien.

"No, surprisingly it's pretty well-preserved. Guess whoever did it to this poor bastard must have done it recently." Mackovoy said matter-of-factly. "There's just one thing." Mackovoy sounded like he was hesitating.

"What is it, Mark?" asked O'Brien, his curiosity up now.

"Well, it's the weirdest thing. The body has a... listen, it's so grisly I can't even say it over the phone, Sarge. Maybe you better come down here as quick as you can."

Mackovoy sounded like a man who was going to lose his lunch. O'Brien could tell he was serious by the way he sounded.

O'Brien hung up and got going down to the river.

* * * * *

A little while later, he pulled up in front of his deputy's squad car. Thank God there was more than one car in the town for them to ride in. It would have been awfully hard for all the cops to ride in just one car.

O'Brien turned off the engine and got out. The sand underneath his feet felt grimy and was still wet from the morning mists. He walked over to where a knot of people were standing around what he guessed was the body.

As he came towards them, they parted and everyone of the men had a sort of ashen look on his face. O'Brien didn't like the looks of this one.

And then he looked down and saw why.

The body of Michael Stipiconti was white and all the skin around him was pale like a fish. It had that look that something gets when waterlogged for a period of hours. Which is sort of exactly how long Michael had been dead.

Then O'Brien saw the little handiwork that Vito and his boys had stuck on the side of his arm. By this time, the organ was shrunken and grey-looking. But there was no mistaking what it was and O'Brien turned away in horror.

Who and what was this? O'Brien didn't even know where to begin to look or ask questions. He forced himself to turn around and look at this grotesque sight again. But he knew that he would have to have the coroner come down and take a look.

He got on the squad car radio and asked for "Ol' Saw Bones," his affectionate name for Doc Considine. He had known the doc for years and in cases like this, he knew he could count on his judgement. This was simply too grisly for someone who didn't have the experience that Considine had.

The doctor responded right away and after some rough kidding about a certain part of the female anatomy, both men got down to business.

"So, what say, O'Brien?" said Doc Considine.

"Looks like a bad one, doc," O'Brien said, wishing that the doc could be here right now.

"How long has the body been dead?" Considine asked trying to get some kind of basic information.

"Doc, I really don't know," said O'Brien rather helplessly. He wanted to help him out, but the truth was—he didn't know.

"OK, O'Brien, I'll be down as soon as I can," said Doc Considine and hung up.

One hour later, Doc Considine pulled up in his battered old station wagon. He walked with a slight limp, the result of an injury in World War II.

After greeting everybody at the site, Doc walked over to the body and peered at it. It would start to decompose before too long and that was what Doc was worried about. A decomposed body would be of no use to anybody.

He got a pair of surgical gloves, then got out his tape recorder and went over the body from head to toe, taking time out to speak into the tape recorder. When he was done, he looked gravely at O'Brien.

"You know, of course, that this has got all the earmarks of a Mob hit?" Doc said to O'Brien.

O'Brien had suspected as much, but had kept silent till he got word from a medical authority such as Doc. Now he had confirmed his worst suspicions.

"You gonna drag it in an do an autopsy?" asked O'Brien to Doc as he was packing up his equipment.

"Guess so," Doc said, shrugging. "Can't just leave the body here. I'll call for an ambulance to pick it up and deliver it to my office. Lemme speak to you for a second over off to the side, privately."

O'Brien dutifully followed Doc over to the side out of earshot of the other men standing around.

"I didn't want the other men to hear this, but you've gotta talk to a certain person, Jack. And you know who that is, right?" asked Doc cautiously.

O'Brien thought he might mean Vito Leone and he dreaded the thought.

The reason he dreaded it was that Vito and O'Brien had crossed swords before, more than once as a matter of fact. O'Brien had brought in Vito for questioning on suspicion of a Mob-related hit. Seems a local city official had just "mysteriously" vanished without a trace and it had Vito's fingerprints all over it.

Nothing had ever been proved and he had been forced to let Vito go. But the animosity lingered between the two men.

With this, though, it seemed pretty dead obvious that someone had taken this poor kid and done a mean job of revenge on him.

To suddenly have your privates cut off like that and then have them attached to you like a dog—well it was a little too much for O'Brien.

But what did he have? He hadn't a shred of evidence, nothing to even remotely resemble sticking to Vito.

That was the dilemna for O'Brien. Vito always made sure that he was too slick and wiggled out of things just before O'Brien had the chance to tighten the noose around his neck.

He nodded without saying a word to Doc and walked back toward his squad car. He'd have to think long and hard before going over to Vito's and having a chat with him.

* * * * *

Chapter 6
Condo's Plan Of Redemption

Condo went down to the river to contemplate things. He couldn't believe things had gotten to this point. Decades ago, when Indians had been forced to rely on manual labor, they were lucky to get any type of throwaway job the white man didn't want. Condo had heard all the charges before: The Indian is lazy; The Indian is unreliable; The Indian is alcoholic.

Now the casinos had changed all that. Suddenly there was prosperity all around. But Condo was no fool. He knew that the Mob had put the money up. And that they were ready to control it through any means necessary. So the Indian had to make do with the arrangement between them.

But the Mob certainly didn't want their involvement advertised. That was definitely bad for business. And so every type of deal that they did, every type of delivery they made, it was all under a phony company name. They didn't want government inspectors down here snooping around. They didn't want the local authorities to start showing up unannounced.

When you really got down to it, the Mob didn't want so much as a parking ticket...

Condo had a theory that with the Mob you knew right out front what you were getting. None of them could be trusted and that was all right. At least you knew where you stood. He kept his involvement with them strictly at armslength.

But what about the Indians around him? Condo never directly suspected anyone who worked with him. That would make things to difficult on a day to day basis. But Condo knew that it was not outside of the realm of possibility that some of the men he worked with had been corrupted by the Mob. The Mob may have not liked Indians personally, but if there was a chance to get them on their side - they would. Particularly those Indians who could be counted on not to talk.

The Supremacy group, now that was another story. The Don Hatchetts of the world were quite prepared to die for their cause. It was as if somewhere along the way, the circuitry had shut off. As if there were wiring defects in their brain. Condo shivered at the thought.

Condo often daydreamed about how he would take down the Mob. Take back control of the casinos and have the control rest with his people. It seemed as if they had everything locked up tight. All ownership was in their name and the Indians were relegated to worker status. That would have to change. But how?

Condo remembered other meetings that the tribe had from long ago...

* * * * * *

The meeting took place at 2:00 p.m. on Friday, July 25. Several of the attendants believed that this was months, even years too late. It was held at the old gathering hall for two reasons. One, they needed to be quite sure no one would be eavesdropping. Two, it would represent what they were doing and who they were doing it for.

The old gathering hall was actually the back room of the trading post. There was access to the room from the post as well as a separate entrance in the rear of the small structure. The room held, at most, fifty people. There was one large table in the middle of the room. It was old and heavy.

The table had an infinite number of knicks and chips from the many knives that had been jabbed into the top of it. There was two long wooden benches on either side of the table. There was one small window next to the door and it produced the ventilation as well as the lighting for the room. The room was musty and reeked of abandonment. Dust covered the wooden floor that dipped in several spots.

Ten men sat at the table. They eyed one another and the seriousness of the meeting was evident. They had agreed to meet here in secret. No one was sure who had called the meeting. They had not been given that information in the letter requesting their presence.

After several awkward minutes of silence, an old man cleared his throat and stood up.

"Gentlemen, may I suggest that from today on, we address each other with our birthnames?"

A whisper began among the group. Excitement was building between them. They nodded in approval. The old man smiled.

"Good. Let's begin the meeting by introducing ourselves."

So the ten men who had known each other for many years began to get acquainted with their new identities. Richard Racine became Running Bear, Jason Strong became Lone Fox, Lucas Horne became Soaring Eagle, Michael Smith became Winding River, Keith Tallow became Tallest Tree.

After the introductions, the old man, Running Bear, stood again.

"Very well, we are born again. Now we must discuss the situation and develop a solution."

The room was silent. Eyes were moving and heads were downcast. The youngest man in the room stood up.

"There is only one solution. Every one here knows it. That is why it has taken so long for us to come together. There is only one solution. No one here wants to admit it. That is why your heads are down. That is the reason for the silence. There is only one solution and that is to eliminate the problem."

This had awoken the group. Voices were rising and the men had temporarily lost their order.

"Lone Fox, what do you mean, eliminate the problem?" someone asked from his seat.

Lone Fox looked at each man at the table and his glare stopped at Running Bear who was still standing.

"I mean kill Frank Palo." He said this and sat down. Now all eyes were on Running Bear.

"Lone Fox has a sharp mind. He sees all sides of the situation. That is why he has been invited here today. I fear he is correct. We must eliminate this problem. But, gentlemen, do you understand all sides of the situation?" Running Bear sat down. He closed his eyes and took a long, slow breath.

"If this begins, there is no end. There will be no bloodshed, ours as well as theirs. We must attack with full force. We must show no mercy. For they will have no mercy.

They will try to eliminate us and will not spare our women and our children. They will, in fact, target them to break our spirit. My brothers, no one can break our spirit if we are one."

Running Bear stood again and removed a long knife from its sheath. He held it up and displayed it to the group.

"This belonged to my father's father's father." He brought the knife down and held it to his left forearm.

"Join me in our quest for freedom." Running Bear ran the sharp knife over his skin and left a two inch bleeding wound. He passed the knife to Lone Fox who quickly sliced his own forearm. Lone Fox passed the knife to Night

Wind and turned back to Running Bear.

"I gladly join you Running Bear." The two Indians locked forearms and were now brothers. This ritual went on around the room until all ten men were related in blood...

* * * * *

Condo explored his options. They certainly weren't going to stage any kind of armed revolt against the Mob. That was for sure. Condo didn't want any bloodshed and to stage a bloody coup that would almost certainly end in death was out of the question.

Realistically, he knew that the Indians didn't really have enough hard, cold cash to buy the Mob out. The legislation that had so greatly benefitted them several years ago was in name only: On paper there were indeed Indian names which would look to the untrained eye as if they were the owners of the casinos.

But Condo knew that the Mob was the real owners. Only they would be very silent, discreet "partners." No, what the tribe needed, Condo decided, was a rich and powerful Indian benefactor. Someone with enough clout to be able to buy out the properties that Vito and his men "owned." A wealthy philanthropist would do just fine, he decided.

Only problem was, as Condo well knew, there weren't too many of those around. What wealthy, powerful Indian businessmen there were, were so discreet as to be invisible. And even then, there was no guarantee that someone would be interested. If he could locate such a man how could he interest him in helping the Indian cause?

For that matter, Condo wasn't entirely sure that an Indian owner would'nt want as much control as the Mob had now. He might have assimilated enough of the white ways to make dealing with him really difficult. There was just no way of knowing. No, Condo had to find another way to get at Vito - and fast.

* * * * *

Chapter 7
THOUGHTS AND SCHEMES

At that very moment, Tonya was sitting in her apartment and thinking of ways she could help Condo. She knew that he had a lot on his mind and wanted to help in any way she could. In a way though, she felt a little frustrated. She could only sit there and listen; the power to do anything, it seemed rested with other people.

She had always been a girl of simple tastes. Tonya had never understood the allure of the city. It held no mystery for her. Perhaps that was the Indian side of her yearning for the wide open spaces and freedom that came with it. In that way, Tonya shared Condo's passions for the great outdoors.

Often times they would pack a picnic lunch and head up to the high country. There she would unfold a huge spread: ham and chicken and salads of all kinds. Ooh, and those deviled eggs that he liked so much. She had watched one day in amazement as Condo had inhaled a dozen of them in something like 10 minutes flat. Whereupon, he got up, took a few steps, thought better of it and collapsed, where he lay for the rest of the day.

Tonya was a natural cook; that is a recipe was merely a starting point, by no means a finishing point. She had to merely take a glance at something once and she could improvise the rest as she went along. Condo had often remarked that someday they could buy a small restaurant and she could supervise the kitchen, occasionally jumping in to whip up a creation of her own.

Cooking was a little like love, Tonya thought. If you were skilled at it, men came back for more. To be fair, Condo had attempted several dinners for her. He approached the stove the way he approached his job; he attacked it. Consequently, while his meals tasted ok, they lacked the imagination that Tonya's had. Still, she had eaten with good humor and appreciated his efforts.

Tonya wasn't too sure about the restaurant idea. She cooked mainly for the enjoyment of it. The thought of standing behind a huge range, under pressure to churn out meals assembly-line style didn't appeal to her. Of course Condo had mentioned just supervising the kitchen staff. But Tonya had enough savvy to know that if things got tight, she might have to jump behind the range and start whipping out the food. No thank you!

Besides, Tonya fully expected to have her hands full with a pile full of kids in a few years. She had the instincts to be a good mother. She could think of nothing more worthy than to guide a child that she had brought into the world through to adulthood. To give that young person a chance to experience the glory and flavor of life as she had known it.

Tonya knew first-hand what it was like to be rejected and unsure of yourself. She knew emphatically that she did not want that to happen to her children.

Perhaps it was the influence of Condo, but Tonya too was a realist. She didn't want to make the mistake that she had seen other women make when it came to their marriages. While her children would be the focal point of her life, she had seen too many unions wither on the vine because the husband and wife had not paid sufficient attention to each other.

It was a sad pattern. In a way, it was as if the children and the husband were both competing for the mother's time. If you gave too much to the kids, the husband felt neglected. Dote on your husband too much, leaving the kids to fend for themselves - and watch them kiss you off when they hit their teen years.

No, the perfect answer Tonya thought, was to work as hard as you could raising decent, well-rounded kids. And when that was done, make sure there was enough quality time for you and your man. Which meant a cozy, romantic getaway every so often.

But all that was far in the future. Tonya was sure Condo loved her, but they weren't married yet, nor even engaged. That would surely change, she was sure of it, but right now, Condo was being squeezed by Vito and Hatchett - and that was the first order of business.

Tonya had no illusions about being able to reason with either of them. To Vito, Condo was just another Indian who could be manipulated. And while he knew that Condo could mobilize support among some of the tribes if push came to shove, he didn't perceive him as a threat. That could work to Condo's advantage, she thought.

Yet Vito didn't perceive her as a threat either. And that was good, very good.

Tonya started to pace around the small apartment, thinking this thing through. The easiest way to get to Vito was to co-opt him. That is, get him on your side where he trusts you implicitly. Tonya knew that Vito admired her looks. Whenever he stopped in the gift shop, his handshake was just a little too intimate, his comments a little too suggestive. Tonya had always smiled at him demurely (even while mocking him as an old fool under her breath). But that was as far as it went.

Tonya knew Vito's wife Sophia only slightly. An attractive woman in her early 50s, she had raised Vito's two sons, Antonio and Marco, but mostly stayed quietly in the background. Tonya tried to picture the scene:

Sophia: "How was your day, honey?"

Vito: "Oh, pretty normal. We had some problems with that plumbing company making their payments. Brasti took care of it; you know, broke a few fingers, some arms, smashed a few heads. It's better now. Say, when's dinner, I'm starved!"

Just normal everyday life in your typical mob family...

* * * * *

Tonya turned the flame under the pot on the stove as she thought of ways to get information from Vito that would be valuable to Condo. She had to find a way to make Vito trust her.

So, start with the obvious. She already had an advantage because he found her attractive. OK. But she had to get him in some kind of compromising position where he would begin to talk freely and openly about his business dealings. But how?

Tonya knew that Condo would never approve of this in any way, shape, manner or form. His soon-to-be fiance keeping time with Vito Leone? There was no way to plausibly explain it to Condo without risking losing him forever. He would never understand that Tonya was doing this purely dispassionately, purely with stone-cold emotion, to elicit information which Condo could then use to get back the casinos.

Ironically, it was one of the core values that Tonya loved about Condo - his traditionalism - that would prevent him from agreeing to this plan. He and his pride were not easily separated. Tonya wouldn't even think to try. It wasn't worth it. So whatever dealings Tonya had with Vito would have to be done strictly in private.

Several problems presented themselves right off the bat. Secrecy was the primary one. Condo could obviously know nothing about this. She knew that if she worked at him enough, she could get Vito alone. But people were bound to talk after a while, and what if word got back to either one?

Tonya tried to picture it: one of Vito's bodyguards casually mentions something to a cocktail waitress, who mentions it to the cook, who mentions it to the doorman who mentions it to ... Condo. But no, they would want to shield him from wild rumors like this. Because it couldn't possibly be true, could it? Not Tonya.

Tonya knew she couldn't afford to take the chance. If she became Vito's mistress - Tonya winced when she thought of it - all of Vito's men, the bodyguards, the lackeys, the gofers, all of them would have to be silenced. She would have to make it clear to Vito that if one word, one syllable got out about this, she would end it.

But what was she going after? Tonya knew from talking to Condo that while it looked as if the Indian tribe was the sole owner of all the casinos - the reality was that the Mob "owned" everything from the bathroom faucets to the lights in the ceiling.

She also knew that since there was a lot of publicity surrounding organized crime's interest in acquiring casinos, Vito sure wouldn't want to have attention drawn his way. Tonya tried to think this through logically. What would law enforcement agencies be most interested in? Illegal activities in casinos of course. But very hard to prove.

On the other hand, Tonya knew that the authorities merely assumed that the casinos were run by Indians. If they suspected that the casino had "partners" they might very well be interested in that. Somehow, Vito was controlling this whole operation through phantom companies, Tonya decided. She had to get Vito to talk about these companies. That was key.

After that, it would simply be a matter of finding out where he kept his records. She would turn them over to Condo who would then have the proof he needed to take everything to the proper authorities.

Tonya knew that Vito liked to stop by the gift shop occasionally. The next time he came there she would be ready.

* * * *

Chapter 8
A Man To Make You Afraid

After that grueling F.B.G. meeting yesterday, all Hatchett could think about was to eliminate the people that did not "belong." You were either in or out. Hatchett knew some of the things he planned in the future would require rigid discipline and cold-blooded determination. For that, he needed men who were going to be on his side. No waffling.

What it boiled down to was that Hatchett could tolerate no dissension in the ranks. Guys that got up and wanted to debate things? What kind of shit was that? There was only one type of thing that Hatchett knew and that was that his orders were to be carried out.

Hatchett was not a yeller or screamer. That just wore your lungs out got you an ulcer. No, thank you. Rather, he ruled with quiet intimidation. That did the trick quite nicely.

The trick was, as Hatchett saw it, the ability to have men who would do whatever it takes. All the way down the line. Hatchett knew from experience that most guys talked a good game at the bar. After a few pops they were ready to take on the world. It was easy to talk like this when the liquor was working inside you.

But in the cold light of day, how many guys had the cojones to actually kill someone? To stalk their prey, studying their patterns. Making sure that the victim was nice and relaxed and completely at ease.

Or better yet. Ingratiating themselves into the person's confidence. Talking with them, drinking with them, eating with them. Sharing good times. And still being able, when the time came, to damp it all down, get hold of that icy cold resolve and pop! eliminate them. Hatchett had always been fascinated by that type of individual.

More importantly, these were the kind of guys Hatchett needed on his side.

He had read with interest the story of the Federal Building that was bombed in Oklahoma City. Hatchett had no particular feeling about innocent people getting blown to kingdom come. Bad luck being in the wrong place at the wrong time was how he rationalized it. He was much more interested in this kid, Timothy McVeigh.

This McVeigh was one cool customer, Hatchett thought. To be capable of planning such mass destruction was truly remarkable. McVeigh was ex-army, a fact that Hatchett could relate to. He had the right temperament that was for sure.

Hatchett wondered whether or not McVeigh had ever murdered someone through assassination. That would be something to see. But he couldn't help the poor bastard now. He had to admit, though, when McVeigh had the guilty verdict come up against him, the boy didn't even flinch. Any way you looked at it, old Tim McVeigh was either going to be getting cooked in the chair or facing a life sentence in some hardass jail. Hatchett had done time once, and believe it: He never wanted to see the inside of a prison again.

He'd managed to get through it largely by plotting what his life would be like after the sentence was over. If he didn't have that to keep him going, he'd have just turned over every morning in his bed and said, fuck it.

He'd also managed to keep his ass to himself. No small thing, when you considered all the guys who turned queer in the joint. All that time with no women, it did strange things to a man's head. Oh, he got rubbed up against enough and more than once he had been cornered. But Hatchett had always looked them right in the eye and said, "You stick it in there; there ain't no guarantee it's going to come out looking the same, partner."

The guys who rubbed up against him and wanted to initiate him, laughed. Then thought: wait, what could he do? Then stood back and looked him up and down - spit at him, and moved on.

Hatchett had faced them down - and won. They simply shunned him, never bothering with him anymore.

Hatchett was fascinated by strength. The kind it took to pull the trigger and watch less than an ounce of lead explode out of the barrel of a gun and tear into the flesh of another human being, mortally wounding them. And then to pull the trigger again and again without remorse or reflection. As many times as it took till the body lay still.

Trying to fill his head with some sort of idea, Hatchett's eyes began to roam over the disheveled room he called his office. He lived about 30 minutes outside of the nearest town, in a small, ramshackle house he had bought with his savings from the Marines. He still remembered the grimace on the real estate agent's face as he showed him the place. Hatchett got the feeling they weren't selling him the place so much as unloading it and fleeing.

Which was fine with Hatchett. The more private and slovenly the place - the better he liked it. Kept visitors to a minimum was how he looked at it.

Upon entering the house, there was a kind of creepy feeling to it. A visitor would be tempted to hold his nose up as if to catch the scent of something. That was accurate, it was the smell of Hatchett's old, musty "office." A better definition would have been a room filled with paper, that threw in a desk and a chair as an afterthought.

Whichever corner of the room you walked to, there were stacks of old, yellowing, decaying newspapers stacked five to six feet high. Reach in deep to the middle of one of the piles, and you might pull out news from 1979. Go over a little further and you'd trip over 1983 or 1991.

Don Hatchett was never someone you'd confuse with a scholar. Hell, he barely got through high school. But he was an omnivorous reader. Only about murder, though. And violent crimes and hijackings, things of that sort. He couldn't get enough of them. But dammit, he just never got around to throwing out the rest of the newspaper. And so they sat year after year, a monument to recycling if ever there was one.

But his "office" wasn't where Don Hatchett was at his most creative. No, that would be the basement.

A trip below revealed a large room almost totally made of concrete. Down a rickety, poorly-lit flight of stairs and you came to a remarkably neat stone lair. Hatchett was as neat and fastidious here as he was slovenly just one flight up.

The place was full of building materials, wood and hand tools of all size and shape. Then there were the rows of alarm clocks and timing devices. Hatchett had quite a collection, yessir. As you got further and further you noticed the spools of wire, all colors all sizes.

You sort of got the feeling Hatchett wasn't using all this stuff for home improvement.

No, Don Hatchett had one thing on his mind. The removal by force or violence if necessary, of the power structures that were oppressing the Indian tribes.

Which wasn't to say that Hatchett was particular when it came to using force or violence. He was an equal-opportunity kind of power supremacist. He was the type that would have fit in any era. It just so happened that he had been born Indian. Had he been born Israeli, he might have joined some of the extremist Zionist groups. If he was born black, he would have joined the Black Panthers. Hatchett basically didn't like authority of any stripe and the Mob was now, unfortunately, square in his sight of vision.

Hatchett didn't have anything against the Mob, per se. These were people who were out to make a profit like everybody else. The fact that they were suppressing his people was incidental. If it wasn't the Mob, it would have been some other group, to his way of thinking.

The Mob just happened to be the latest group that had figured out a foolproof method to cheat the Indians out of their hard work. In the parlance of casinos, history had dealt the Indians so many bad hands it was as if they came to expect it after a while.

No, he had nothing personal against anyone in the Mob. That is, with the exception of one gray-haired old bastard.

One Vito Leone, that is. It seems that Vito and Hatchett's paths had crossed years ago when Hatchett was working as a low-level flunky for Vito. And it all involved a woman...

Val was her name, a sexy, smoldering piece of ass that belonged to Hatchett. That is, until Vito got his hands on her.

She had started hanging around the casinos years ago when Hatchett was toiling away for Vito as a glorified errand boy. But even then, he gave off a kind of brute-strength aura that Val had picked up on. She started waiting around till he finished his shift and one night surprised him in the parking lot with the offer to have a drink.

They had settled in at a local hangout frequented by young Indians. Right from the git go, Hatchett noticed that while she had Indian blood in her, there was no particular love lost for the white man.

"I'm kind of surprised to be sittin' here with you," he said, as he settled into a booth opposite her. He was pleased to see that she could hold her booze as well as a man. The shots of Wild Turkey and beer chasers flowed freely.

"Well, I've noticed you around," Val said, as she took off her jacket. She was a beautiful girl who had raven-like hair that she wore long. And she had the body to match: Generous, full breasts, a slim waist and beautiful legs. What surprised Hatchett was that she was interested in him.

Donald T. Hatchett was, to be charitable, not exactly what you'd call a ladies man. He had a trim, muscular physique - but it was his eyes and granite-like stare that repelled women usually. The eyes of a serpent, cold and dark. But Val hung on every word. And Hatchett kept on talking.

He saw that she had two qualities right away that he liked. One, she disliked authority in all forms. (A plus for the lady). Number two, she seemed interested and more than willing to go to bed with him. Perfect woman, as far as he was concerned. But then Hatchett had never been interested in taking the time to discover the mystery of a woman.

When they came together it was with a roaring fury. After the third outing at the bar, Hatchett said, rather casually, hey, why don't we take this shindig over to my place?

Once inside, they could barely contain themselves, ripping and clawing at each other, mouths locked, hands snaking over hips and chests and asses and tits. It was a race to the finish line to see who could get the other's clothes off faster. Hatchett grasped Val by her back legs, hoisted her up and threw her on the bed.

So much for foreplay...

He entered her immediately, savagely and brutally, pounding away for all he was worth. Val arched her back and took it, soft moans giving way to screams of pleasure. Their rhythm pounded together over and over till finally there was a shudder and a blessed release.

Afterward, Hatchett lay quite still. Catching his breath, he thought, shit, this chick is good.

And then an odd thing happened to him. For the first time since he began doing the dirty with Cindy Krause in 9th grade, he reached over and smoothed his partner's hair. He adjusted the blanket around her naked shoulders so she wouldn't be cold. He kissed her softly on the cheek. And then, in the ultimate sign that he had lost his mind, he snuggled close to Val.

Something clearly had moved Donald T. Hatchett.

He got her a job as a hostess in the casino, partly because she needed it and partly so he could keep an eye on her. The truth of it was, when it came to women, Hatchett didn't trust any of them.

Val, though, Val was different. She measured up to him in many ways and always told him the truth. For the first time in his life, Hatchett relaxed the tight coil that he always kept himself under and let Val in.

They began dating. It was a good thing Val liked the same things as Hatchett because their "dates" were usually confined to bars and racetracks. The kind that cars went around on.

Hatchett was a nut about cars and motorcycles. He had haunted the local racing track for years. Stock cars or motor cross, it didn't matter. He liked the action and he liked the speed. Hatchett at one time had even tried his hand at motorcross racing. But man, those bikes bruised your kidneys and shook your brains something awful!

He liked the sport because danger was always around every corner. It was man pitted against machine and that was fine by Hatchett's way of thinking. To prove to the world that you could guide a mechanical machine around lap after lap - and walk away with not a scratch on you, hey, that was pretty heavy-duty stuff. And it was far better than some other sports which guys liked for some unknown reason to Hatchett. He considered some of them sports for pussies.

Val, for some odd reason, was also drawn to the track. She liked the action and so when Hatchett asked her to come along, she more than willingly went. Of course it was out of the question to hang out with some of the drivers -

Hatchett was way too jealous for that.

He couldn't stand it when guys in the bar would make a pass at her, sometimes when he was no more than two feet away from her! Some guys had balls, that was for sure. When that happened, Hatchett had more than once just stood up, fists balled, veins in his neck bulging out, and the guy got the message - fast. Val always looked up at him beseechingly as if to say: cool out, it's ok.

Hatchett thought a lot about asking Val to move in with him. He was by nature a loner, but that could change. Truth to tell, he was getting a little sick of living alone. With Val it might be possible to have a life together. They both liked the same things, and man, that chick was wild in the sack! After a time he might even be able to confide in her his dream of having a little business as a mechanic, fixing motorcycles.

Hatchett had it all figured out until Vito came into the picture.

* * * * *

It had started when Vito and his boys walked into the casino late one evening when Val was on her shift. They went into the lounge and sat around ordering drinks. It was really the first time Vito had noticed Val, and his eyes followed her discreetly around the room.

And Val, it seemed, was doing nothing to discourage the attention. And just about this time, Hatchett walked through the door over to the table.

As Hatchett crossed the expanse of carpet toward the group he very clearly saw Vito hand her a one-hundred dollar bill - and a white note underneath with something scrawled on it. Val palmed the money and the note, gave him a mischevious smile and turned to go. It was at that moment that she saw Hatchett and her face reddened.

"Mr. Leone, your wife asked me to tell you that... uh, well, she's going out with her friends and she'll, uh, see you later on tonight," stammered Hatchett, who had to control his temper in front of his boss.

"Uh huh. OK, kid, you delivered the message," Vito said, never taking his eyes off Val. He then turned to face Hatchett. "That's it? You got anything else?" he asked.

"Uh, no sir," Hatchett said as Val walked off with the tray of drinks. He couldn't even look at her as he hurried out.

Later on that night at the bar, he confronted her about Vito handing her the note.

"Hey, I didn't ask him to, your boss man surprised me with it," she said somewhat defensively.

"I don't want you fuckin' around with him, you hear me," Hatchett said angrily, grabbing her by the arm and shaking her.

"It's no business of yours what I do, asshole! You don't own me," she said as she got out of the booth and ran toward the door.

Before he could catch her, she ran out to the parking lot, got in her car and sped out, scattering gravel in all directions. Goddamn her, he thought. He had no idea whether or not Vito had gotten to her.

A few nights later, his questions were answered. Hatchett had been on his way up to Vito's office to deliver some receipts from the cashier. He usually just picked them up and dropped them off to Vito's secretary, not really looking at them.

But tonight when he ascended the stairs and walked towards Vito's office, he noticed that she was not there. For that matter none of the muscle that Vito customarily surrounded himself with were there either. The hallway was dimly lit and as Hatchett tiptoed to the door, he heard a woman's laughter. He felt a cold flush.

It was Val all right. And she was inside with Vito.

Hatchett crept around to the other side of the window that framed Vito's large office. He could dimly make out two figures on the couch through the slit in the blinds. Vito was reclining on the big leather couch, still dressed in his suit and tie. Between his legs was Val, crouched on her knees, her head bobbing up and down rhythmically.

He could hear Vito saying, "Yeah, that's great, baby. Oh, that mouth - that's where your talent is, baby."

Hatchett felt all the sinews of his muscles go taut with uncontrollable rage, as he slowly backed away from the door. Taking a quick look around to make sure he wasn't being watched, Hatchett crept back down the hallway, revenge on his mind.

All the while, the surveillance cameras watched him watching them.

* * * *

Chapter 9
RUSSIAN DREAMS

Hatchett lay there in bed thinking about that night. Vito had taken the one thing from him that could have made Hatchett whole again. He had used his money and his power to seduce Val. Oh, she may have been a willing participant all right. Women could not be trusted as Hatchett well knew. But it was Vito who set his sights on her. And she had succumbed.

Well, fuck her. And fuck him too. They'd both pay. But none more than Vito.

He fell asleep and dreamed. In his dream, he is walking into the office of the Russian leader.

Hatchett is sitting waiting to go into the Russian leader's office. All around him are photographs of the Soviet Union. Photographs of Moscow, shots of the tremendous Russian factories and the wheat fields that seem to go on for miles and miles. Hatchett has flown here on a mission: to secure nuclear weapons for mass destruction. Finally, he is ushered into see the Russian leader:

Hatchett is momentarily awed at meeting such a famous world leader. Russian leader sits behind a massive desk, which looks like any powerful CEOs desk except for one ominous thing: A red phone sits squarely to the right of the chair. There are no buttons on it, and it seems to glow. Hatchett wonders what it could be for, but he has a pretty good idea. The launching of missiles from Soviet silos buried far out in the fields. The solemn expression on the Russian leader's face wipes all thoughts from Hatchett's mind about asking what the phone is. Russian leader gestures for Hatchett to sit down and places his arms in front of him as he gets right to the point.

"Don Hattchet, my advisors tell me you are from America and you have flown a great distance to purchase nuclear arms from country. Is that correct?"

"Yes, Russian leader. I think we both share a common interest, you need money and I need nuclear technology."

"No, Mr. Hatchett, let me correct you about that. Our common interest, as you say, is that your government destroyed your nation by stealing your land. Now in my country, the government was destroyed but we had been a very powerful country for years. Now we are reduced to relying on handouts by the United States. But let me tell you that I do not believe in my new government, so I still run the red army and our special forces."

"We could have had a deal with the government of Iran to sell them nuclear weapons but your government put a stop to that. Now I am interested to know just exactly why it should be in my interest to sell nuclear arms to you?"

"Russian leader, I will avenge all the atrocities the United States has done to your country and mine."

"And how exactly do you proposed to accomplish this, Mr. Hatchett. That's rather a tall order wouldn't you say? Even for someone as determined as you."

"Russian leader, I can transport any item into my country because of the Indian fair act that was signed in 1988, so it won't be hard for me to smuggle in these arms. It will be easy to bribe someone at customs. For that matter, we can pick the weakest port of entry and use it. It's done all the time in the United States."

"Secondly, my people and I are in the process of building bomb shelters in my country to be able to withstand a nuclear attack. I will set up the nuclear bombs in Washington, New York and all the major areas in the United States."

"Very well and good, Mr. Hatchett. I do have other questions, though. For example, after you ignite these nuclear weapons, what are you going to do?"

"Russian leader, it is true that it will take some time for the nuclear radiation to dissipate. It could take as long as a few weeks. Once that is over, I can take my party out in nuclear suits and take back my country. We will be in a position to start over."

"The leaders in power are dangerously naive, Russian leader. They thought that once the Cold War was over with Russia, no one would try and take their country over."

"The leaders have short memories, Russian leader. They should read their history books. If they did, they would remember that even Rome, which was the greatest civilization on earth, got fat and lazy. And they paid the consequences for it."

"It was the same thing with Greece. They had all the culture and all the armies and all the advanced civilization. There was no greater or more advanced country of its time than Greece. But they got fat and lazy. Every great nation has gotten fat and lazy and has been taken over. Now it is the Americans turn for they are fat and lazy. They let their national defense get slack."

"All right, very well, Mr. Hatchett. These are my terms: I will need $100 million dollars before I deliver, and another $100 million on delivery. For this you will get a dozen of the most powerful Triton nuclear warheads manufactured. Where and when do we transport your weapons, Mr. Hatchett?"

"Russian leader, I am going to set up delivery of the weapons before the fourth of July on the year 1997. We will give the Americans a fourth of July they'll never forget. That will give me a year and eight months to build my bomb shelters and get my tribe ready. I will give you $100 million on commencement and $100 million on delivery."

"Mr. Hatchett, we have a deal. Thank you for coming in. Have a safe journey back to the United States."

* * * *

Vito Leone walked through the front door of the gift shop and fixed his eyes on some of the beautiful things on the shelves. Tonya had seen him walk in and whispered to her part-time assistant, a young college student named Mary, to watch the register for a second. She was going to help a customer.

"Mr. Leone, how are you today! So good to see you," said Tonya in a seductive tone of voice that even surprised her.

Vito straightened as she came over to greet him. Tonya had on a leopard-print miniskirt, high black heels and a Danskin top which perfectly accentuated her beautiful breasts. Her flowing hair was styled just perfectly.

She was dressed to kill - and had one Vito Leone in her sights.

Vito took the whole view of the sleek, sexy Tonya in, and unconsciously his hand found his silk tie and smoothed it. He then ran the palms of his hands along the sides of his hair. He was a little surprised. Up to this point, Tonya had only hinted at her potential with clothing that revealed just enough and usually came down on the side of prim.

But the girl who slinked towards him was definitely giving out some powerful body language. What was this?

"Tonya," he nodded to her. "How are ya. It's been awhile. I, uh, just stopped in to pick out some stuff, ah, gifts, for my wife's folks. They love it. Any suggestions?"

Tonya stood there and thought: I know damn well you didn't come in to browse through all the cheap crap on these shelves, mister. No, she thought.

She went up to him and picked out some glass figurines from the middle shelf. "Here, you might like these," she said. "They're blown in the shape of cats. Do you like cats?" she asked in a light tone of voice.

"Yeah, they're great," Vito said, thinking that he despised the little bastards. Tonya was standing very close to him, and Vito could feel the heat she was giving off. What gives, he thought? This had certainly never happened before. He then pulled himself together and remembered who he was and where he was.

"Well, listen, Tonya, it was nice seeing you," said Vito, conscious of the time. "Give Carmine here a half-dozen of these, uh, figurines. He'll pay you for them. Wrap 'em up nice, huh?"

Tonya called over her shoulder for Mary to come over and take the order. As she walked over, Tonya said: "I was just on my way out to grab a bite to eat. Would you... care to join me, Mr. Leone? There's a marvelous little Napolitan restaurant called Dante's not too far from here. Excellent calimari. But I'm sure you know it."

He did know it. But Vito Leone was a man who lived with a very highly-tuned antenna. He had the equivalent of a mental surveillance going on all the time. Meaning that whenever a situation presented itself, the first thing Vito thought about was who was going to find out. In this case, his dear wife Maria came quickly to the forefront of his mind. Uncomfortably quickly, he thought.

"Let me have a word with Tony here, ok?" Vito said.

"Sure, I understand," Tonya said with a mischievous smile. "I'll help Mary get the figurines for Carmine," swiveling to walk back to the counter, giving Vito a discreet view of her curves from the back.

Vito motioned for Tony to come over. A short, tightly-wound, muscular man, Tony sprang from his position lounging against the door and came over. Vito told him he wanted him to go over to Dante's and case the joint. To see if there were any "surprise visitors."

* * * *

Thirty minutes later, they were motoring over the short distance to Dante's. The limo ride had been at Vito's insistence.

While Vito talked on the car phone to one of his lieutenants, Tonya took the time to plot out what she would say. For her plan to work, it was essential that she convince Vito that she and Condo were finished. Or at least that his attention wasn't wanted anymore. There could be not the slightest hint of suspicion on his part. Tonya had no illusions about Vito's power, or his vengeance if double-crossed.

"So, the last I heard, you were involved with one of my main dealers, Condo Cherokee. I don't suppose he'd like to join us, whaddya think?" Vito said with a slight chuckle as Carmine and Tony laughed along with their boss.

"Well, that would be difficult, Mr. Leone, particularly since we're not involved anymore. No, I can definitely say Condo Cherokee wouldn't want to be within 100 miles of this joint." Tonya sat back and took a long sip of her iced tea, waiting for his reaction.

"Not involved, huh?" said Vito. His ears pricked up at that.

"No, Condo doesn't understand the realities of the casino business. He still thinks the wealth should be spread out among the tribes. He doesn't understand that the casinos are there to make a profit. Putting it bluntly, Mr. Leone, he's just naive." Tonya was surprised at how easily this was rolling off her tongue!

So, in fact, was Vito. This was a surprise. He had heard through the casino gossip mills that Tonya and Condo were very much an item. So now to hear that she was interested in dropping him like yesterday's news—well, that made him sit up and take notice.

Personally, he didn't care one way or the other about Condo. Vito knew that the other Indians looked up to him and respected him - which meant he was valuable to keep around to help keep down mini-revolts from time to time. Beyond that, he didn't care if the guy lived or died.

Although now that he thought about it, Vito had had his own problems with the bastard. Like the time he got into it with a member of his crew. Vito would remember that incident for a long time...

It all started the day that Vito had sent Condo over to talk sense to a couple of rebellious Indians. He had been hearing stories about work stoppages and so forth, largely because the Indians were unhappy with their working conditions. This had been a sore spot for as long as Vito could remember. He depended on cheap Indian labor to keep things running smoothly.

The problem was that his crew was cracking down a little too hard on them. Pushing them to work longer hours, withholding pay for sick days, things like that. Vito was certainly no humanitarian when it came to Indian rights—but he knew it was bad for business to have them so unhappy. So he had sent Condo over to smooth things out. Condo could communicate with them directly where a member of his crew would just have lost patience.

Just to be on the safe side, however, he had Joey Vitale and Marco Vignetto keep Condo company—just to make sure he didn't give away the store. Later on that day he was sitting in his office when Marco was suddenly buzzed in:

"Excuse me, boss, but I think you better see this downstairs," he said, slightly out of breath. "Joey and that crazy Indian Condo are ready to square off."

"Now what the hell..." Vito stood up, smoothed his lapels and strode out of the office as Marco held the door.

When he went downstairs, he saw an angry Condo and an equally angry Joey Vitale nose to nose, jawing at each other. Surrounding them were a few Indian braves nervously backing Condo up. They were outnumbered, though, by his crew of at least 12 guys. Vito was half afraid that at any moment, his boys would reach for the hardware and come out blasting. This had to be stopped—and quickly before he had a full-scale riot on his hands.

"Hey, HEY!," Vito yelled. At the sound of his voice, both men snapped to attention and the room fell silent. You could hear a :44 magnum shell casing drop.

"All right, I want some answers. Cherokee, I sent you over to straighten out your people and now you're in Joey's face? You'd better back off, boy, or I'll come down on you so hard you won't know what hit you."

Condo took in Vito's words, but his eyes never left Joey's. "Mr. Leone, I don't start trouble. But if some comes looking for me—well, I'm going to protect myself. Joey here should really learn to watch his mouth—before it gets him hurt."

Joey's eyes lit up anew with fresh hatred at this crack. He made a motion to grab Condo's shirt, which Condo deflected with a flick of the wrist, nearly knocking Joey sideways. He recovered quickly and this time pointed his finger at Condo. "Listen, you dirty Indian asshole. I'll talk to you anyway I want, anytime. Far as I'm concerned, it would have been fine with me if we'd massacred you years ago! Save us all a lot of trouble!"

Vito stepped between the two men. "All right, since you both can't wait to get a piece of each other, there's only one way to settle this."

Condo and Joey looked at him expectantly.

"You're gonna settle this man to man—in the ring."

* * * *

Condo gazed around the gym till his eyes located the worried face of Tonya. She sat huddled in the fourth row of the tiny amphitheater. He couldn't believe this was actually going to happen.

At first he thought Vito was kidding—but one look in Joey's eyes told him Vito was dead serious.

He'd gotten the word for the time and the place a few days later when he picked up the phone at Tonya's place.

"Cherokee?" said a low voice filled with menace.

"Yeah, it's me," Condo answered.

"Atlas Gym. 7:00. Thursday night. All the equipment you'll need'll be in the locker room. You're the main even, redskin."

"Alright," Condo said.

"Don't forget to bring your balls with you."

"Hey—"

The line went dead.

So here he was, exactly one week later, feeling faintly ridiculous in his boxing trunks, shoes. mouthpiece, and what seemed like the most enormous pair of gloves ever invented.

Condo was worried sick that Tonya might do something to stop the fight. To that end, he had instructed all his friends to make sure she didn't leave the stands. If that meant gluing her to the seat, so be it.

He looked across the ring to where Joey was yukking it up with all his goombas. In terms of weight and height, Joey was at a definite disadvantage. Condo had at least 4 inches and 40 pounds on him. A heavyweight vs. a higher class middleweight.

He could see the talking and occasionally gesturing to him. They seemed to be speaking in low, intense tones, difficult to make out. Probably wondering how many rounds this was going to go. He wished he could hear them.

Actually, he should have wished for headgear.

For Joey's part, at that moment, he as wishing for a smaller opponent.

"Man, he's a lot bigger with his shirt off," said Joey anxiously as he looked across the ring at Condo's sculpted shape. Some of the cocky bravado fell away when he realized Condo might actually hit him. And keep hitting him.

Vinnie slapped Joey's face lightly to get his attention. "Hey, bro, pay attention. Now listen, this ape is way too big for you—I don't know what the hell you were thinking when you got into it with him—anyway, you ain't gonna beat him, so we gotta think of something else, fast!"

Joey gestured impatiently. "What, what?"

"I'm thinkin', I'm thinkin'."

Joey's other buddy, Petey, leaned in suddenly across the ropes and snapped his fingers. He kept his voice low. "I got it! Give it a round or so and then do a bites his ear off on him. Chomp a piece of his ear off!"

Both of them looked at him in amazement.

"Yo, that's disgusting, man!" Joey said. "Hey, it's one thing for Bites his ear off to play cannibal—but he's an animal anyway. No way am I doing it!"

Vinnie and Petey both looked at Joey solemnly. "Hey, not for nothing, Joey," said Vinnie. "But from the looks of this, this Cherokee is gonna pound you into raw hamburger meat, bro. I saw him pound a heavy bag at a gym one time. He's got a hell of a left hook for a nobody. My advice: Go for the ear."

At that moment, they were interrupted by Vito who came by to wish Joey luck.

"Hey, Joey, are you all right?" Vito asked.

"Sure, boss," Joey replied. He didn't sound very certain, but managed to stitch a grin on his face.

Vito looked at him for a long moment. He sighed. "Alright, let's get this over with." He stepped down from the ring and took his seat. By this point, the amphitheater was filled with a small but determined band of braves silently cheering Condo on. The other side was filled with assorted crew members and other wiseguys who had wandered in for fun.

Hansen, who was acting as referee, motioned for both Condo and Joey to approach the middle of the makeshift ring. They came to the center, both a little unsure of what the other one would do. Stripping a man of his street clothes had a way of reducing him in size and threat: Joey looked like a midget next to Condo.

Vito thought: This sure ain't Ali-Frazier.

Hansen motioned both men. He put his arms around them and said in a low voice, out of earshot of Vito: "Look, I don't know shit about this. Just come out swinging and get it on, alright?"

"Yeah, that's alright with me," said Joey, grimacing through his mouthpiece. "How about you, redskin?"

Condo made no reply. Instead, he reached over and tapped Joey on the head with his glove.

Hansen blew a whistle and the bout began.

Tonya wrung her hands nervously in the stands.

Both men came out, bobbing and weaving slightly. Joey tried to land the first punch, a wild roundhouse right that glanced off Condo's shoulder. He looked at it like a lion might look at an annoying flea. Condo cautiously threw a left-right combo which landed on Joey's shoulder and stomach. It wasn't hard, but it rocked Joey. He looked up in consternation and anger.

Joey bounced on his feet and tried to aim for Condo's jaw. He missed by a foot. When he was wide open, Condo clocked him with a short right. Joey stumbled and nearly went down. For the next minute they circled each other warily and no more punches were landed by the time Hansen blew his whistle, ending the round.

Condo walked back to his corner, where a brave named Frank Proudfoot tended to him, wiping off the sweat.

Joey walked back to his corner where Vinnie and Petey immediately got in his face.

"What the fuck is going on, Joey?" asked Vinnie. "This guy's gonna pound you into stromboli, you keep up this crap. Do what we said, do a Bites his ear off on him!"

Joey was breathing hard. Damn, he didn't know he was this much out of shape. He tried to protest: "Hey, I can handle this putz. I just gotta... just gotta find—"

"Shutup, Joey," Petey said. He grabbed his head with both hands. "Take him out."

Joey nodded and squared himself.

Hansen blew the whistle for the second round.

Joey came out and immediately went in for a clinch. Condo shook him off.

One or two weak exchanges were landed, and again Joey went right for a clinch.

Only this time, Condo could feel his face probing into the side of his...

This time he felt Joey's teeth scraping against the side of his face close to his ear...

Condo shook him off, this time more angrily.

He started to feel uneasy. The tempo was different. Joey was different. He was—he was—Condo tried to clear his head.

And then it came to him: Joey was trying to bite his ear off! The little shit was actually going to turn cannibal on him!

Condo looked up and everything suddenly seemed in slow motion. He looked at Vito, he looked at Vinnie and Petey, he looked at all the goons surrounding the ring. Looked right into their eyes and suddenly had the terrible thought that if he died in here tonight, they would just as soon lock the doors on the rest of his people.

Condo gave a silent warrior ROAR to himself deep within his proud chest. They would not kill him!

As Joey came in for the clinch for a third time, his teeth bared, the hatred showing on his squirmy little face, Condo took dead aim and launched a right uppercut that cut right through Joey's pathetic stance and rocked him backward on his feet. He followed it with a left hook that slammed into Joey's body and then a right cross that took him out on his feet.

As Joey went down, and the small crowd erupted, Condo heard that one magical voice soaring above the din and the smoke, the voice of Tonya screaming: "Knock him OUT, baby!!!" He looked out into the crowd to see her raising her fists triumphantly as if he had just knocked out Evander Holyfield. He blew her a kiss and then went to a neutral corner...

... Yeah, Vito reflected as he shook his head at the memory, he didn't care if Condo Cherokee lived or died.

He remembered where he was. "And you, Tonya, what are you?" Vito asked as he leaned across the table and looked into her face.

Tonya composed herself and said in a voice filled with pure honey: "Someone who is very attracted to men with power - and know how to use it."

She left Vito to chew on that as she pushed back her chair and excused herself to go to the ladies' room.

Once inside, she paced and thought furiously. It's going well, she thought. But I have to be just the right mixture of pathos, intrigue and ambition. If I overstep my bounds, Vito will smell a rat and I'll be toast, she thought. She squared her shoulders and said to the mirror: In that case, just make sure you don't, girl!

When she stepped out of the ladies room, she was composed and ready to go back to the table. She did not want to draw so much attention to herself that she took it away from the business at hand. That was a concern.

She was not prepared for what happened next...

As soon as she sat down, Vito launched into his sales pitch.

"You like this restaurant, Tonya?" Vito asked as he casually slid his chair a little closer to hers. A little TOO close for Tonya's comfort.

"Yes, Mr. Leone, it's great," Tonya said warily. What else could he want, she wondered.

"Yeah, I come here a lot," Vito said reflectively. "I mean, I could go pretty much anywhere I want in this town. But I always come back to Dante's. You know why? I'll tell you. Cause' they got good food and good service. That's it, nothing more. And more importantly they deliver the goods.

Hey, when you get right down to it, Tonya, in life that's what it's all about, you know? Delivering the goods. And for that, you gotta have talent. Oh, everybody's got talents. They just gotta know what they are. You get what I mean?"

Tonya had no idea where Vito was going with this, but just to keep the conversation moving along—and possibly to keep attention off her real plan—she nodded. "Sure, Mr. Leone, I know what you mean," she said carefully with just the right touch of eagerness in her voice.

"I'll tell you why I'm thinkin' these thoughts out loud, Tonya," Vito said expansively.

He lined up his chair so that he could look her square in the eye. He measured his words carefully.

"To tell you the truth, Tonya, I've been thinking a lot about the casino business. Oh, I still love what I'm doing, don't get me wrong. And believe me, it provides a very nice living for me and my family. It's just that, well... I guess you could say this all started when I went to the movies a couple of weeks ago."

Tonya looked at him blankly. The movies? What the hell was this shit. She sighed inwardly. She still had no idea where he was headed with any of this.

"So I'm sitting there watching some picture that you'd forget in about 2 minutes once you left the theater," he said as he motioned to the waitress for another drink. "With a couple of real losers in it. All this noise and explosions and everything in it, enough to give you the mother of all headaches.

And all I could keep thinking was how people go to the movies every day of the year, and continually have to see the same crap over and over," Vito said excitedly. "I mean, it's unbelievable. And the thing is, you're like held captive there. What are you going to do? Get up and walk out? Well, you can do that but kiss your money goodbye!"

Tonya nodded and for the first time, she felt a tiny scrap of sympathy for what he was trying to say. Yes, she felt the same thing. People were sort of held captive to the stuff that was put out. But the way Tonya viewed it, there wasn't much you could do about it.

As if reading her mind, Vito launched into the second half of his speech. "Well, Tonya, this is what I mean by doing something about it. I've decided to expand my repertoire so to speak. I'm going to produce and finance my own movie. What do you think about that?" he said like a pleased father who is asking their child something.

Tonya sat there speechless. In her wildest dreams she didn't think she would hear this. Of course, part of it made perfect sense. Vito was simply a man with a little too much money and a little too much time on his hands. But she hardly expected to hear about a movie. She leaned forward.

"Uh, Mr. Leone, what's it about?" Tonya asked inquisitively.

Vito sat back. "Well, what's that old expression: Write about what you know? Me, I know about two things: what it's like to come over here as a kid, and the casino business."

OK, thought Tonya. This oughta be good.

Vito leaned over the table trying very hard to do his best Francis Ford Coppola imitation.

"I thought about it and well, it's gonna be very hard to do a movie about coming to America," said Vito as he smacked his hand down on the table lightly. "On account of, number one, there's been a lot of stories like that already that have been made into movies. You know, like with Robert DeNiro and so on. Maybe you seen them?"

"Sure, sure, Mr. Leone, I've seen them. And you're right the genre has been done to death," said Tonya carefully.

Vito looked at her blankly. "Genre? Come again," he said rather thickly.

"Um, it just means a particular type of movie, Mr. Leone," she said quickly hoping not to make him look stupid.

Vito grunted affirmatively. "Whatever," he said with a wave of the hand.

Whew, thought Tonya.

He shifted in his chair and got more comfortable. "So now I'm thinking, well, I know a lot about the casino business and how that runs. Perfect idea, no?" Vito said this with the air of a perfectly satisfied man who was very impressed with himself.

Hoping to move the conversation along, Tonya asked him carefully: "So, Mr. Leone, what's the movie about?"

Vito brightened at this show of interest from Tonya. "It's sort of going to be based on what I do at my casino," Vito said very grandly. "But I plan on having a lot of different, uh, like elements in the movie. So people don't get bored and fall asleep and want to walk out."

Like I'm doing now, thought Tonya.

"Oh there's going to be murder and intrigue and mystery in it," said Vito, sounding like an excited teenager as he talked. "The lead character's going to be based on me, of course, but after that, things are pretty much open. And that's what I wanted to talk to you about Tonya," he finished, staring right at her.

Oh, God, here it comes, Tonya thought. The proposition.

She wasn't far off the mark...

Vito leaned back and as he did, casually let his arm brush against Tonya's back. Tonya willed herself not to flinch, but rather to sit and smile pleasantly.

"Now, Tonya, the movie, in part, is going to contain guys who threaten my life," Vito said. Hey, can you imagine someone doing that. Ha, ha." Vito slapped the table at the thought of someone trying to rub him out.

"Now the way I see it, my character has to present himself as a very proper married man," said Vito. "I mean, let's face it, I'm a little long in the tooth to convince the audience that I'm a young swinging guy with chicks hanging all over me, you know?" When Vito said this, he said it with the arch of an eyebrow, as if to say: Well, Tonya, what do YOU think about that? As if he was daring her to disagree with him.

Tonya caught on and said quickly, "Oh, no, Mr. Leone, I could see you as someone that younger women would desire. Yes, I could, uh-huh." Tonya basically sat there and lied through her teeth to this guy who could crush her like a grape if he wanted to.

Vito straightened up his tie a little at that. Hhmm, he thought inwardly, this babe's knows class when she sees it. Not bad.

"Well, glad you feel that way, Tonya," said Vito warmly. Now, as I was sayin' my character in the movie, he's married, got the wife the kids, the whole bit. OK, so far, so good. But he has needs outside of marriage, you know?" Vito said with a wink and a nod to Carmine and Tony, who tried to suppress the grins sliding across their fat Italian pusses.

Tonya groaned once again inwardly. She spoke: "So, what would, uh, these particular needs have to do with me, Mr. Leone."

Vito smirked and nudged Carmine. "Hey, that's good, Tonya. I like that." Then he cocked his head at her and said, "Hey, you really don't know, do you?"

"Well, I have an idea, Mr. Leone," Tonya said warily.   Vito leaned forward again. "Tonya, hey look at yourself in the mirror, ok? I mean, not for nothing girl, but you're built like a blonde bombshell. If you don't mind me saying so. The role that I had in mind for you was the role of my mistress."

Tonya sat back and smiled weakly. Oohh, she'd give anything for Condo to be there right now. Just to see the look on his face as Vito smoothtalked his way into her dress.

Now, how to play this? If she protested, Vito would not be pleased. Humor him too much and he would smell that and still not be too pleased. The answer, she thought, was to play along and hope that things just quietly died on the vine. If that could happen.

"Is that all I should know, Mr. Leone?" Tonya asked, praying to God that it was.

Vito smirked again, but quickly hid it. He cleared his throat and tried to look serious again. It was an uphill struggle for him, Tonya could see that.

"Actually, Tonya, I was kind of hoping that when it came time for your scenes that we could display some of your more natural, uh, assets, you know?" Vito said very mysteriously.

She decided to play dumb. "Like what, Mr. Leone," she said innocently.

"Well, for starters nudity." said Vito.

Tonya nearly dropped her glass.

"I mean, I'd handle it with class, you know? Nothing cheap or out of line," said Vito quickly to cover things up.

Tonya played the blushing girl: "Well, I should hope not, Mr. Leone!" she said primly.

"I mean, it's not like I'd ask you to do a lesbian scene with another woman, or something like that," Vito said, proud of himself for explaining things.

"I'm going to have to think about this one, Mr. Leone," Tonya said quickly. "I'm flattered and all, but really—when did you plan on doing this movie?"

"We're going to start shooting anytime, Tonya. I already have the locations set and the money behind it. But it really needs someone like you. Are you sure I can't persuade you to do one little tiny nude scene for my movie?"

"Mr. Leone, I really couldn't," she said with hesitation in her voice. "I mean... I'm flattered that you'd ask me to do it (Tonya felt like throwing up), but it takes a special kind of girl to do that, and I guess I'm not it."

Vito sat back in his chair, his eyes like granite. Tonya could see the clenched teeth behind the barely forced smile. Suddenly, he leaned forward.

"I don't like anyone to say no to me, Tonya," he said thoughtfully stroking his chin. "But I guess that's your answer." "For now..." He sat back, the hard stare never leaving Tonya's face.

Tonya knew she had just made a big mistake

* * * *

Chapter 10
THOUGHTS OF REVENGE

Condo pulled into the parking lot of Tonya's building deep in thought. He was still in a quandary about what to do to get the casinos back from Vito.

He opened the door and held out his arms to her. As she sailed into them he thought once again about what a lucky man he was.

"Hi, Big Chief," said Tonya, employing the teasing little nickname she had for Condo sometimes.

"Hi, babe," said Condo, although his spirit wasn't in it at all.

Tonya sensed that something was wrong, and the "something" had to do with an Italian gentleman they were both familiar with.

"What is it, sweetie?" asked Tonya, "As if I don't know."

Condo smiled. "You read my mind. It's just Vito. You know, more than once I've thought about rallying the braves, but what would I use for firepower? Violence is not an answer to anything, but I know Vito would not hesitate to use it against us."

"And that would just mean needless bloodshed and casualties. Mostly on our side. And I couldn't live with that. With the knowledge that I helped get some of our best sons of the tribe killed."

Tonya hesitated before saying anything. Her heart ached for Condo, yet she had to be careful from now on about how she talked about Vito. Careful, safe statements, that was the way to go.

But Condo was not finished. "You know, that there is not enough money for some people here in the tribe, don't you? I mean, it's all very well and good for people like me. I make enough to provide for everything.

"But what about the cooks and the waiters and the parking garage guys and the waitresses. The Mob pays them shit, and they don't care."

"Tonya, honey, I'm telling you, we need to have things like they were in the old days. When ethics and loyalty meant something. Our people were proud people and even though on paper it says we own the land and our casinos, the deal we have with the Mob, that was forced on us, well, that really says it all!" Condo continued to pace around the room as he said these words, he was so mad.

Tonya tried to get a word in. "Sweetie, look maybe there's a way to —" That was as far as she got.

"I'll tell you what I'm going to do," Condo said excitedly. "I'm going to look up an old friend of mine at the town newspaper, Tom Bighorn. We go way back. I've got some stories to tell him that a whole lot of folks would be interested in. In fact, I'm going to see him right now." With that, he went flying out the door.

Tonya realized she had to do something fast. The idea of going to the newspapers would only make Condo look like some sort of half-baked redskin. What was he going to back up anything with. She ran to catch him, but he was already gone.

* * * * *

Tom Bighorn leaned back in his chair and stared with disbelief at Condo. They had known each other for years, but he could not believe what he was hearing. Condo was actually willing to talk to him about all the corruption that was rampant on Indian land, involving the Mob.

Several times over the years, Bighorn had attempted to broach the subject with Condo, but all he got for his efforts were polite refusals from his friend. He supposed he couldn't blame him in a way; after all, it wasn't his neck that was going to be stuck in the noose.

Still, Bighorn had attempted to make Condo see that it would be in his best interest to put the information in the papers. That way, the authorities could step in and right some of the terrible wrongs that were being done to Indians.

Condo had a number of things going for him: 1) He was inside the action as a dealer in the casino. 2) The braves respected him as their leader.

Bighorn had to admit that he had met with failure the few times he thought about infiltrating the Mob. He had thought about going undercover more than once, getting some kind of low-level flunky job and just observing what went on until he felt sure he had enough material for a series of newspaper columns.

The plans had never come about in part because Bighorn could never find an easy way to infiltrate the Mob without calling attention to himself. He was half afraid that there would come that one day that someone would recognize him - and his cover would be blown. And if that happened, it would be goodbye Mr. Newspaper Editor, for they would make sure he disappeared.

"Now, Condo, old buddy, you're sure you want to do this?" Bighorn had asked with his finger poised on the RECORD button on his tape recorder.

"Yes, Tom, I'm sure," Condo replied. "It's time someone took these bastards on. Our people are getting the shaft eight ways from Sunday and there is no one to speak for them. The Mob has us under such tight control that there is no way we can ever get out from under them."

"What exactly are you talking about?" asked Bighorn.

"I'm talking about loansharking, I'm talking about extortion, I'm talking about the Mob freely having their way with our women. Do you really think any of the braves would be crazy enough to expose this? Of course not. They know what would happen to them."

"But what about proof, Condo? After all, just playing devils' advocate - the case could be made that it's simply your word against theirs. How do you prove it in a court of law?" Bighorn leaned forward anxiously as he said this.

"Hey, it may not get that far, Tom. But if it does, I'm fully prepared to testify under sworn oath about all this stuff I'm about to tell you."

"So you can supply me with exact names, dates and instances," Bighorn pressed.

"Yes sir," Condo replied. "Anytime you're ready."

"OK, then, let's get started," Bighorn said as he pressed the button and watched the tape spool around and around, a metaphor for the tale that was about to weave around him.

Condo sat back and thought for a minute about the time that he had caught someone card counting. That had been some night.

He had had no idea about what card counting was until after his shift one night, someone told him the whole story of how it was done.

The guy's name was Michael Navarro and he was apparently a full-blooded Navajo. He had just wandered into the casino one night and started to play and one thing had led to another.

After he had lost another hand to Condo, he sighed and said: "OK, partner, I give up. You win. Damn, I had a streak of bad luck tonight."

Condo smiled at the guy. He seemed friendly enough.

"So where are you from, friend?"

"Oh, I've lived in quite a lot of places over the years, you know. Say, when do you finish your shift? Have I got a story for you?"

Condo glanced up at the clock. "In about 30 minutes, I'll be done. You want to get a cup of coffee?"

Navarro smiled. "Sure, that'd be great. Meet me over in the coffee shop."

A little while later, Condo came strolling into the coffee shop. Proudfoot was already there with a cup in his hand.

"Pull up a chair friend."

"Condo Cherokee is the name"

"Michael Navarro."

"Pleased to meet you, Michael."

"Likewise."

"So, I understand you have some story to tell me?"

Navarro sat back and smiled. "Yes, I do. The strange thing is I don't know why I'm tellin' it to you. I mean, I don't really know you that well. But I guess it'd because I don't want to see it happen to your casino."

"So tell me." Condo sat back to listen.

"Well, the easiest way to explain card counting, which is what this is about, is to tell you my experiences with it and then kind of go from there. You know?"

The story Navarro told was unbelievable...

He had been playing one night and things were going well, when all of a sudden he heard someone try to get his attention behind him. The first thing that Navarro had thought was that they recognized him from old surveillance pictures.

He had been playing in a sort of sealed-off section that was only for players of a certain, shall we say, clientele.

All of a sudden, he felt a tap on his shoulder. He had been playing straight old regular one-on-one with a dealer at the table. It was a good game for him. In no time at all he had whizzed through the six-deck shoe.

Navarro had gone through the shoe like a hot knife through butter. He felt strong and confident.

From playing here many times, Navarro had developed sort of a code with the dealer. He had only to feint slightly or move his hand in the slightest motion. He would either stand pat or call for more cards.

No words were spoken except when Navarro started playing the green chips which were worth $200. Then the dealer said "Green chips." This was a sort of signal to the supervisor that Navarro was playing with green chips.

He felt naturally elated when he won, but to sort of show off for the surveillance cameras he would clench his fist and gesture. Or some such thing like that.

It was then that the security people from the casino had walked over and greeted him and congratulated him on his winnings.

After that, he slowly turned around and went back to his game.

What I'm telling you, Condo, said Navarro, is that I am part of a professional team of card counters. We call ourselves the "Brave Hearts." Because believe me, Condo, you have to be brave to take on the mob in their own house and count cards on them.

* * * * *

Condo sat there transfixed. What this guy was saying was unbelievable. He pressed him for more details. Navarro's story got even more amazing...

There were ten members of the Brave Hearts. When the local casino had opened, they made their first killing. Their winnings were modest at first; they won about $10,000 over several weeks. But they knew they had to be careful. One wrong slip and they could find themselves looking upward from a cement overcoat.

Casinos are naturally touchy about players who win high stakes. Not that they want to discourage that; it's just that there can't be TOO many high-stakes winners. That's bad for business.

But there has to be just enough so that people want to come back and gamble there.

Otherwise, soon there is no more casino.

But in the case of card-counters, Navarro explained, they were sometimes asked not to come back. All done very politely, you understand—but the message was clear: don't gamble in our casino any more. You're winning *just* a little too much...

The one thing that you have to keep in mind, Condo, Navarro said, is that counting cards is *not* illegal. No way.

But how did you learn this? Condo wanted to know.

Well, said Navarro, years ago, there was a book written called "Tips For Beating The Dealer." That was one of the first books which touched on the subject. It was a landmark book, because it meant for the first time that someone was saying that, yes, blackjack could be beaten.

Naturally, the casinos were not too keen on the notion that blackjack could be beaten consistently.

Navarro explained that blackjack, or 21 as it used to be known had become the most popular casino game. But even with that, Navarro explained, the house always has the advantage.

Over the time he talked with Condo, Navarro kept returning to this point again and again. Casinos are huge business, he said. (As if Condo didn't know that). As such they control vast amounts of money and power. So it was only logical that the casino would have a sort of mathematical advantage where the house would always win.

Oh, a good player might win some, Navarro explained. But over the long haul, the house would always win. The only exception to the rule was blackjack.

That was because the game was based on numbers and odds, and a player who learned how to pay attention and skillfully count cards could make a killing...

This was not, for example, the kind of thing that would make one Vito Leone very happy, thought Condo...

Winning at blackjack consistently over the house was like cutting into a casino's lifeblood. And that would not be tolerated not in this lifetime, never.

Can they spot you when you walk into a casino? asked Condo.

Oh, yeah, came the reply.

In fact, Navarro said, there is even a private security agency that specializes in this. They know the names and faces of most of the card counters around. It would not be too hard to place him at the scene where there was suspected card counting going on.

Couldn't you wear like a disguise, asked Condo. If it was me, I'd shave my head.

Navarro laughed and fingered the flowing locks of his hair. No, that's not quite my style. Although he has, on occasion, taken to wearing a wig or a moustache of some kind.

But it's weird, because this agency always seems to find him.

Navarro found himself in the strange position one time of reading a classified memo from the agency. He was surprised to learn that the agency did not take sides one way or the other when it came to card counting. If anything, it was sympathetic to the card counter.

Still, that wasn't going to cut any ice with the casinos, and Navarro knew it. It was like they looked at him like Al Capone.

He knew from experience that you had to be careful about whose casino you plied your wares in.

Some were more cool than others. But beware the ones that weren't.

He recalled one time he and part of his team were in one smaller venue. It had been tipped off that they were doing a number on the casino.

The next thing Navarro knew was that he was in a back room. Some very large and very threatening men were going to make things very unpleasant for him if he didn't come clean.

But Navarro managed to hold on, and not give away any of the secrets.

After all, he was smart enough to know that if he did that—well, they might as well close up shop. And that was that.

Condo was curious how a seemingly nice guy like Michael Navarro could get involved with all this stuff. Didn't he want to lead a normal life?

Sure, Navarro replied. I went to college and have a degree in economics. Which may explain, though, why I'm so interested in beating the system. Numbers and odds intrigue me.

What does your family think about this, Condo asked.

Well, they're not exactly wild about it, he explained. But you can't have everything, he said. My parents enjoy the money I make, especially when my winnings help pay for a vacation for them.

But beyond that, they just wish I'd clear the hell out. You know?

Condo was still curious about the basic precepts of card counting. Didn't you have to be some kind of brain to learn how to do it?

Not really, replied Navarro. In fact, I've heard of cases where people have used computers to study how to beat the game. Computers can do calculations much faster and it's a hell of a lot easier.

There were some games, explained, Navarro, that were basically one-deck games. These were very slow games and the odds could be controlled so that you could win a lot.

Now, Navarro cautioned that while you won, you weren't going to become a millionaire by any stretch of the imagination. No, most of what you won was enough to be a little comfortable, you know for buying dinners and so forth, but that was about it.

There were two things, Navarro said. One, the act of counting cards itself was separate. I mean, anyone can count cards if they have a sharp enough memory and can see what's plainly before them.

The trick was to be able to count cards, *and* have your wits about you enough to be able to do it consistently. You had to be able to withstand a lot of things that would throw you off...

Like the dealers who looked at you with watchfulness in their eyes...

Like the security people and bouncers who were always looking for you to trip up somehow...

Like all the yahoos craning their necks and talking out loud when someone was making a big score.

Little distractions like that...

The only way that he got good at it, Navarro explained, was to practice constantly. So everywhere he went he took cards with him. He had to be able to breathe, eat and dream about card counting.

Many people would have assumed that card counters just count all the cards as their way of doing things. But they would be wrong.

What card counters do is keep track of one number. And how that number always changes. Through this method, the card counter has a ratio of cards that have already been played. In general, the low-numbered cards are not good for them. High-numbered cards yield much better results.

Basically, low cards which are two through six count as one, and the middle cards which are seven, eight and nine, count as zero. Now the higher cards, meaning ten and the face cards and aces, are considered minus one.

The trick is to look for a count that is positive. So what you want, Navarro explained, is a situation in which there are a lot of low cards that have been played and then you have an abundance of high cards left over in the deck.

This way the player had a statistical advantage over the dealer. Very strictly speaking, the higher the count, the greater the advantage was.

All the player had to do then was increase the amount that was bet.

However, there were several things that could go wrong...

For example if the bet was raised *too* much, it created havoc because the pit boss became suspicious.

One thing you did not do was make the pit boss suspicious...

That would sort of be analogous to making Vito Leone suspicious. Definitely not done!

The ideal type of casino, to Navarro's way of thinking was one in which you had blackjack tables that had large betting limits. Which was good if you wanted to bet a lot; but also had an advantage of allowing you to lay off if the count was negative.

Perfect, in other words.

Although the one thing that Navarro had to keep in mind was to make sure that no one did anything stupid. Like for example raising the stakes too much when they knew they had a chance to win. You just suddenly couldn't zoom upwards and expect no one to notice!

After that had happened once or twice, the hotel was a little different in their welcome the next time.

Navarro noticed a lot of clenched teeth when they went there again.

Navarro told Condo that it was not unusual for card counters to work in teams. Although the people he played with was relatively minor league compared to some of these operations, he knew of guys who made a lot more money doing this.

Condo was curious. How did you make sure the guys on your team weren't slacking off?

Navarro said there were checks and balances to the system which would make it as fail-safe as possible.

For example, before any of the guys he worked with would go to a casino, Navarro and the other guys ran them through their paces—just to make sure. Strict accounting was kept of the money that went in and went out, so there was no funny business.

It was almost like being in school, Navarro said. Sometimes the guys bitched and moaned, but everyone generally agreed that these checks and balances were necessary.

Navarro leaned forward and tried to emphasize his point with Condo: A team is only as good as its individual members. And they had to pool their money so that when they had losses along the way, they had some backup.

But how could you lose with such a failsafe system? asked Condo.

Oh, you'd be surprised, said Navarro.

* * * *

It got later and they just continued to talk. Condo found himself fascinated by the things that Navarro was saying. He never realized that the game which he thought was so simple, could be so complex.

Navarro said that it was funny to watch some of the people who were beginning at the game, sidle up to the table and basically have no idea what they were doing. They would get a little stake going, which they thought would carry them over for a long time and—poof! all their money was gone very soon.

He said that in some casinos, they even had what was known as an instructional table. This was where the players could get what amounted to a "tutorial" on how to play the game. The older people, basically those who had retired, were the most eager to learn.

Navarro said he knew this one dealer named Victor. Victor instructed a lot of people there, and was very sympathetic to the people's questions.

One day, Navarro remembered, he was sitting at the table when this old lady had a pair of two's in her hand. Victor could tell she was deliberating about how to play the hand. Victor told her, well, maam if you split them up you'll be playing strategy.

The woman's eyes lit up when she heard that—because she thought it would make her seem like a pro. All strategy was in essence was studying the game from a sort of mathematical viewpoint.

Navarro claimed that if you tried to play blackjack that way sometimes you had a better chance of winning. So many people were just basically throwing their money away by playing lousy hands because they weren't paying attention. Such a shame, he said.

So, if everyone counted cards like you, Condo said, they would win more?

Well, that's true, Navarro said. But there was a certain skill level to counting cards that many players would just never get.

Didn't the players ever wonder how they could gain more knowledge, Condo wondered.

Of course they did, Navarro answered. And if he had to take a guess he would say that most players were lazy. All they had to do was buy a decent book on the subject and study up on it.

Navarro shook his head. The average person, he said, started socializing at the table after one or two wins. Suddenly they felt the game was fun and so they relaxed a little.

You never relax, said Navarro. You want to relax, go home and turn on your VCR and watch television. When you're playing to win money—you never relax. Cause you gotta treat it like work, he said. It is work.

Hey, whatever happened to that woman who had the pair of twos, Condo asked?

Oh, said Navarro, she won. It turned out to be good advice.

Still, Navarro said, for as many people who think they could be potential hotshots after a few go-arounds, there were that many more who studied up on it and wouldn't even dare dream of going near a table until they were good and ready. So it could work both ways.

He remembered one old guy, he told Condo, who did the whole gamut from watching videos to taking instructional courses. He had even gone so far as to take a course in gambling at a local college! That was dedication, said Navarro.

He practically could deal himself, he was so fluent in the rules of the game after that, Navarro remembered.

So did all casinos have these instructional type tables, Condo wondered?

Not all, said Navarro. It all depended on what the management of the place said. That was pretty much basically it.

If the general managers of some of these places felt that their dealers and supervisors could help the customers then that was the direction they took. Of course, not every dealer was pleased to hear that his boss wanted him to help some old lady with strategy, Navarro said.

For that reason, Navarro said, a lot of times, people got scared and intimidated by blackjack, because they thought, hey, I'm going to lose my shirt here.

Indeed, after a couple of losses, that was *exactly* the mindset for some people. They just couldn't handle it, and they got up and went to play the slots.

Navarro had to chuckle about that one, though. He said that many people thought, hey, it's just putting quarters in and pulling. No big deal! That was, until their losses started to mount. Because those quarters sure could add up in a hurry!

So what help was the casino to you if there were no instructional tables, asked Condo?

Well, Navarro said, not much. See, what they usually did, he said was give you a written guide that basically just outlined the rules of the game. But if you're looking for help with any of the odds—forget about it, Navarro said.

It was a very odd philosophy, he said.

How so, asked Condo.

Well, the way I figure it the casino is sort of like a factory that produces products, you know? And well if you want to touch, feel and handle that product then you have to pay the price. So the money that was lost is the price paid for handling that particular product.

Wow, that's really something, Condo said, nodding.

Which brings things back to me he said. All casinos want to know if card counters are paying what amounts to a fair price.

Navarro went on to explain the in blackjack, a casino can have quite an advantage over a novice player. Some estimate it at 2 or 3 percent. Now a player who just uses good basic strategy can take that house advantage down to almost zero.

And that's just for someone who is only fair at counting cards.

A really good card counter can gain an advantage over the casino of approximately one percent.

Condo interrupted: But that seems like really small money, doesn't it?

Navarro said, well, yes it does, but over time they can add up to a lot of money.

Navarro gave an example to Condo. Let's just say you strolled into a casino and are strictly new at all this. You bankroll yourself say, a $100 and you sit down at the $5 blackjack table. Now if the casino is ahead of you by 2 percent does that mean that you should only lose $2?

No, it does, not, Navarro said.

What it really means is that over time, you should only lose two percent of the money you bet. Think percentages, not dollars.

Now let's just say that you sat there for a couple of hours. Over time, you'll win some hands and lose some hands. And let's say you wind up betting around $500 in all. Now the expected two percent loss is $10. And what is that? It's ten percent of the bankroll you started with, which was $100.

How much money are certain casinos making on games, Condo wanted to know.

Well, Navarro replied, certain casinos don't really release figures on what they make at blackjack or other games. But there are certain states where a commercial casino is required to file a financial report.

Now Nevada and New Jersey are two big states for gambling. What they usually do is keep close to 16 percent of the money that customers change into tips at the blackjack tables. This is what is known in casino parlance as a win.

And believe me, Navarro, said, this type of blackjack money is big money.

How big, Condo asked?

Well, I know it's over a billion dollars.

Wow, Condo whistled.

Wow, indeed said Navarro. Hey, it's just the price that people pay for playing blackjack.

Condo sat back and took it all in. This was really something. But again he had to ask: Aren't the casinos paranoid of people like you who count cards?

Well, Navarro replied, like I said before, there are certain ones that are a little more quick to act. They'll just flat out ask you to leave the tables. Which can be pretty weird especially if you're in the middle of a winning hand.

But how can a casino be sure, Condo asked. What happens if there is a mistake made. What then?

It happens, Navarro shrugged. The casino has sometimes chased away perfectly innocent people who were winning good and weren't counting cards.

Don't they get mad?

Navarro smirked. Get mad at the casino, he said. Well, you do that and you cut off your chances of ever coming back. Who wants to do that?

The casinos, as you can imagine get a little touchy when it comes to the subject of card counting, Navarro said. Some of them don't have a policy of just not talking about it at all.

Besides, Navarro said, the casinos readily acknowledge that it's hard to spot card counting teams sometimes. They're too busy looking out for other things. So many times, card counting teams slip away undetected.

Navarro leaned forward and tried to emphasize something important to Condo. That is that most card counters were in for the long haul. Which is a lot different from someone who walks into a casino with the express purpose of cheating.

That, Navarro said, is far worse for the casino, because it means that someone is out and out trying to steal their money right out from under their nose.

But card counters play the long-term percentages. Which means that players simply practice and practice till they get good. They work to earn that one percent advantage over the casino.

And the one thing that card counters NEVER count on is that they're going to win every day, Navarro said. That just ain't gonna happen.

Now, if a casino's smart, Navarro said, they will simply ask a player to play another type of game. This way everybody stays friendly and no one gets hurt. And most always, players will be good about it and find another game.

The smartest thing you can do when a casino supervisor approaches you is just to leave, Navarro said. Don't try and argue with anyone cause you'll lose. Don't show them a license or any other piece of identification.

Has that ever happened to you, Condo asked.

Sure, Navarro said. And I was smart. I just turned on my heels and got out.

One other thing you want to watch out for is when a casino tries to take someone's picture, so they can "have it on file." As soon as they start to mention that stuff, you know it's time to leave.

Was there ever such a thing as someone bringing a lawsuit asked Condo?

Navarro shrugged. It happens, he said. But more often than not, it's just an idle threat. Someone shooting their mouth off. But it does happen where someone can get money from the casino for just such a thing.

Finally, it was time to go. Condo and Navarro got up from the table and shook hands. Condo knew that he had heard an incredible tale, one that he would always remember.

* * * * *

Chapter 11
THE TRAP IS SET

Don Hatchett stared through the window of his kitchen with eyes of stone. All around him were piles of dirty dishes and general mess. That was something else he was going to have to get used to. Val wouldn't be over to take care of things anymore. No siree.

Right now, the only thing that Hatchett was thinking about was how to rotisserie Vito Leone over a fire, letting him cook good and slow until his flesh popped and oozed and turned nine shades of black.

Other than that, he was doing fine...

Hatchett knew that his first loyalty should lie with his men in the Supremacy group. Yeah, well, this was personal. He didn't exactly get all warm and sentimental about that crew, though. They'd survive without him fine for a time until he took care of this business with Vito.

The only question was how to do it.

Hatchett knew from past experience that Vito always traveled with a few sides of beef never more than a foot from him. A man in his position couldn't afford to do it any other way. So the answer was to look for that one moment when Vito would be utterly, completely alone and vulnerable. Think, think, dammitt!

Vito was a man of routine. He basically had five or six places you could always count on him being: At the casino, at home, on his boat, or at Carmen's. Carmen's...

If Carmen called him, he'd come.

That is, if she had a little coaxing. Like say, with a .45 Automatic pressed against her creamy white temple.

Hatchett knew her condo well. Shit, he had delivered enough messages to the head man. Hatchett had things to take care of. He wanted Vito nice and relaxed and suspecting nothing. A cruel smile crossed his lips and the thick vein in his forehead throbbed at the thought.

First, though, there was a little matter to take care of. One that involved an old Indian bastard who had outlived his time...

* * * * *

Tonya was nervous. Since their last lunch, she had thought that things between them were going to be chilly because she had basically said she wouldn't appear nude in Vito's movie.

But it hadn't come up and she and Vito had gone to dinner at another Italian restaurant, Giordano's. After the meal, Vito had said, ah, it's getting a little too close for comfort out in public like this, you know. He asked her if she knew of another place that was a little more intimate, a little less public. Basically, a place where his wife wouldn't catch him screwing around.

Tonya had him convinced about Condo, she thought. She had laid it on good and thick, never missing the opportunity to give Condo a few digs. She said just enough to be convincing, but not enough to raise suspicion.

Tonight was the night she would plant the bugs.

Tonya was a woman of resource. And working at the casino put her in contact with a lot of, shall we say, people with very different occupations. Such as Vinnie, the wiretap expert.

When she coyly mentioned that she was interested in getting another person on tape, Vinnie had at first demurred, mumbling the usual pieties about wiretapping being illegal in certain situations, and what if the police were to find out. And so forth.

Vinnie changed his tune when the first big bill with the President's face on it flashed before his eyes.

He regaled her for the next hour with the merits of dry-cell listening devices. You could use the TR-581 model, he said. Or the RX-432 Superbug. That one would pick up the slightest whisper. Or there was the...

Tonya cut him off there. All she wanted, she said, was a bug that would pick up normal conversations. Simple, and easy. GO with the TX-581, he said. I'll have one sent over to your shop this afternoon.

Now came the hard part. . .

Tonya basically needed to know the names of phantom companies where Vito had his holdings. After that, it was simply a matter of supplying the information to the authorities, and Mr. Leone would soon be getting a surprise visit from the local magistrate. Simple, right?

She thought about this as she watched Vinnie installing the bugs. He had offered, as an extra bonus, to come over and do the job. Tonya didn't tell him everything - like who the "buggee" was going to be. He installed one against the underside of a lamp, one in the sofa backing and one in the hidden compartment of the dining room table.

He had coyly asked if she needed one in the bedroom and Tonya smacked his arm good-naturedly but the look on her face told him to keep his trap shut after that. The bugs were voice-activated, and there was no telltale hiss or whirring on the tape.

Tonya was all set. Bugging Vito was the easy part. The hard part would be to keep his paws off her the entire evening until she got enough evidence on tape.

Tonya thought it through carefully. The trick was to be fluid, keep moving, laugh at his jokes - but above all, keep moving. Finally, the door bell rang. With a deep breath, she let him in. Let the fun begin, she thought.

"So tell me, baby, why are you so interested in the casino business all of a sudden?" They were on their second bottle of Pino Grigio and Tonya had to concentrate on keeping her wits about her - even while she was pouring down the wine.

"I'm interested. I mean, what you do from day to day is so fascinating - Tonya was really pouring it on now - that I'd like to know how things operate." "I mean for starters, you don't open a casino with money from your Christmas Club, I know that much!"

He chuckled. "Hey, that's a good one. I've got to tell that to Tony. Now where'd he - "

"Tony's not here, Vito. Remember. You sent him out. It's just you and me, handsome. So tell me how do things operate?" Tonya leaned over smoothed his jacket, running a long, naked arm smelling of Guerlain's "Ode" across the side of his cheek.

Vito took notice and tried to reach over for a little kiss. But Tonya patted him firmly on his chest, which had the effect of pushing him back slightly on the couch.

He shrugged and yawned slightly. Christ, this was good wine. He preferred Scotch, but this was good. "Hell, it's not as complicated as you might think. A couple years back, we heard through the grapevine that Indian land was going to be the next hot thing with gambling. So we had he accountants siphon money out of our other, uuhh, activities and we - "

"You mean like loansharking, stuff like that?" Tonya leaned forward, all ears now.

"Hey, hey, I never said that," Vito protested with a laugh. "But yeah, we got cash coming in from a lot of other areas. So the first thing we did was have the accountant run all sorts of numbers on what the potential was. You know, crowd size, number of games and so forth. He comes back and says, Mr. Leone, we're talking huge numbers in a few years."

"So then we have the engineers and architects come out. They draw up floor plans and the builders and contractors set to work, and -"

"Who are they?" Tonya interrupted. "Would I know them?"

"No, don't think so," Vito said, puzzled. "I don't get it, what are you so interested for? They're just companies."

Tonya stood up, hands on hips. "Suppose I want to be a casino manager some day? I need to know everything about the business!" She hoped her strident tone would not put him off. She desperately needed names - and quickly.

"Ok, ok," Vito threw his hands up. "Uh, well, we use a building company named Caruso Builders. Tommy Caruso, I've known him for years. See, you start with the builders and they recommend everybody else. Tommy says use Palomento Plumbing Supply, I use 'em. He says you want the best electrical work done, use Vitale Brothers. For all the supplies we need like chips, cards, dice, we go to Carbone Inc."

"What about the liquor license? I've heard something like that could take years," Tonya said with her eyes wide open and innocent.

"Naw, not if you know the right people," Vito said with a smirk. "See, for booze, I got a friend on the state commission, Mark Pugliese. Some pirated paperwork and zing! A license that costs a couple of hundred grand suddenly costs one dollar."

"Of course, Mark gets a nice little envelope every two weeks delivered by Tony personally. As a token of my appreciation, you understand." Vito sat back with a satisfied smile. He then sat back up and said in voice silky smooth with threat: "You know, Tonya, all this stuff - we're just talking, you know? You heard the expression, 'herkos odonton?' Means 'behind the hedge of the teeth.' You get me?"

Tonya sat very still and thought: Got you, you bastard! She hoped everything was caught on tape.

She smoothed his lapel again, gave him a smile that purred, and said, "I feel like some champagne. What do you say?"

* * * *

Chapter 12
A Time For Killing

    Hatchett waited until he saw Running Bear come slowly out of the convenience store. He watched as he fumbled for his keys taking his time, shifting items around awkwardly. No, there wouldn't be any problem, Hatchett thought. Running Bear would start his beat-up old pickup truck, shift the rusty ancient gearshift, and blend creakily into traffic. It would be then that he would notice the gas gauge.

    Hatchett could almost see the old man's face twist into a frown, confused now, scratch his head and stare once again at the needle hovering anxiously on E. Hmmmnnn, thought I had more gas than that. Guess I'll have to get some more.

    Except that the convenience store was the last stop for miles, as Hatchett knew. He had left the old man just enough to get him maybe two miles before conking out.

    Kaacchhuunnk... kaacchhuunnkk. With a last desperate buckle, the truck clunked to a stop. The horizon was just starting to lose the last vestige of orange light and already the sky looked as if it were encased in black velvet.

    Running Bear wearily put the gearshift into park and stared out at the darkening sky. Now what, he thought? He considered hitching a ride although he knew that this road was off the beaten path. Indeed only one car had passed in 10 minutes. He pulled his blue denim workshirt tighter around his body and got out to stand by the truck and give it a shot.

    Hatchett observed all this through his night binoculars from a vantage point a few hundred yards away, shrouded in the gloom. Alone and vulnerable, he thought. Perfect.

    Condo looked anxiously out the window. It wasn't like Tonya to be gone for this long, he thought. Whatever she was doing, it sure was taking a long time. I hope everything is all right, he thought.

    At that very moment, Tonya was popping the champagne cork in her kitchen and fetching some long-stemmed glasses. Yessss! Everything was going strictly according to plan. Vito had unwittingly supplied her with all the information she would need to bring to law enforcement. Perhaps they would even convene a grand jury. The main thing now was to finish this thing off smoothly, and get Vito.

"Hey, babe, what's keeping you in there?" came the sound of Vito's slightly slurred speech.

"Be right out," Tonya lightly yelled back. God, she thought, can this night ever end!

* * * * *

Hatchett left his truck parked on the side of the road and walked the short distance to where Running Bear was standing forlornly by his truck. He was hidden by a shadow of darkness, which was the way he wanted it.

Gradually, his eyes made out the form of the older man peering down the road, looking in vain for a car to pass. Finally, one did. Running Bear stretched his thumb up in the air hopefully; the car hesitated a moment, and then zoomed on. His thumb came down with a sigh and a resigned air.

Hatchett advanced on Running Bear till he was 50, then 40, then a mere 10 yards away. The night air was slightly chilly and Hatchett's breath came out in small clouds. He didn't want to kill the old guy, but he couldn't trust that Running Bear would be on his side anymore—and Hatchett knew he still had enough influence with other members of the tribe. Now it had to be done.

The scuffling of Hatchett's boots on the road gravel was the sound that made Running Bear turn his head and stare in Hatchett's direction. He watched him approach as he stood on the other side of the car, the headlights giving his face a spooky quality.

Hatchett didn't waste any time on small talk. "Get rid of the lights, old man."

Running Bear reached through the window and pushed the knob. "It's been awhile, Silent Wolf," he said, referring to Hatchett's Indian name.

"Yeah, well, it's ain't gonna be long now," Hatchett said impatiently. "Let's move away from the car out into that field." He gestured towards the now dark expanse by the side of the road.

Running Bear felt an electricity build up in him, but he just shook his head and meekly complied. He walked out slowly into the field with Hatchett behind him, nervously looking around the for the sound of oncoming cars.

When they were a good distance out, Hatchett said, "Stop. Turn around."

Hatchett drew the long barrel of the gun with the silencer out of his coat and eased back the hammer.

Even though it was dark, Running Bear could clearly make out Hatchett's face. He concentrated on looking into his eyes for he wanted him to hear what he had to say, if these would be his last words on earth.

"You don't have to do this, Silent Wolf," he said slowly and distinctly. "Ask yourself - is it worth having my spirit - dipped in blood by your hands - haunt your soul for all eternity?"

Hatchett raised his gun, pointed it at Running Bear's forehead and spoke in a growling whisper: "Ain't got no soul for you to haunt, old man."

Running Bear closed his eyes and waited.

The sound - three times - was swallowed up in the night, which held its breath for one terrible moment, and then slowly began to breathe again.

* * * *

Chapter 13
RACE AGAINST TIME

Vito tried once more to kiss Tonya. He was weaving slightly and trying to focus his lips on to hers. But Tonya quickly sidestepped his outstretched arms and set the champagne glasses delicately on the marble-topped table.

"Now, c'mon, big man," she said admonishing him. "Let's drink up a toast now. Here's to you. May that cash river never run dry!"

Vito shrugged, took a sip and sat back. He didn't seem to be getting anywhere with this broad. Most girls would be eager, offering their bodies to him. This one, though, with that incredible body, she keeps ducking me. For a moment he tried to decide if it made him angry. Fuck it, he thought. I'm too tired to deal with this shit now.

(It was lucky for Tonya that Vito had this change of heart. She had been a nervous wreck all night at the thought of having to go to bed with Vito. When he shrugged and sat back, she breathed an inward sigh of relief.)

Vito yawned and looked at his watch. "Thanks, doll. Listen, I'm gonna leave. That grape knocked me for a loop. Whew. Here, beep Sal, alright? Tell him, bring the car round front and get up here. I'm ready to go."

He walked the couple of steps to the door, then turned to look at Tonya quizzically. "You're a nice chick, Tonya. But you ask too many questions, you know that. People that ask a lot of questions about my business, I get nervous. You know?" He stared at Tonya thoughtfully, narrowing the black gun muzzles of his eyes.

Tonya felt a shiver of fear run up her body as Vito looked at her. Just reassure him, she thought. Nice and easy is way to play it here.

"Now, now, I told you before, suppose I want to become a dealer some day. I want to know everything. And besides, you'd help me out there, wouldn't you?" Tonya stood very close to Vito and smoothed the lapel on his jacket, all the while batting her eyes seductively at him.

Vito shrugged. What the hell. "OK, you put it like that, I could maybe make an opening appear." Yeah, he thought. Not bad. "Course you know, Tonya, one hand washes the other." He held her eyes. "And baby, with curves like you got, I'd let you wash me any day. You get my point?"

Without waiting for a reply, Vito took her hand lightly, brought it to his mouth and kissed it. He looked at her one last time, and then knocked once for Sal to open the door and escort him to the waiting limo.

Tonya shut the door, nearly hyperventilating. She then ran over to the sofa, kicking off her high heels on the way. Digging deeper into the recesses of the pillows, she came up with the bug. Holding her breath, she nervously flicked the PLAYBACK button. As the tape flicked to a stop, she pushed the ON button. Vito's deep, wiseguy voice came to life. Whew, she thought. Now there were only two things she had to take care of.

The first was to run, do not walk, to the police, F.B.I., hell the C.I.A., with these tapes! Tonya racked her brain. Yes, there was her friend, Paula Noel, who worked over at the 82nd precinct. Tonya knew she could trust Paula to get her boss to make the tapes top priority. And Tonya desperately wanted to get the tapes out of her apartment and into police custody. She was half convinced Vito would find out, come back and kill her.

That was problem number one. The second problem was Condo. She just had to find a way to convince him that the tapes were real and that she had done the right thing by handing them over to the police, and then Condo would be abel to regain control of the casinos. She couldn't wait to see the look on his face.

* * * *

Tom Bighorn couldn't believe his luck. The sessions with Condo had gone so well, stretching into hours that he had enough material to write a book. But he would of course settle for some good, hard-hitting newspaper-type exposes.

One of the questions that was bugging Bighorn was the issue of confidentiality. If he came outright and named Condo - that would be a death sentence for him. He'd have to use a pseudonym of some kind. Chief Big River, well, that was something at least.

He would plan the columns so that they would run for one week. Seven days worth. Enough to make the public aware of what was going on. He could only hope that his office would be flooded with calls and that questions would be raised. These types of exposes were always a crap shoot, Bighorn knew from experience.

The problem was that you never knew when and if you were tapping into a subject of genuine interest - or merely tapping into the public's apathy about the subject. The danger with this was like the proverbial tree falling in the forest - if it fell, would anyone CARE that it fell? That's essentially what Bighorn was facing.

Still, with the mountains of material he now had, he couldn't very well sit on it. It was a large part of the reason he went into the newspaper business. To tell the truth to people. He felt honor-bound to do so. So it was with relish that he now sat before his computer and started to write. He knew the words would flow off his fingertips...

* * * * *

It was now two weeks later. The stories had run as page one exclusives for the entire past week. And he could not have anticipated the reaction he was receiving. Midway through the week, Bighorn received a call from the state's attorney general.

The attorney general's name was Paul Atkinson. He had read with interest the stories of mob corruption in the paper the same way as everyone had. Paul Atkinson knew two things:

a) He wanted to bring down the Mob
b) He wanted to bring down the Mob

It could not be emphasized enough. Atkinson had tried to get his hooks into the Mob's control over Indian gambling for several years now. And now he was presented with an opportunity to do just that right now.

The only problem was how could he make sure that the charges that this Indian guy was making were accurate. I mean it was understandable that he had an ax to grind with the Mob.

But what if he wasn't on the level?

That had happened to Atkinson more times than he cared to remember. It was not pleasant to put months of work into something only to find out that it backfired on him.

So the answer was first to make sure that this kid Tom Bighorn wasn't being taken in.

"So, Tom, again congratulations on the stories. There sounds like there could be a bunch of corroborating evidence that we can make stick."

"Thanks, Mr. Atkinson. That's very nice of you," replied Tom Bighorn.

Of course, two can play at this game, he thought...

Bighorn knew what Atkinson was REALLY saying. He could almost read his mind that he thought Condo might be lying, or at least making tall tales that he couldn't back up.

So actually, both of them were kind of dancing a little minuet with each other, not quite trusting the other one.

"Now, Tom, what I am concerned about in my position as Attorney General, as you can well understand, is the veracity of this, er, Condo's statements. He makes various claims about extortion's and payoffs and many other things. Can he really back this up?"

"Well, sir, he has been on the front lines, so to speak for quite a long time," replied Bighorn. If there was anyone that I would trust it would be Condo."

"What is your background with this man, Tom?"

"Oh, Condo and I go back a long way. I think of him almost as a bloodbrother. Ha-ha."

Silence came from the other end of the phone.

Bighorn cleared his throat. "Uh, what I was trying to say is that I trust him with my life. And I trust completely what he has to say."

He heard the silence on the other end of the phone. He started to think that he would have to explain all over again, but the Attorney General suddenly said: "OK, Tom, that's what I wanted to know. So you think then that I should give these charges credence?"

"Oh absolutely. You can take Condo's word to the bank."

"Goodbye then, Tom."

"Goodbye, sir."

After the Attorney General hung up, he thought for a moment before rolling back in his chair. There were a couple of things going through his mind:

1) He could put a tail on Condo and see what the goddamn redskin was up to.

2) He could just ignore the charges, pay lip service to the newspaper columns and do nothing.

Both were tempting, he had to admit...

He pressed the buzzer on his desk and said to his secretary, "Sophie, get Frank DeLuca on the phone for me. I need to speak to him"

"Right away, sir," came the answer.

A few minutes later, he was speaking with the person he considered the finest private investigator around. Frank DeLuca was a throwback to the old school.

Meaning he knew how to conduct an investigation without getting his fingerprints all over everything. That was valuable to someone in Atkinson's position.

"Yessir, what can I do for you this fine evening?" came the smooth-as-silk question from DeLuca.

"Thanks, Frank. Listen, I may have a job for you."

"No problem, sir. Who, what and where?"

"Have you read the papers in the past week?"

"Sure, I keep up."

"Well, then you know about this Condo Cherokee guy?"

"A little bit."

Atkinson sat back. Where to begin? Not many people knew the exact nature of what the Mob was up to. Least of all people that weren't in on it specifically.

Atkinson just wondered how much of this he would have to explain to DeLuca. He decided to start somewhere in the middle...

Ten minutes later when he was finished, DeLuca gave a long pause over the phone. Atkinson was sure that he had lost him for a moment. But then he came back on the line.

"So, sir, what is it exactly you want me to do?"

"I want you to tail this guy Condo, find out if he's 'got the goods' if you know what I mean."

"I assume the fee will be acceptable."

"Yes, it will."

"Very good, just have someone send me the particulars about where to find this Condo and I'll get started."

"That's what I like to hear, Frank."

"Goodbye, sir."

"Goodbye, Frank."

After Atkinson hung up, he looked at the wall. He hoped he was doing the right thing by getting DeLuca involved. There was certainly no way of knowing until things got rolling—and that wouldn't be for a while until he heard from him and got his report. He hoped it would be a good one.

* * * * *

Bighorn had plenty of reason to be worried about the Attorney General's sudden interest in Condo. He knew it was only a matter of time before he would want to meet with the state's star witness should this come to trial.

Bighorn was hesitant to do this. He knew Condo could be put in grave danger if he agreed to the attorney general's wishes. Yet, how did you say no to the state's top cop?

He decided the answer was to stall for time until he could at least talk to a lawyer that he knew, Bill Cooper. Coop would give him the answers he needed.

Circulation was also building because of these stories. The numbers that he was getting from the circulation department on the daily purchases of customers were encouraging. He knew now that the public was responding to the stories.

And then there was the praise he was receiving from members of his own tribe. They would stop him on the street and congratulate him for telling a story that badly needed telling. Bighorn knew that he wouldn't have been able to do any of this without Condo's cooperation.

He wondered sometimes if this was going to put a strain on the relationship that Condo had with Tonya. He didn't know Tonya that well, but from what he knew, he was aware that she was very private. And perhaps she wouldn't want to have her man's story splashed all over Page One of the biggest newspaper in town. Unwanted fame has a way of causing strain on relationships, Bighorn knew.

He thought that perhaps he could set up some kind of clandestine meeting with the Attorney General and Condo. He'd have to preserve Condo's identity; that he knew. Maybe there was a way that he could get Condo to wear some type of hood or have his voice disguised like he'd seen done on TV. Bighorn had to chuckle at the thought: This big mountain of a man disguising himself. But he knew it was necessary.

* * * * *

Sal stared at the headline and turned white. There in big bold letters was the headline: THE GAZETTE WEEKLY SERIES: A PROUD PEOPLE UNDER THE THUMB OF ORGANIZED CRIME. Christ, when Vito sees this he's going to burst an artery. But he knew that if he was really doing his job, he would have to bring it to Vito's attention. Because if he found it somewhere else, he'd have Sal's head. He bought a copy and tossed it on the seat next to him.

As he drove over to the casino, he tried to figure out who the informant was. Could it have been one of the boys? Sal wondered. Loyalties being what they were these days, nothing would have surprised him. All Vito's men were well-paid and had their pick of beautiful women whenever they felt the need to satisfy their urges. He turned into the lot, parked the car and walked quickly to Vito's office.

He saw Ginger sitting there talking on the phone. From the looks of it, the conversation was about nothing of consequence. She could have been talking with one of her girlfriends about the Home Shopping Network for all he knew. Sal loomed in front of her desk and drew his index finger across his throat impatiently, the signal for Ginger to stop yapping.

She got the message quickly, uttered a quick, "Talk to you later," and hung up.

"Hi, Sal," she said nervously. (This was not due simply to the present moment. The truth of it was that Sal did make her nervous all the time).

"Knock on his door - now. I need to see him," Sal said with as much urgency as he had ever said anything.

Ginger hopped to it.

Sal walked in and very quietly laid the newspaper on the desk. He crossed his arms and stared very intently at Vito.

It was the last moment of silence he was likely to hear in this office for a very long time...

Vito stared at the words and his mouth started to move but nothing came out. Finally, he ran a hand through the side of his well-coifed gray hair, not caring now, and brought the same hand down to the desk with a shuddering crash.

"WOULD SOMEONE TELL ME HOW THIS SHIT LANDED IN THE NEWSPAPERS??," he roared, his voice seeming to rattle the pictures on the walls.

All Sal could do was raise his eyebrows to the ceiling, shrug - and wish that he was in Bermuda right now.

"I want to find out who the rat is, and I want to find out quick, you understand?" Vito said to Sal with his finger pointed directly in his face. "If the cops ever get ahold of my records we, us, you, this operation is FINISHED!"

"Boss, it's not going to be as easy as that," Sal said, hoping to bring some sense to this crazy situation. This turned out to be the wrong thing to say.

Vito got up from his desk and came around it to confront Sal face to face. "I don't want to hear that, Sal, you got that?" Vito said in a voice that was the very whisper of death itself. "You make it that easy," he said, poking his finger in his chest. "You call in whatever favors you have to, you shake down whoever you have to - only find me a rat!"

"I already got enough problems with the cops. Remember? Or did you forget who was here the other day?" Vito said in a disgusted tone of voice.

He was referring to the little chat that he had had at the station house of one Sergeant Jack O'Brien. Yeah, the prick had come down here and picked up Vito right then and there and asked him to come down to the precinct.

Vito knew that they were trying to put the squeeze on him for information about the killing of that Stipiconiti kid. Fat chance, thought Vito. They ain't got nothing!

And he was right for the most part. O'Brien admitted to being frustrated when he thought of all the headaches involved with this. Christ, what did he have to go on?

Nevertheless he had paid a call to Vito in the early evening and was greeted with all the warmth of an igloo.

When he had walked up the stairs, Carmine had sarcastically said: "Hey, boss, hide the bodies. The police are here." Then he had chuckled openly in O'Brien's face.

Vito looked over his desk at O'Brien with hooded eyes. "Well, well, O'Brien—or sorry, sergeant, what can I do for you on this early evening?" Vito then leaned back in his chair like he hadn't a care in the world.

O'Brien stood stock still in front of Vito and said: "Mr. Leone, you wouldn't be able to tell me your whereabouts the last two days would you? No, of course you wouldn't. Why would you do that? So, I think I may have to ask both of you to come down to the stationhouse with me to answer some questions, if that's not too much trouble. Whaddya say?"

Vito looked up at O'Brien again and then looked over at Carmine, who stood there in disbelief. But Carmine was trying to mask a growing anxiety about this. What the hell did the police know? They couldn't know that much, could they?

As if connected to the same thought process, the same thing was running through Vito's mind. And at that moment he decided that he had better be a little cautious. Better to error on the side of caution, then not. Just take it nice and easy, answer the guy's questions, then he would be out of there.

O'Brien held the door for Vito and Carmine as they walked out.

When they were safely inside the precinct, O'Brien waited until they were seated in the interrogation room before he started in.

"So, Mr. Leone, or can I call you Vito, you do know what we found on the body today that we fished out of the river, don't you?" O'Brien said casually, as if talking about a ballgame.

Vito looked over at the cop. "No, I don't," he said in a relaxed manner. "Why don't you tell me."

O'Brien took his time. "Oh, it was real interesting. I mean, for starters, we find this guy, young kid actually, who obviously shows signs of having been thrown in there against his will."

"The funny thing is," he continued, "the first thing we see is something so disgusting, so vile, that the medical examiner actually almost got ill. Followed by me, of course. We see a human penis, a guy's dick if you will, nailed through his arm. Now what, I wonder, could something like that be doing on this poor bastard's arm?"

As he was talking, O'Brien tried to gauge the reactions that Vito and Carmine were having to all this. They were pretty cool customers he had to admit.

Mostly they just sat there and nodded their heads. "Really?" their expressions seemed to say. Like they were totally surprised to hear about this for the first time. Like they could never imagine anything like this EVER happening. It was weird, O'Brien had to say.

... So what do you think, Mr. Leone?" O'Brien finished up with.

Vito turned his hands up toward the ceiling in the classic shrug. Again, he had to remind himself, take it easy. The cop thinks he is on to something—but he doesn't have squat.

"Gee, Sergeant O'Brien, that's horrible," Vito said. "I can't imagine someone doing that to another human being, can you, Carmine?"

"No, Mr. Leone I sure couldn't," piped up Carmine, right on cue.

Oh, real cute, thought O'Brien.

"Well, the reason I ask, is because, unless I'm mistaken that's usually the signature of the Mob, am I right?" asked O'Brien slyly.

Vito put his hands lightly over his chest. "How would I know, Sergeant? I'm just a plumbing contractor. I would have no idea how something like that could happen." He sounded just as nice and sincere as you could ever think.

O'Brien decided to move on for a moment.

"Vito, where were you the night before last?"

"Home, sweet home, Sarge," Vito said.

"Can you prove it?" asked O'Brien.

"Do I have to?" came back the retort.

"Not yet, but you might have to if you become a suspect," replied O'Brien.

At this point, Carmine got up and said: "Prove what? Mr. Leone ain't done nuthin—"

Vito silenced him with a wave of the hand. Stupid, he thought. What the hell was Carmine thinking?

"Now, now, Carmine, what the good sergeant was merely saying was that if things start to get sticky, then he'll want to haul me in and things will proceed from there. Or something like that," Vito finished.

O'Brien knew he was skating on thin ice with this. He didn't have shit to go on and he knew he couldn't hold Vito and Carmine for very long until they started demanding to "lawyer up." He knew that he needed time to build a case and yet he knew that part, if not all of the case could be sitting right in front of him. He just couldn't prove it, dammit!

Vito got up carefully from the table. "Now, if there is nothing else, Sergeant, I'd like to go home, as would my associate here. Do you think that would be possible, or do you want to turn the screws to us somemore?" Vito said this last sentence as half smirk, half threat.

O'Brien tensed a little and said: "OK, Leone, you and Musclehead can go—for now. But I'll be waiting for you to screw up."

He watched them roll their shoulders and saunter out. All that was missing was for them to give him the finger over their shoulder as they left.

O'Brien felt very discouraged.

That had not been a pleasant experience for Vito and the look in his eyes told Sal he had better find a rat but quick. You could say that Sal got the message.

* * * * *

Chapter 14
THE NOOSE TIGHTENS

Tonya just sat there as Condo paced the room.

"You actually expect me to believe that you bugged Vito Leone, the top mob boss, and he didn't lay a hand on you?"

Tonya couldn't believe this. Earlier in this day, she had met Paula for lunch at the most secluded, out of the way hole in the wall you could imagine. Tonya was so nervous that she grabbed Paula by the arm, after a meal in which she spent the better part of the time looking over her shoulder, and steered her towards the ladies room

Once inside, she locked the door, braced it with her back and handed the tapes over to Paula in a whisper. Paula nodded and promised to get them immediately to her boss.

Tonya had driven to Condo's apartment, rehearsing her little speech all the way over.

Tonya sought to calm him down. "Condo, the reason I did it was so we would have corruption and extortion charges against Vito that would stick. Don't you understand? You can't go to the authorities with no evidence. He's on tape naming phony companies that are just a cover for all the illegal stuff that goes on. Jesus, money-laundering, extortion, it's all THERE!"

"And you're telling me he didn't lay a hand on you?" he said with real concern in his voice. "It's important for me to know this, babe."

She smoothed his face. "Honey, I'm telling you nothing happened."

"He tried to kiss you though, right? Condo said.

"He TRIED to sure, but I pushed him away," she said, batting this away like a fly.

"Well, you do know that Vito Leone is the biggest hound there is, don't you?"

"Condo, honey, look calm down, ok? Nothing happened, and that's that."

Condo looked at her one more time, shrugged and said, "Well, ok, if that's what you say then that's it. I'll never bring it up again." He reached over and kissed the top of her head. "Now listen, sweetie, I gotta go, I'm gonna go scout out locations for the new youth center that your mom's money is going to help build. I'll call you later, alright?"

Tonya went over and kissed Condo long and deep.

"OK, big chief, whatever you say," she said sweetly.

* * * * *

Hatchett walked quickly back to his truck, started the engine and got going. It would be hours before the body was discovered. There were no identifying marks, no footprints, nothing for police forensics to get a handle on. And the gun, which Hatchett was about to dispose of after one last stop, was sheared of its i.d. number.

In short, Donald T. Hatchett was clean as a whistle.

The last piece of business was to stop at Vito Leone's. He had some business to settle. But he would wait on that. No, he wanted to be good and ready.

* * * * *

Chapter 15
AN OFFICER OF THE LAW

Condo got into his truck and thought about what Tonya had said. He trusted her completely

* * * * *

Vito sat back in his chair and looked at Sal with a puzzled expression on his face. "I can't figure it out. I'm over there, what 3-4 hours, and all this broad and I did was TALK. Jesus, I felt like I was a college professor or something. Questions about operation, about our cash flow, about the plumbing contractors and the builders and, I don't know, it just never stopped!"

Sal looked over at his boss. "And she never spread her legs, not once?" He suddenly realized how that sounded. "Er, sorry, boss. I didn't mean it like—"

Vito was too distracted to take offense. He waved his hand. "No, she didn't do anything but talk. Strange." His voice trailed away.

Sal ran that through his mind. It did seem strange. But he said nothing. Vito Leone was the type of boss that liked to take credit for his own ideas. Which was another way of saying he didn't appreciate brainstorms from the hired help. No, if Vito suspected something, better to let him figure it out his own way.

Vito snapped back to reality. "How many of the other boys are on duty?" he asked Sal.

"Just me. I let Rocco, Sammy and Vinnie off to go get some food. It's Vinnie's birthday, and he kept talking about this one stripper over at the club. He's in love—at least with her pussy." He laughed. "Anyway, I told 'me to be back by 10 sharp, boss, so you don't have to worry."

Vito frowned a little. "I don't like going light on the security with so much weird shit going down, Sal. Give 'em another half-hour, then beep 'em. And next time, check with me first, understand?"

"OK, boss," Sal nodded and turned to leave.

"Sal, one more thing," Vito voice commanded as Sal had his hand on the knob.

He turned back around. "What is it, boss?" he said.

Vito swung his feet up to the desk, took out a fine Cuban cigar and prepared to torch it up. He fetched a small pearl-handled knife from his breast pocket and carefully cut the tip. "Did you find me a rat, Sal?" Vito asked with deadly precision. His head with its fine mane of wavy hair tilted back slightly.

Sal walked over to his desk and cooly replied. "You won't have to give it another thought, boss."

"Talk to me," Vito said as the blue wisps of smoke curled around his chair.

Sal reflected on the hit, thinking, IT HAD BEEN SO EASY The poor fool never even saw it coming...

... As Tom Bighorn left his office that day, he had mixed emotions. The articles were generating an outpouring of response from the Indian community, where now it seemed there were braves nearly tripping over one another to get at Vito or any of the bosses he employed.

The problem was two-fold, as Bighorn saw it. One, he would have to protect Condo as much as he could, particularly by stalling the Attorney General. He had gotten a few more calls turning up the heat on him. He didn't know how much longer he could stall.

The second problem was how to separate the calls that were legitimate grievances with specific allegations of abuse from crank callers who just had a hard-on against the Mob with nothing to back it up. Particularly if the Attorney General was now going to step into the act. He would not take kindly to having to wade through this morass of stuff.

Actually, a third problem that presented itself was having the people actually testify if such a thing ever came about. He could just see the crowds.

So there were indeed issues that had to be solved and quickly. Bighorn sighed as he trudged to his car in the empty parking garage. It was late at night and there was not a soul around.

It was then that he felt the first vague tingle come up his spine. He stopped for a moment and listened intently. There was still no sound, wait... there it was, someone or something rustling. Bighorn called out anxiously, "Hello, anybody here?"

Nothing. He shrugged and kept going to his car. Must be my imagination he thought.

As he rounded the darkened concrete corner of the garage, he never felt Sal until he was right on top of him administering an old-style Mob killing.

Bighorn's eyes bulged out as he was swept backward by the force of the silver wire being wrapped tighter and tighter around his throat, choking the life out of him. The wire sliced first through skin, then cut through the delicate tendons around his larynx as easy as a knife through butter. A gurgling sound came out which was quickly gone as his lifeless body crumpled to the ground.

Sal reached into his pocket, clicked open the stiletto and took a copy of a newspaper article from his pocket. He placed the article very delicately in the middle of Bighorn's chest and then plunged the knife in quickly and with such a thrust that it seemed perfectly straight sticking out of the dead man's heart.

He got up quickly, stripped gloves off which he transferred to a plastic bag in his pocket, and walked out of the garage as silently as he had come in...

... "Yeah, boss, you don't have anything to worry about. You know those stories you been reading? Well, they're going to need a new editor there."

Vito nodded. Now that that was taken care of, if he could only get this cop O'Brien off his ass. But that was for another time. Right now, Vito had something else on his mind.

"You know, Sal, you may have gotten rid of this guy, Bighorn, but that ain't the whole problem. Not by a long shot," said Vito pointedly. "Cause the way I got it figured, he had to have gotten his information from somebody. And that somebody had to be pissed off enough to want to cross me. Now, who do you think that would be? Maybe someone who's been very quiet for awhile—but knows all sorts of things about my operation, you know?"

Carmine stayed quiet, knowing that the boss liked to come to these brainstorms on his own. And sooner or later, the cloudburst would hit this room.

"It was Condo Cherokee, Carmine," Vito said pounding his hand on the table for emphasis. "I'd bet anything on it. Well, you know what. I'm going to pay Mr. Cherokee back in spades."

Carmine spoke up. "How you gonna do that, boss?" he asked, half afraid to hear the answer. He hoped it wouldn't mean whacking anybody again.

"Well, we're gonna see how old Condo feels when he hears about a certain former snatch of his being snatched," Vito said with a chuckle.

Carmine was confused. "What do you mean, boss?" he asked cautiously.

Vito looked at him levelly. "What I mean is, that bitch Tonya turned me down when I offered her a part in my movie. I don't like being told no, Carmine," he said coldly.

Vito sat back and got comfortable. "The way I figure it, Carmine, if Tonya won't get nude for me in my movie, she'll get nude for guys that would be willing to pay a lot for the pleasure. She'll be a good addition to the other girls" he said with a smile. "You know what to do, Carmine," he said as he extinguished his cigar. "Now go bring her to me."

* * * * *

... As if by mental telepathy, Jack O'Brien was sitting in his office thinking of Vito Leone and wondering about the strange visit he had had today from one Glen Wallace.

He had been sitting in his office after lunch ruminating on what an excellent meal he'd just had over at the diner when his phone rang. A very excited young man was on the other end of the line.

"H-e-llo... have I reached the police department?" asked the quavering voice on the other end of the line.

"Yes, you have. This is Sergeant O'Brien. What can I help you with?" said O'Brien.

"Uh, listen, I don't want to say anything over this line. Could I, like come down and talk to you in person?" said the voice again.

"Sure, son," O'Brien said. "You got the address, right?"

"Yeah, I got it," said the kid.

The line went dead.

One hour later, Jack O'Brien was sitting across from a very scared, petrified actually, Glen Wallace. He'd never seen a kid so scared. It made him take his time.

O'Brien dutifully took out a police report form, filled in the appropriate information, then smiled a half-smile at Glen. "So, why don't you tell me why you're here?" That would help as a start.

Glen ran a hand through his hair. The thing was he wasn't sure at all why he was here. He just knew that Michael had been found dead yesterday, and when he saw the picture, he'd nearly collapsed with fright. What if these two goons were the guys who had done this to him? Jesus Christ, Glen thought. I've gotta tell somebody.

So he had hesitated for awhile before calling the cops (not among his favorite activities) but eventually he had broken down.

Now as he sat down across from O'Brien, he felt almost a surge of relief at finally being able to pour out everything that was on his mind. In an odd way he didn't look at the cop as an adversary—now he looked at him as a friend. Which for Glen Wallace, was really strange.

"OK," he said, drawing a large breath. "The other night me and my friend,

Michael Stipiconti, were at this bar. You know, just drinking and watching the babies—"

O'Brien broke in. "Excuse me, maybe I'm showing my age—the babies?"

Glen just rolled his eyes. "Yeah, girls, you know—babies. Anyway, we were just hanging there, when all of a sudden, Michael starts telling me some really weird shit. In fact, it was so weird I can't even barely bear to repeat it."

"Why not?" asked O'Brien.

"'Cause I like livin' that's why, Sergeant," said Glen, cautiously.

O'Brien considered this carefully, his pulse quickening at what he was about to hear. If he pressured the kid, he might get nothing. On the other hand if he didn't exert some authority, the kid might get nonchalant. It was a tough call.

The other possibility was that the kid might ask for a lawyer. That presented another set of problems. Because with that type of situation, anything could happen. The lawyer could be one of these smart-ass types who would step on everything his "client" said. O'Brien hated those kinds of guys.

His thoughts were interrupted by Glen, who suddenly said: "Hey, can I get police protection if something goes wrong here?"

That must mean something was up, thought O'Brien. If you're that scared that you want the cops to protect you, something was really weird.

"Yeah, we can have somebody watch you, if that's what you're thinking, kid," said O'Brien.

"OK, I feel better then," sighed Glen.

"Now what is it you gotta tell me?" asked O'Brien, waiting now to hear this blockbuster tale.

"Well, like I said, we were just sitting there when these two guys walked in over to me and Mike. Goons is more like it. They were huge...

... Carmine is huge, thought O'Brien excitedly.

...and they started in on Mike," continued Glen.

"What do you mean, 'started in on him'," asked O'Brien.

"I mean, the one guy came over and put his head down real low and asked Mike to come with him. Actually, the both of them kind of escorted him out the door, if you know what I mean.

"Well, did you see what happened after that?" asked O'Brien anxiously.

"No, I didn't," said Glen.

Well, that was ok, O'Brien thought. Because even if he didn't see what happened, there was still enough circumstantial evidence to start the ball rolling on some kind of case.

Why, for example, would Carmine bother to come into the bar and search out Mike Stipiconti? O'Brien wondered if he possibly had a connection with the kid some way, but quickly ruled that out.

Unless he was working on orders from his boss, Vito.

OK, then why would Vito be so interested in one little pipsqueak, Michael Stipiconti?

O'Brien decided he needed to seek out people who knew both Vito and Stipiconti. And the best place to start was with the quivering, nervous wreck sitting here right in front of him.

He decided that it would be better to take a fatherly approach, rather than come off like a hard-ass. Something in his experience told him that the kid would respond better to that.

Let's start small, he thought.

O'Brien came around from his desk and sat on the side of it facing Glen.

"Let's go back aways, ok, Glen?" said O'Brien in a soothing voice.

Glen immediately sensed something was up.

"How far you want to go back, Sergeant?" he said warily.

"Well, for starters, how well do you know this Mike Stipiconti?" asked O'Brien.

"A couple of years," came the reply back. "You know, it's one of these things where you start hanging with somebody, pretty soon, before you know it—they're your running buddy."

"OK, then, has Mike always been a good kid, far as you know," probed O'Brien, slowly taking his time.

"Mmmnn, yeah, on balance, I'd say he had it wrapped pretty tight, if that's what you mean," said Glen, leaning back in his chair, getting comfortable.

"What were his habits, like what did he do for a job, things like that?" asked O'Brien.

Glen looked surprised. "He was a car mechanic. I thought you knew that," he said, not sure whether O'Brien was putting him on or not.

O'Brien knew; he just wanted to throw a little curve at Glen, see how he responded. OK, so they were both on the same page. That was good.

"Alright, so, car mechanic—probably makes average cash. Nothing fancy. What I mean is, unless he was a player and had the kind of money that would make loansharks nervous cause he didn't pay them back—why would someone want this kid dead?"

Glen knew what he was getting at. And at the same time began to feel a crawling feeling in the pit of his stomach.

Because he knew that sooner or later, he'd have to tell the cop everything.

But would he? He could evade, stall, and just kind of tell a few white lies forever, but what good would that do? Sooner or later, the cop would find out.

He was still trying to determine if the cop was on the level about him getting protection from Vito, if and when it came to that. From what he knew about Vito, he'd need it.

He remembered how he'd felt when he heard the news about Mike. Christ, he thought, they couldn't possibly have done to him what the paper said, could they?

The danger, as Glen saw it here, was that if he spilled the beans about Mike raping Vito's daughter, the cops would immediately target Vito as a suspect from the revenge angle. And in the process, old Glen Wallace would be forgotten about. And so conveniently might the offer of protection. And then it was simply a matter of time till Vito or one of his goons found out about how the cops came to know so much about Mike Stipiconti.

He'd better play dumb for now, he thought.

O'Brien continued to sit there, looking for all the world like he was concerned about the fate of poor Glen Wallace. But inside he was thinking that this kid held the answers to a couple very key questions.

The key was to draw him out.

"So as far as you know, this Michael didn't have any outstanding gambling debts or owe any other money, anything like that?" O'Brien asked quietly.

"No, I don't even know if he gambled," said Glen truthfully.

"So just a quiet kid who went to church, a regular altar boy, eh?" said O'Brien sarcastically.

"No, I didn't say that," said Glen. "Mike knew how to party, he could set 'em up, then set 'em back."

"So he was a drinker?" asked O'Brien.   "No, not with a problem" came back the reply.

"Alright, let's move on to sex," said O'Brien. "Did he have a girlfriend that you knew of?"

Glen decided that if he said, yes, he knew Mike's girlfriend he would not technically be lying because he certainly knew *of* her, and that was what the cop had asked.   He took a deep breath.

"Yes, I knew her," he said.

Indian Nation 143

O'Brien perked up a little bit at that. Alright, if he could establish a link here, he might be on to something.

But what? All Glen was saying was that he knew the guy's chick. Big deal.

But there might be more, he just had to be patient.

"What was she like?" O'Brien asked, carefully looking into Glen's eyes.

Glen shifted in his seat. He did a sharp intake of breath. This was it, he thought. Just play it casual, straight down the line.

"Oh, she was ok," he said. "Good looking, you know the whole nine yards," Glen said, giving O'Brien sort of a male conspiracy wink. It came off looking slightly dopey, since O'Brien was practically old enough to be Glen's father.

"What was her name?" he asked.

"Oh, he might have had a couple, you know," said Glen, desperately trying to get off the subject.

O'Brien was not to be shook off that easy. "OK, so what were *their* names?" he asked pleasantly.

Glen found himself sweating. What was he supposed to do, make up names?

O'Brien looked at him again and said, "You're sure you don't know their names? Let me remind you, kid if you withhold evidence, that's a crime."

"Well," Glen said, "There was Pamela Smith and there was Angela, and there was Karen Vigigonti, and—"

"Just a second. Does Angela have a last name?" asked O'Brien, watching Glen closely.

This was where Glen felt like he could easily throw up. He had never thought it would come to this, man! Here the cop practically had him nailed! If he gave up Angela's last name, it would be no time at all before the cop put two and two together. But if he didn't, he might be committing a crime.

"Her name was, uh, Angela Leone..." Glen said, the last name barely trailing off his lips.

O'Brien felt his heart stop. Could it be possible? Mike Stipiconti dating the daughter of one Vito Leone? O'Brien couldn't believe it. The question was, how could he tie things together. That's what he wanted to do. And once again, the answer was sitting right in front of him.

O'Brien wound up and sent a high fast pitch over the plate aimed directly at Glen Wallace's head.

"What do you know about these two, Glen? And why would a certain fellow be interested in coming into a bar and hassling Mike Stipiconti?" O'Brien asked, knowing the answer. "What happened to cause this, Glen?"

Glen shifted nervously. He leaned forward and whispered, "Look, I'm serious about this police protection, if this gets out and it gets back to me, I am a dead man!"

"If what gets out, Glen?" O'Brien said.

"Mike sort of, well you know, went a little nuts on Angela," Glen said, again in a whisper.

"What do you mean, 'went a little nuts,'?" O'Brien asked. "I don't know how to take that."

"He like... assaulted her, I guess you could say," Glen said.

"Did he rape her, Glen?" O'Brien said, leaning forward hard now.

"Yeah," came the one word answer.

"You heard him say that?"

"Yeah, I mean, yes... I did."

"And you'd be willing to testify to that?"

"Whoa," Glen said, suddenly alert now. "You never said anything about testifying."

"Alright, forget about that for now," O'Brien said, not wanting to lose the good stream he had going with Glen here. He was satisfied with the way things had gone.

He had never heard or read anything about Vito's daughter being raped. But it didn't take much of an imagination to understand what he was looking at: If Michael Stipiconti **had** raped Angela, Vito had him killed in an act of revenge. That much he was certain of.

But how to prove it?

* * * *

Tonya sat back and thought about Condo and their conversation. He had big plans for all his Indian brothers, and she wanted to support that in any way she could. If only he wouldn't get so crazy about other things, everything would be fine.

She knew that he suspected that Vito was trying some funny business with her. That was ok, she could handle that. She just hoped that it wouldn't come between them eventually. That would not be good.

Tonya had always hoped to marry Condo and she could feel that the day would not be that far off. But he was preoccupied with other things, that she knew. Even when they had babies, she could never be quite sure what he would do. Would he be the type of father who would be there for their child, or would be the kind of father who was always gone? Tonya had no way of knowing, although she did have a good sense about Condo.

She didn't know quite what to expect from motherhood herself. Poca Daisy had talked to her about it, but only very little. Tonya had a feeling that she would find out the way every woman did—through trial and error.

She herself was very inclined towards children; she felt they added something you couldn't measure to your life.

If it was a daughter, that would be good, nothing like a little girl to play with. But a son for Condo would be just as well.

Tonya still had the tapes in her possession of that evening with Vito. She would hang on to them for awhile until the moment was completely right. She didn't want Vito slipping away from her.

It was while she was having these pleasant thoughts that she decided to luxuriate in the bathtub. She went into the bathroom and bent over the tub, turning the knobs to fill it. She stood up and started to stretch her arms above her head to take off her top, when suddenly her breath was sucked out of her in a soundless scream...

Carmine was standing just outside the doorway with his arms folded across his chest.

He put his fingers to his lips, then brushed past her as he bent over the tub and turned the faucets off.

"We don't want any water spillin' over, now do we?" he said in a soft, menacing whisper. "No, we don't. Now get dressed."

Tonya decided not to wasted time screaming. And in that split second she decided to go for it. She put her head down and took two steps and launched her her head straight at Carmine's chest.

Oooommmppphhh!!! came the sound as his chest exhaled its breath as Tonya crashed into him and he went sprawling.

Tonya scrambled to her feet and got going lickety-split down the stairs. She figured she had 30 seconds at best before Carmine came pounding after her. She searched around wildly for a pair of shoes and her handbag. Got the shoes, where was the goddamn handbag? She forgot it and snatched her keys up from the table by the door. It was at that moment that she felt herself being yanked back by her hair with a force that nearly tore her head off.

Carmine was pretty quick for a big man, she had to give the bastard that.

"WHAT THE HELL DO YOU THINK YOU'RE DOING, BITCH?" he roared. He still had her head pulled back and finally released her grip and she slumped to the floor.

Carmine composed himself, smoothing his hair back and straightening his jacket. His hand went to the small lump at the back of his head where he had fallen. She's lucky my orders are to bring her in one piece, he thought. Cause otherwise she'd be picking her teeth up off the floor.

He leaned over her and said, "Now, we're gonna try this again, alright Tonya? And if you run on me, I'll shoot you—and take my chances with the boss."

Thirty minutes later, Tonya was sitting handcuffed to the chair in Vito's office. She couldn't believe this. They had kidnapped her from her apartment! It was like some old cop show on TV.

She looked around for Vito. Where was he? She knew he had to be around somewhere.

"Where is Vito, Carmine? I know he's around here somewhere. And that he is behind this."

Carmine thought to himself. Hey, the bitch doesn't have to know anything. Which is the way the boss wants it.

"What do you want with me?" asked Tonya in a defiant voice, wishing she could only reach Condo now.

"Me?" "Oh, I don't want anything with you, Tonya," said Carmine, sounding slightly mystified. "I don't ever touch any of my girls, no never. That's bad for business."

Girls? What girls? Tonya gave him a quizzical look.

"You don't know what's going on do you?" Carmine chuckled. "Well, it's simple, Tonya, you're going to become one of my girls. See, this is my little action here. Vito don't have nothing to do with it. Now, as I was sayin'. We're going to find you some nice clothes, get your hair done, get you all dolled up, so you'll be presentable for my clients."

"You're going to make me a whore?" she raged at Carmine. "Is that what you're telling me?"

Carmine shook his head. "Tonya, Tonya, tsk.. tsk," he said, clucking his tongue. "Whore is such a dirty word. You are an escort, Tonya. And believe me, there is an art to being an escort. In fact, we have someone who is going to work with you on the more cultured stuff you need to know."

Tonya shook her head. "OK, since I have no choice and no one can find me, I'll play your game," she said with venom in her voice. "But no one of your 'clients' better touch me. Cause I'm not having sex with any of these dirtbags!"

Carmine got real close to Tonya now. He bent down and lifted her chin up. "Oh, that's where you're wrong, Tonya.

You'll do whatever they want. If they want to watch your pretty mouth go down on them over and over, you'll do that. If they want you to spread your legs and play with yourself, you'll spread 'em wide. If they want to see you do it with another girl, you'll do it. You'll do whatever my clients want. Your body is bought and paid for." With that Carmine got up and left the room.

Tonya sat there dumbfounded. What the hell could Carmine possibly mean "bought and paid for?"

She was soon to find out.

And Vito Leone watched all these proceedings from behind a two-way mirror.

* * * * *

O'Brien pulled his unmarked car into the parking lot of Victory Hospital. The best place to start, he reasoned was the hospitals. They would have records of all patients who had come in for any type of procedure within the past few weeks. The way O'Brien figured it, Angela had been taken to the hospital, examined, and then released. After all, there was no reason to keep a rape victim overnight or for a few days unless they had been injured.

So, the thing to do first, was to check to see if she was an inpatient.

He was familiar with the hospital, having visited it many times over the course of his career. He'd always found the staff to be very courteous to cops. And he needed information right now.

He walked over to the desk and flashed his badge and asked if he could talk to the admissions nurse.

"What's this about officer?" asked the nurse.

"Would you mind stepping around to the side of the desk, miss?" O'Brien asked. He didn't want any four alarms going off.

She shrugged and complied. They walked a few feet away from the desk.

"I'd like to find out if there has been a patient who has been admitted here," O'Brien explained. "However, this isn't just any old patient, you understand."

The nurse started to get impatient. "Look, Sergeant, they're all the same to me," she said. "They come in and go—"

O'Brien cut her off. "Do you know who Vito Leone is, miss?" he asked quickly.

The nurse's eyes widened. "Well, I've heard his name mentioned in the papers, and—well, that's about all I know about him. What does this have to do with Vito Leone?" she asked, suddenly a little afraid now.

"I need to know if there was a patient named Angela Leone in her sometime within the last couple of days to a week," said O'Brien, hoping the urgency in his voice would get him the needed info about Angela.

The nurse got official. "Sergeant, how many times have you been around here. You know that I can't—"

O'Brien pleaded with her. "Look, nurse... Mitchell, I'd really like your help on this," he said in that paternal way he had. He lowered his voice. "We have reason to believe that whatever Angela came in for—has to do with another incident, in this case a murder. So I'd need to talk to the examining physician, if you don't mind."

The nurse hesitated. Right away, you could see the mind clicking her options like pinballs. "Well, that may be a little difficult to do, Sergeant," she said primly. "You see according to hospital regulations—"

O'Brien again cut her short. "Nurse Mitchell, if you impede an official police investigation, I can also haul you in for questioning," he said, hoping to scare her. "And the doctor, too, I might add."

"Oh, my," said nurse Mitchell, her hand going to her mouth.

O'Brien stood back and folded his arms. "Now then, where can I find the good doctor?" he said calmly.

"I'll have him paged," said nurse Mitchell meekly.

Ten minutes later, Dr. Sanford was sitting across from O'Brien. He seemed a little annoyed at the nurse having paged him.

"What is this, Sergeant?" he asked brusquely. "As you can see, I'm trying to do my rounds. And I need to finish."

"This won't take long, Doctor," O'Brien said, attempting to calm the man down. "I just need information on a patient named Angela Leone. To be more specific, I'd like to find out if she was brought in here because she had been raped."

The doctor adjusted his stethoscope. "Well, even if I could tell you that, I can't. It would have to do with the ethics of the hospital, you see," he said in a tone meant to imply that the conversation was over.

O'Brien wasn't about to be put off. "I understand, Doctor. However, as I told nurse Mitchell, you don't want to be put in the position of impeding a police investigation, now do you?" he inquired pleasantly.

The doctor looked at nurse Mitchell. She shrugged and looked at the floor.

"Well, um, no, of course not," he answered. "But why is this so important?"

"Doctor, we have reason to believe that Angela's condition may have been the trigger to something much worse—possibly a murder."

"Do I need to call a lawyer, Sergeant?" asked Dr. Sanford with hesitation in his voice.

O'Brien shook his head. "No, just tell me if in fact she was raped, doctor," he said.

"Yes, she was. I did the vaginal swabs on her and saw the semen count," said Dr. Sanford in a small voice.

"Dr., did the parents of Angela bring her in here?" O'Brien asked.

"Yes they did."

"And how would you describe their behavior after you told them?"

Dr. Sanford hesitated. "Mr. Leone seemed extremely upset," he said.

"Would you say at that point he was capable of anything, including violence?" asked O'Brien, holding his breath.

"Um, on balance, yes, I would have to say so, Sergeant," Dr. Sanford replied.

"Thank you, doctor. And now, you can go," O'Brien said, snapping shut his notebook.

O'Brien drove back to his office in silence. What he had was unbelievable. The doctor had virtually told him everything he wanted to know. By telling him Vito's mental state when he found out that Angela was raped, he had unwittingly told him that Vito was capable of anything.

Including murder... Maybe.

O'Brien knew it was out of the question to try and get to Angela. She would be guarded like the crown jewels. He wondered if there was a way that he could make her talk to him. It didn't seem very likely. But before that, he had a problem.

Even if Angela did tell him everything, he still had to tie Vito to the murder of Michael Stipiconti. No easy task! Vito would of course say that, hey, he had no grudges against the kid. Stipiconti, huh? Name rings a bell, I guess. Yeah, he went out with my daughter once or twice officer, what about it? And then O'Brien was dead.

    O'Brien knew he had to find a way to get a witness who had seen them together. The word of this kid Glen was good, but maybe it wouldn't stand up in court. He had to talk to people who may have seen them together at any time. He'd start with the bartender and work his way back down.

* * * * *

Chapter 16
TONYA'S DESPERATE HOURS

The next few days were a nightmare for Tonya.

After initially scoffing at Carmine, she had slowly come to the realization that he meant to basically enslave her. It was like she was living out some sort of movie. She had struggled and finally Sal caught her by the hair and yanked her back, pinning her on the ground. He then fed her a couple of nice pink pills that would help her sleep very nicely, thank you.

She woke up, not sure what time it was, hell what day it was. She was in a small room. Her clothes had been stripped from her and she was dressed in a smock that came down below her knees. She peered out the window. It was obvious she was being held in some type of hotel room. She tried the window. Bolted shut. She ran a hand over the glass. Very thick, which meant it was probably bullet-proof.

She felt ravenous and couldn't remember the last time she had eaten. As if by mental telepathy, the key twisted in the lock and Sal came in with a tray of food. He set it down and then stopped to look at her a minute.

"So, do we understand each other, tootsie?" he said.

"You're here for the duration so forget about runnin' anyplace. Won't do you no good anyway."

"Where am I?" Tonya asked.

"Don't worry, the doc'll explain everything when she comes in."

The doc?

Without another word, Sal got up and walked out, locking the door behind him.

Tonya went over and examined the food. Some kind of sandwich and a piece of fruit, and a coke. Prison grub. She gulped down the sandwich and fruit, then sat back and took a long drink of coke, and examined her situation.

She had no idea where she was, or how long she was going to be held for. God knew if she could ever get a message somehow to Condo, who probably right now would be going out of his mind with worry, poor guy. Well, she'd just have to ride it out for now. See what they had in store for her. One thing was for sure, though. When this was through, she'd find Vito and kill him.

Her thoughts were interrupted by the key turning in the door. In walked a tall, slender woman of indeterminate age. She was dressed casually, but the clipboard she held and her demeanor suggested anything but casualness. Her hair was pulled back tight in a bun.

She came directly over to Tonya and said, "Hello, Tonya, I'm Dr. Taylor. I see you've eaten. Good, we can get started."

Tonya broke in quickly. "Look, whoever you are. Where am I and how can I get out. I was brought here against my will and that's all I know."

"But of course you were," Dr. Taylor said, smiling a little at how naive Tonya was. "It's how you conduct yourself from here on out that counts, now."

"Alright, first things first," Dr. Taylor said. "I am here to explain exactly what your duties will be and your schedule. After that, if you have any questions, I'll be glad to answer them."

"Mr. Leone has personally asked that I take charge of picking out a nice wardrobe for you and explaining the duties that you'll need to know when you entertain our clients," she explained.

"Basically, you'll spend time in the hotel here during the day until we come for you a little after 5:00," Dr. Taylor said. "You can sleep as late as you like, swim in the pool in the hotel, shop in the little mini-mall, eat in the restaurants. The only thing we ask is that you be available for the evening's entertainment. Whatever form that takes you understand."

Tonya couldn't believe it. "First of all, Doc, where am I? And secondly, what kind of doctor are you anyway?"

"You're on the other side of town," Dr. Taylor said. "We had to take at least some precaution that someone would recognize you. But you might as well be in China for all the good it will do you. Because you're not going to run, are you? That's a good girl.

And the answer to your second question is, I am a licensed sex therapist who has been brought in to supervise your orientation."

"How do you mean entertain the clients?" Tonya asked.

"Whatever they desire," Dr. Taylor explained patiently. "If they choose to sit and talk, that's fine. If they choose to have sex with you, that's fine. If they choose to just sit and look at you, that's fine also. Now, stand up."

Dr. Taylor then spent the next couple of minutes getting Tonya's sizes. She finally capped her pen and put away her clipboard.

"The clothes will be delivered by Sal later today," Dr. Taylor said. "At that point I will come back and inspect you in them. But I'm sure they'll be fine. You have a beautiful body, Tonya, you should feel proud." Dr. Taylor took a step towards her and ran his index finger from Tonya's neck down through the valley of her breasts to her stomach. "In fact, if things were different between us... who knows?"

Tonya flinched visibly and stepped back.

"That's all right," Dr. Taylor laughed. "In time, you may come to see me as your best friend. In fact, I'm sure of it."

* * * * *

Condo paced up and down the apartment. He could not understand this. It was not like Tonya to take off like this. He tried to comb his memory to see if it was something he had said to make her angry, but he couldn't think of anything. Everything was right on target between them.

Of course Tonya was a strong-willed girl, so anything could be possible, but still... this was awfully strange.

Condo thought about possibly going to the police but decided against it. What were they going to do? Tell him to fill out a form and go home. Great, he thought.

He also thought about other things:

Like rape...

Like murder...

Like - hell, the list was too gruesome to go on.

Nothing could have happened like that to his Tonya, that he knew. Still, he had heard about other women who just one day vanish, never to be heard from again.

There were a few people he could talk to about this, but no one that he could confide his true feelings too. For all the braves that Condo had befriended and done the right thing for, not many of them were what he would call his bosom buddies.

That was strange because they shared the same brotherhood, the same bond. But when push came to shove, well, some of them just couldn't step up to the plate for him.

So Condo would shoulder on alone with this one. Trying to gather whatever strength he could along the way.

The first place he thought about looking were over some of her old friends. After all, Tonya might have gone there for a day or two. Or they might have talked to her. He decided to try Pat Clarkson, a good friend of hers.

He bounded over there in his truck and 30 minutes later was knocking on Pat's door. A small, petite woman, she answered the door and smiled when she saw Condo.

"Hi, Condo, what's up?"

"Well, Pat, I was hoping you could tell me that, he said."

"What do you mean, Condo?"

"It's Tonya. I haven't heard from her or seen her in several days. Well, a few anyway. Actually a day and a half."

"Oh, it's probably nothing. You know how Tonya just likes to drop out of sight sometime."

Did he? He couldn't exactly say that about Tonya, he thought.

"Well, no, actually Pat. She, uh, really doesn't just kind of up and leave."

"So you think maybe she's broke down somewhere with her car and just never called?"

"The funny thing is—her car is still in the parking lot," he said.

"Hhhmmm, that is a strange one. What are you gonna do?"

Actually, Condo was stumped. Again he tried to picture the police station and the various responses:

... "and that's all we know, Mr. Cherokee."

... "and we'll keep you posted if anything turns up."

... "are you sure **you** didn't have an argument with her, Mr. Cherokee? After all, 8 out of 10 domestic quarrels end up with the woman walking out..."

Condo got the creeps thinking about the reception he'd get from the police.

Still, what to do? He had struck out with Pat Clarkson. Maybe she would have some helpful tips that he could use. But somehow, he doubted it.

He brought his mind back to Pat who was hovering over him with a cookie tray and a cup of tea. That was nice of her but right now, he wasn't in the mood. He told her thanks and got out of the apartment.

He walked back to his truck lost in thought. Where to go now? Tonya wasn't known to hang out in bars or bowling alleys so those two venues were out. And she certainly had no family to speak of, since Poca was dead.

Maybe she was visiting Poca's grave?

Well, if she was, it was a long time to be spending at a gravesite.

Condo decided he would have to start at square one again.

* * * * *

Hatchett looked in the paper and saw that the murder had indeed been investigated. That was alright. There was no way they could tie it to him.

He sat there and thought about how he would put things to Vito when the time came. Hatchett had always felt that the element of surprise worked really well with certain people.

To just kind of walk in and pop Sal or Carmine or whoever was there... and then just to walk in further and confront Vito would be good.

Hatchett could see him start to sweat. That awful moment when he realized that all his muscle was no longer there to help him. Good, he could hardly wait.

* * * * *

Tonya looked up and saw Dr. Taylor standing there, with a whole bunch of new clothes hanging from her hand. OK, she thought. What kind of nonsense is this now?

Dr. Taylor walked over and laid them down on her bed.

"Now then, Tonya, here are the clothes that you need to try on. Take your time, but I need to see each one."

Tonya thought, what the hell, and went into the bathroom.

She came out and paraded around in the silk dress. Dr. Taylor nodded her approval...

She came out in the leopard-print mini-dress. Dr. Taylor nodded her approval...

She modeled at least 10 pairs of shoes, one by one, all of which Dr. Taylor liked...

Finally, just when Tonya thought she was all done, Dr. Taylor said, "OK, now we'll start with the lingerie."

"Hold it, lady," said Tonya. "If you think I'm parading around in skimpy little nothings, you can forget about it."

"Tonya, it's just me," Dr. Taylor protested. "I'm a girl, remember?"

"Good, let's remember that then."

A few minutes later, Tonya came out with the first of the pieces of lingerie. It was a red silk Teddy number.

Dr. Taylor said, yes, that will do.

She then went back and modeled a corset that accentuated her breasts. Dr. Taylor nodded her approval, but her eyes and mouth were watering a bit too much for Tonya's comfort. She decided that would be the end of the fashion show for Dr. Taylor today.

* * * * *

After she tried on her last piece of lingerie for her, Tonya sat back and heard what Dr. Taylor had to say about her "duties."

"Well, that depends, Tonya," Dr. Taylor said, as if discussing some arcane piece of literature. "Some of our clients like certain things, others don't. You just have to sort of feel them out to make sure."

Tonya felt that she had to say something, or she would scream. This woman was painting her into a corner that Tonya was not sure she could get out of.

"Dr. Taylor, can you listen to me for a second?"

"Well of course, Tonya, that's what I'm here for."

"You know they kidnapped me?"

"Well, I'd heard something to that effect, yes."

"And so you know that I'm here against my will?"

Dr. Taylor got up and took a walk across the expanse of carpet in the room. She came back and sat down and looked at Tonya squarely in the eye.

"Tonya, to be quite frank, I don't give a rat's ass why you came here, or how you did. Understand?"

So much for a quiet, bedside manner...

"But the fact is you are here. And as such, you're under my supervision. Carmine is expecting to see a high-class lady come from here. So remember that."

Tonya felt as if she would explode.

"LOOK, YOU CAN'T FORCE SOMEONE AGAINST THEIR WILL TO BECOME A WHORE! DON'T YOU KNOW THAT?"

Dr. Taylor became quite indignant.

"If you don't sit back down I'll call Sal."

Tonya let out her breath. What was the use?

For the next few hours, they went over the things she was expected to do and the things she was expected to say.

What type of businessmen she would be entertaining and so forth.

Tonya again felt like she was going to be ill.

This woman actually expected her to go through with all this.

Tonya's first "client" was scheduled to see her the next day. She was curious to know who it was.

But all Dr. Taylor would say was that the gentleman was an Asian man who preferred blondes like Tonya. And that he liked to go to dinner and loved small talk.

OK, she thought, that doesn't really give me much to go on. Of course, it didn't really matter because eventually Condo would find her and they would be together again. Or so Tonya thought. Or so she could only hope.

Dr. Taylor suggested that Tonya get a good night's sleep...

Promptly at 6:00 the next evening, Tonya was dressed and ready to go. She had on a low-cut red dress and high heels. Feeling faintly ridiculous, but determined to ride this out, Tonya presented herself for "inspection" by the good doctor.

Dr. Taylor came in and asked Tonya to turn this way and that way. "Hhhmmnn-hhhmmnn" was all she murmured.

"Very good selection, Tonya, I like it," she pronounced.

"Uh huh," piped up Tonya in a monotone.

"Now just one more thing Tonya."

Dr. Taylor reached over and brought her hand up sharply under Tonya's chin so as to not to disturb her makeup.

"You will do what we tell you to do, Tonya or else."

"OK, ok," Tonya said through clenched teeth.

Ten minutes later she was on her way to the restaurant where she was supposed to meet this "client." Sal drove her and was silent the whole way. She didn't really have much conversation in her anyway, so it was no big deal.

Once inside the restaurant, she was led to a table where sat a smallish Asian man of indeterminate age. Sal brought her over and introduced her.

"How do you do, miss?" the man said to her. His english was perfect despite having complete Asian features.

"I'm ok, I guess, Mr.?"

"Oh, please, call me Mr. Wang."

Tonya chuckled at that one. The Asian guy with the phallic-sounding name.

Mr. Wang's face became concerned. "Is... is anything wrong, miss?"

Tonya tried to stifle herself from laughing more. She was urged along by a glare from Sal.

"No, no, nothing's wrong, Mr. er, Wang."

Mr. Wang's face lit up again. "Good, very good."

"Would you like something to drink, miss?"

Tonya had never wanted a drink so bad in her life. But she had been warned against the use of alcohol by Dr. Taylor.

"No, thank you, just an iced tea would be fine."

Mr. Wang seemed disappointed. "No champagne? Come, come, I was hoping for a bit more."

Sal broke in from the back. "No, really Mr. Wang. Mr. Leone figures that the girls don't perform so well—I mean they don't do well with booze. You know? So Tonya here will just have an iced tea. Won't you, Tonya?"

"Sure, Sal," smiled back Tonya.

Mr. Wang shut up after that.

The drinks came and Mr. Wang loosened up after a few minutes with some kind of daiquiri thing in front of him.

Tonya suddenly remembered that she was supposed to make small talk.

But before she could do that, Sal excused himself, walking up and giving Mr. Wang a hearty clap on the back, and a broad wink.

He gave the cold fish eye to Tonya, however, a look filled with menace...

Tonya got the message.

It turned out that Mr. Wang was some kind of commodities broker (what else?) and he was here in town on business, and boy didn't he like American girls.

Mr. Wang explained a thing or two about Asians.

It seemed that a lot of Asian women, while they looked real passive, were actually not very much fun, at least as far as Mr. Wang was concerned.

So, it seemed that Mr. Wang liked American girls he could laugh with and joke with, without having to be constantly reminded that he was from the Orient, and as such, he had to watch his manners—or risk embarrassing his country.

Mr. Wang had had quite his fill of that.

Oddly enough, Tonya found the little guy amusing. It was weird. She even felt a little sorry for him.

The second round of drinks came and Tonya changed her mind. The hell with their rules.

"Mr. Wang—order that champagne."

Mr. Wang frowned. "Yes, but Sal was very clear. He said—."

Tonya leaned forward. "I KNOW what Sal said. But I'm asking if you want to have a good time with me."

"Yes, yes, of course I do. It's just that—"

"OK, then. Waiter!"

A little while later they were just sitting there getting pleasantly smashed when Mr. Wang suddenly announced, "Perhaps we should go to my hotel room."

Tonya suddenly seized with panic. It was as if the alcohol suddenly just drained from her. This was the moment of truth.

She leaned forward. "Listen, Mr. Wang. I'll be straight with you. You don't know anything about me, right? Well, of course not. The truth of the matter is, I've been brought here against my will." She lowered her voice, "I've been *kidnapped*."

Mr. Wang was either very drunk or just simply didn't comprehend. He sat there with this stupid look on his face, not saying anything.

It was as if Tonya had not said a word.

"Look, Mr. Wang. I've gotta get out of here. I'll find a way to pay you back if you'll help me. I've got money, I've just gotta find a way to get back to my boyfriend, and he'll help me."

Out of sight of Tonya, Mr. Wang's hand found its way to his beeper. He pressed it once.

It was plain from Mr. Wang's silence that he wasn't going to help her. So Tonya stood up and decided to make a run for it.

"See you, Mr. Wang."

With that, she plunged for the door, hoping to lose herself in the crowd.

She got about a dozen feet before she ran into a brick wall.

Actually, to be more precise, a brick wall named Sal.

He hustled her over to the car quickly. Twisting her arm, he brought her up straight and said, "You stupid bitch, I told you not to try and run."

Sal's hand went into his pocket...

...and the next thing Tonya felt was a flash of pain across her face. Sal stepped back and removed a velvet glove from his right hand.

Tonya's face felt like it was on fire. She raised a hand to her face and looked at it. No blood, no nothing. No, the velvet glove would leave no marks. Smart boy.

Sal yanked her arm again and threw her in the front seat. They sped off in the car.

He started to chuckle. "Boy, are you in for it."

"What do you mean?"

"Oh, when Vito finds out, boy will he be pissed." Sal could barely contain himself.

Tonya just sat there and scowled silently to herself.

As soon as the car hit the garage and they were parked, Sal got out and pulled the door open. He reached in, grabbed Tonya who twisted away from him. He let her go and they walked upstairs.

Dr. Taylor was waiting.

"Well, well, Tonya. I see on your first attempt you failed miserably."

Just that minute the phone rang. Dr. Taylor went over to answer it.

It was Vito...

She took it in the other room.

"Yes, Mr. Leone. I understand. Well, the girl just didn't cooperate. What I would suggest..." She turned her back to Tonya and began whispering into the phone.

Finally she hung up.

She came back over to where Tonya and Sal stood. "Carmine is making a personal visit down here. He wants to have another talk with Tonya."

Tonya scowled again inwardly.

* * * * *

Frank DeLuca swirled the drink in his glass and stared blankly at the back of the bar. He had been on this Indian Condo's trail for a few days now and had come up with nothing.

The problem was that it wasn't like your typical case. Trying to follow an Indian around was pretty slippery. It was like they led different lifestyles.

He had thought at first that he would try to see if there was any way he could tie what the Indian had to say about mob corruption into some of the mob guys he knew.

That was a lot easier said than done...

The problem was that like most private detectives, DeLuca worked both sides of the proverbial street. Meaning that while he had no allegiance to the Indians, he definitely had some to particular mob guys.

That made things doubly tricky.

Fact was that nosing *too* much around certain mob business made them nervous.

It could also potentially be bad for your health.

DeLuca had no illusions about guys in the mob. He knew plenty about the days when people like Lucky Luciano roamed the earth. And like everyone else he had heard stories about things that would make you shudder.

Like horrible garrotings and stabbings too grotesque to witness...

Like guys winding up shot with their genitals stuffed into their mouths...

Like disfigurements with acid...

As far as he was concerned, he didn't even want to *think* about what would happen if they started to dislike *him*.

So, he was in a bit of a rough spot. He had to find a way to investigate all this stuff quietly without arousing too many suspicions that he was poking his nose in where it wasn't wanted.

DeLuca thought about his options.

He knew that if he found things that were out and out illegal and reported them back to the Attorney General that the guy would want to shut down operations immediatlely.

And if they shut things down suddenly, the mob guys would come looking for a reason.

So he had to come up with something that he could feed Atkinson to keep him quiet, but not something *so* bad that it would blow everything out of the water. That was key.

Let's see, now what were some of the things that this Condo guy was alleging in the articles...

DeLuca came up with something right away. Condo had said that the Mob was moving a lot of stolen merchandise and basically having his blood brothers do all the stealing and the dirty work.

It was simple, so simple, he couldn't believe it...

Now, it wasn't just enough to *say* that all this activity was going down. No, he had to *prove* it somehow.

And how does one prove things in this world?

With photographs, that's how. Lots and lots of photographs. The kind that impatient Attorney Generals would just love to get their hands on.

But he would stage it so that it was just so hard to actually get these guys caught in the act that the Attorney General would eventually give up on that and set his sights somewhere else.

Or so DeLuca hoped...

He sat there and ordered another round. The way to do it was simple. He knew plenty of guys who would be willing to shall we say *pose* for certain pictures.

Guys that could be made up to look just like Indians...

DeLuca knew just where to stage this little caper to. There were empty warehouses down by the docks that would be perfect backdrops for what *looked* for all intents and purposes like stolen goods being unloaded.

Only if the Attorney General went down to visit those docks, he wouldn't see anything. Gee, I don't know what happened, sir. They were here last week. Must have picked another location.

Oh, yes, this was good, DeLuca thought. So good that he almost felt like ordering champagne. Then thought better of it. Better not get so cocky, he thought. The job ain't even begun yet.

* * * * *

Condo pulled over to the side of the road. The search for Tonya was definitely not going as well as he had hoped. He had exhausted so many possibilities, he didn't know where to turn next.

He was missing something, but he didn't know what...

Tonya could not just have vanished into thin air...

He tried to think what he could have missed. He had been over every inch of space and still it turned up blank.

As far as he knew Tonya was not disliked by anyone. If that was true, it would be news to him.

Who then could possibly have it in for her?

He actually had summoned up the courage to try the police department. And, as predicted, he had come across a desk sergeant that was sleepy and bored.

And graduated to being pissed off at Condo for interrupting his routine.

The bottom line, though, was that they had not heard a word from anyone even resembling Tonya.

So that avenue was closed.

There was one other avenue that Condo thought about trying but even he had to laugh at.

He thought about going to a psychic.

What the hell, he thought. It was worth a shot. Everything else had turned up empty. He drove over to the library.

Thirty minutes later he was on his way over to "Madame Rose's Psychic Parlor." As much as Condo was worried and concerned about Tonya, he had to chuckle. If Tonya knew he was doing this, she would have laughed out loud.

Condo parked his truck and walked up the steps to Madame Rose's. He rang the doorbell and instantly Madame Rose was greeting him. Whew, he thought, that was pretty fast service.

She ushered him in and nodded as he repeated again why he was here.

"I am sure that I can help," Madame Rose said in some kind of weird east european accent.

"Now, you are looking for a girl, uh, woman about how old?"

"Early thirties," Condo replied.

"OK, now you say that she was last seen several days ago?"

"That's right."

"Did you have some kind of fight at the time?"

"No, there was no fight."

"Well, had you argued a day or two before that? Sometimes these things fester and then—"

"No, we don't fight." Condo was starting to get a little irritated.

"I see. I see." Madame Rose was starting to feel Condo's impatience so she decided to switch gears. She went into a trance all of a sudden.

Then didn't speak for what seemed like an eternity...

Finally, after five full minutes of silence, Condo suddenly looked at her and said, "Uh, Madame Rose, can you see anything. Anything at all?"

Ssshhh... came the reply.

Condo shushed.

Madame Rose opened her eyes.

"I can't help you," she announced.

Condo was struck dumb. "What do you mean, you can't help me? You've got to, Madame Rose, you've just got to. I'm really getting to the end of my rope here."

Madame Rose sighed and looked deeply at Condo. "I know, my son, I know. It is just that sometimes these things don't pan out. I mean, I'll give you your money back if that's what this is—"

Condo cut her off. "It's not the money. I just really want to know what happened to my Tonya. That's all. Can't you see that?" He was nearly on his feet now shouting. He controlled himself and sat back down.

Madame Rose looked at him and sighed inwardly. This was typical. So many people came to her seeking their loved ones.

But sometimes, as in this case, things just didn't pan out. She wasn't some toy manufacturer where you got a money-back guarantee. Either things came to her, certain visions and whatnot, or they didn't.

In this case, she had tried really hard, but could not raise the spirit of Tonya...

She looked up again at Condo standing there looking so defeated and so alone. She reached into her cigar box, withdrew the $10 he had paid her, and handed it back to him without a word. She nodded sympathetically.

Condo thanked her and walked back out to his truck...

* * * * *

DeLuca again thought about where to stage this little caper. He knew of an empty warehouse that he could get into with no problem.

Now the only problem would be to recruit enough men and he knew just where he would start. He needed guys he could depend on, guys that would be able to understand what the plot was without a lot of *explanation*.

He thought of bribery but that was way too complicated. What he could do was put the word out that he needed a bunch of reliable guys who knew how to disguise things well.

And what better place to start than the Greek lounge.

"So how much I get for this little thing you doing?" asked Markos Semetra.

DeLuca leaned back and contemplated his drink. This was going to be easy. The great thing was that old Markos and his boys *looked* enough like Indians to pull this thing off.

All they had to do was be very convincing in the photographs.

Let's see, DeLuca thought, what do I need...

Couple of pairs of old shabby clothes should do...

Wigs, so it looks like they have long hair...

A little dark, oily makeup which they rub on their skin to make their skin look Indian...

That ought to do it, he thought. Now, just settle on the price and the time of day and he was set.

DeLuca leaned back towards the conversation. "Tell you what, Markos, I'll give each man $100 bucks for a few hours work. How's that?"

Markos looked at DeLuca in the gloom of the Greek Lounge. "Is ok, I guess," he said with a shrug. "You can't make it a little higher?"

DeLuca laughed. "OK, you got guts, Markos. $125 a man it is then."

They shook hands.

"So what is it my men going to be stealing?"

DeLuca winced. Jesus, did he have to phrase it like that? He said patiently to Markos: "You're not going to be *stealing* anything. It's only going to *look* like you're stealing. Get it?"

Markos shifted his toothpick. "OK, what it is we *look* like we're stealing?"

That was a good question. Actually, DeLuca hadn't got around to quite figuring that out yet.

"I'll let you know. Now, let's go meet your boys."

* * * *

They drove a short distance to a diner where four men were sitting. DeLuca couldn't get over it. It was amazing how these Greek guys could look Indian with so little trouble. Must be something in the genes he thought.

There was Alexi, Arista, Trocas and Phillip. They looked pretty much like a silent bunch, not very prone to yakking.

Which was fine with DeLuca.

Alexi, though, was a little cocky. He acted like this caper was the recreation of the Bulgari jewel heist.

"So what we gonna be doing, Mr., er, DeLuca?"

"Same answer I gave your boss, Alexi, I'll let you know when I find out."

DeLuca hoped he wouldn't get this from every one of these yahoos. That was all he needed. Basically they were to show up and mind their manners.

"You guys do any prison time?"

All four of them shifted their eyes.

DeLuca glanced at Markos. "OK, is there something I should know?"

Markos looked uncomfortable. "Well, as long as we're getting into this—yeah, one or two of my boys have done time in the big house. But they were framed though."

DeLuca thought: Of course, same old story.

"OK, where and when?"

"Trocas did a short piece up at the State Pen, and Phillip did his time in Rockingham Prison."

"What were the charges?"

"Petty theft on both counts."

Great, DeLuca thought. Just what I need. Ex-cons.

"Everything is all right now, right?"

"Oh, yeah, it's fine," said Markos.

"Allright, well, stay out of trouble when you're around me." DeLuca stood up. "Allright, that's it. Markos, I'll be talking to you."

* * * *

A day or two later, DeLuca was standing on a loading dock shivering slightly. The guys that Markos had assembled were all ready.

The night was clear and the moon had come up. That was perfect, DeLuca thought. It's going to give me some dynamite pictures.

The better to send to one very anxious Attorney General, who was already bugging DeLuca.

His questions were so weird. Like hey, Frank, do you have any evidence yet? He actually thought that DeLuca just stumbled across evidence of the mob's illegal activities just as easy as you ordered breakfast.

Unbelievable... thought DeLuca.

So here he was ready to send these guys into action. He had the fake boxes all ready. Everything was set to make this look like a real heist.

The plan was this: Markos would direct his men to start unloading boxes and crates from a huge semi that was parked here. (It had cost DeLuca a bundle to get this semi. Things like this did not come cheap.)

Now all Markos' guys had to do was make it *look* there was a shipment being unloaded. The boxes and crates were actually filled with paper. But they had to do it in such as convincing way that it convince the District Attorney.

He had the camera and the tripod all set up. A Pentax 4000SL. It was a honey of a camera and took great night photos. The images were so clear, there is no way Mr. Attorney General would not immediately think of illegal activity going down.

He walked over to where Markos was standing.

"OK, let's go. Now remember. These guys are to take their time until I get all the shots I want, ok?"

"OK, Mr. DeLuca."

DeLuca walked back to the camera and then stopped a minute. He walked back a little ways out of sight of the men.

He wanted to check for any pain-in-the-ass cops who might be loitering around. That would be all he needed. Tonight was definitely not a night to have cops nosing around.

He didn't see any, so he walked back to the group.

He peered through the lens. Everything was coming into focus just fine. He could make out all the forms and figures.

DeLuca gave Markos the thumbs up sign.

He waited a minute until all the men formed a kind of line that stretched from the back of the semi down the long loading platform onto the dock. He wanted a long line of men.

"Wait a minute."

DeLuca walked over to the guys and took one last look at their costumes. Markos had certainly made all his men look like Indians that was for sure. There were more headbands and long hair than DeLuca had ever seen at a rock concert. The instructions were to make them look Indian, but not like comical Indian—and Markos had obeyed.

DeLuca walked back over to the camera, got behind the lens again and did the hand sign to Markos again.

The men started moving real slow and passing the fake boxes down the loading platform. Nice and slow, thought DeLuca.

He lined up the shot, got the flash ready.

Kkkkccccchhhttt...

He focused in on the long hair and headbands of the guys, but not the faces. No, DeLuca wasn't *that* stupid.

Kkkkccccchhhttt...

This went on for quite a while. DeLuca shot a roll of 36 pictures. When he felt that he had enough, he said, "OK, that's it."

The men just stopped and looked up at him for instruction. One or two of them yawned, as though they did this type of thing every day.

DeLuca was satisfied.

He walked over to where Markos was standing. He gestured with his hand for Markos to come and join him for a little walk.

In his pocket, he felt for the piano wire with the two walnut handles on each end. It wouldn't do for Markos to go blabbing all over about how they had pulled off this fake heist just so DeLuca could look good to his boss.

No, DeLuca had to take out a little personal liability insurance. Nothing personal to Markos—he had done a terrific job.

Markos came over and they walked a couple of hundred yards away. DeLuca wanted to make sure they were out of sight and also make sure that the moon was not so bright that it would pick up any reflection.

"So, Mr. DeLuca, you like, yes?" Markos said.

"Yes, Markos, you did a fine job," DeLuca said, totally disarming Markos with charm. He wanted him nice and relaxed...

"So, now you pay me and my men the money and we be gone, yes?"

"Sure, Markos. Why don't we just go over to my car."

They walked over to the car. DeLuca got in the driver's side and gestured for Markos to get in the passenger side.

Just as he had planned, Markos could not get in. DeLuca reached across and attempted to pull open the lock. It wouldn't budge.

It would have taken a very strong man to open a lock that had been glued shut with industrial strength glue. DeLuca had seen to that earlier in the evening. Markos could tug and tug but the door wouldn't open.

DeLuca got out of the car and went around helpfully. He gestured as if to say, see what happens with stupid car locks?

Markos was still standing with his right hand gripped on the door handle. So DeLuca was able to come around directly behind him.

"Tell you what, Markos, give it a *really* good tug this time. You're stronger than I am. Maybe what the door needs is good brute strength."

Markos smiled modestly at this compliment.

He bent to the task.

Perfect, thought DeLuca.

In that moment that Markos had all his concentration on opening the door, DeLuca slipped the handles of the razor-sharp piano wire between both his hands and in one quick, neat move slipped it around Markos' exposed throat.

He could feel the wire cutting through the soft tissue of the man's throat until it grew taut when it had sliced through an inch of tissue and came to rest on the windpipe. DeLuca tightened his grip and all he heard from Markos was a sort of hissing sound as he collapsed to the ground.

He was dead instantly.

Just to make sure DeLuca knelt down and felt a pulse. Perfect...

He looked up and made sure no one had seen him. He removed the garrote from Markos' throat and wiped the wire in a handkerchief, which was then transferred to a plastic bag, which was *then* sealed tightly and put inside *another* plastic bag. He put this item neatly into his coat.

Now all he had to do was wait for the garbage truck to show up as he had planned, for a little nighttime pickup...

* * * *

Carmine walked in the door of Tonya's room and stood in the doorway. He shook his head with disapproval and sort of tut-tutted as he walked over to where Tonya sat.

"Well, I don't know what we're gonna do with you, kid. You try any more stunts like the one you pulled today and that could get you in a lot of trouble."

"Carmine, I seriously don't know what you expect me to do. I mean, I'm not some whore you can just toss out to anyone."

"Hey, did anyone ever use that term, Tonya? I mean, even once?" Carmine was insulted. How could Tonya think such as thing.

"Oh, come on. Everyone knows why you snatched me up."

"Well, it don't help that you don't wanna play ball."

Tonya felt ill again. What the hell was with this guy? Was he *so* far gone that he didn't get it. He apparently had Tonya mixed up with one of his whores. She decided to strike a deal.

"OK, since it seems like I'm destined to remain here, what if I just kept some of these guys company? You know, and didn't, like, do anything um, sexual with them? Would that be all right?"

Carmine laughed. "Sure, Tonya. Like anyone's gonna believe that somebody could resist your body."

Carmine turned around to Sal who was standing behind him and started to laugh more.

"Hey, you hear that, Sal? That's good, no?"

Sal chuckled. "Yeah, boss, that's a good one."

"Tonya, you know where I would be if I allowed that?"

Tonya wasn't sure she wanted to hear.

"Bad idea?"

"Yes, it's a bad idea. Listen, if a guy wants to go to bed with you, just lay back and think about something else. That's all you gotta do. It'll be over soon. And listen. You got my word if any guy tries any rough stuff, he's out of here!"

Yeah, fat chance thought Tonya.

"So really, you have nothing to worry about," Carmine kept on saying.

At that moment, Dr. Taylor came in and stood next to Carmine. She smiled pleasantly at him and frowned at Tonya. Tonya felt like a little schoolgirl who was being reprimanded.

Carmine turned to Dr. Taylor. "So, Doc, do you think our girl here can be trusted?" His implication was clear: either Tonya had better shape up or Dr. Taylor would be held accountable.

Dr. Taylor looked at Tonya as she talked to her. "Perhaps what she needs is a little coaching from some of the other girls."

Other girls? thought Tonya.

As if reading her mind, Dr. Taylor said: "Yes, that's right, Tonya, you're not the only one. We have several other women who are more than ready to provide an out of town businessman with a suitable escort for a lovely evening."

Carmine said: "Ok, it's settled then. Get her started."

Dr. Taylor nodded her approval.

The next day, Tonya was brought to a medium-sized conference room. As she walked in, she saw to her amazement that the room was filled with 10 ravishing-looking women, one more beautiful than the next.

Dr. Taylor introduced them:

There was Monica, a pretty blonde from California, who could pass as a dead ringer for Jennifer Aniston...

There was Tiffany, also a blonde, from Phoenix, who looked like she had spent her whole life at the beach...

There was Karen, a brunette, who was from Houston, and looked rather like the prettiest flight attendant there was...

There was Ingrid, an exotic Swedish girl, who had a killer body and a very generous mouth...

There was Crystal, a sexy black girl, who hailed from Chicago...

There was Connie, an exotic Oriental girl, who was very petite, with perfect Asian features...

There was Barbara, a fiery redhead that had a ready smile and a beautiful shape...

There was Kristen, another blonde, who hailed from Florida, and looked like she had been a cheerleader in another life...

Finally, there was Lisa, a curly-haired bombshell who had a mischievous look about her...

Dr. Taylor looked across at Tonya, to see how she would take it all in. What she saw was Tonya just staring and staring at all these beauties lined up in a row.

Dr. Taylor smiled. That had been her first reaction too when she saw all these girls. But she knew that it would pass and they would just become everyday normal girls to Tonya after a while.

Finally, she spoke: "Ladies, I would like you to make Tonya feel welcome. She is the newest addition to our family and therefore, I want you to spend some time answering any questions she might have. But above all, impress upon her what her duties are. OK? I'll be right outside here if you need any help."

Duties? thought Tonya.

Then she left.

Tiffany was the first to come over. She offered her hand to Tonya, who shook it and then looked away.

"So, this is your first time here, huh?" she said. "Well, don't let Dr. Taylor scare you. She doesn't me, anymore."

"So what is it exactly that they want me to do besides go to bed with all these guys?" asked Tonya with a bewildered tone.

Tiffany sighed and said, "Yes, I can see it's come to that. Well, honey, for my money you just have to try as hard as you can to resist having some of these guys go all the way with you."

"Is that possible? I thought Vito was watching over everything. He would know, wouldn't he?"

"Not really, if you play it right. All you have to do is say to the guy 'Look, what goes on in this room is between me and you. I don't want anyone else knowing.' And that should usually do the trick."

"So what else do I do?"

"It's simple. You put off having sex with the guy as much as possible. Get him to want you to do other things. Like, for instance, start rubbing him down there, then when the time comes, excuse yourself and go into the bathroom for a minute."

"Why?" asked Tonya, totally mystified.

"Because that way he'll become distracted and you might be able to get out of it."

Tonya looked at her like she was weird, but kept her mouth shut.

She couldn't figure out what to do that would distract a guy *that* much.

The other girls chimed in with variations on the theme of how to make the guy *not* have sex with you.

Slowly, something started to dawn on Tonya.

And that was that not many of the girls here had ever had sex with these guys!

She could stand it no longer: "Alright, girls, let's level with each other. How many times have you actually had sex with any of these creeps?"

There was not one hand that shot up into the air...

Tonya couldn't believe it. Wouldn't the customers complain that the girls weren't "putting out?"

In fact, she voiced this very concern to a few of the girls. They just smirked and said, well, you know how it is. Just got to roll with the flow sometimes.

Finally, Ginger spoke right out to Tonya and put it on the line: "Tonya, honey, what you got to get good at is making the man so hot, so bothered that he'll shoot his load. As long as it's not in you, honey-what do you care?"

"Yeah, but again, won't they complain to Vito that that is not what they paid for?"

"Uh,uh. Not if you handle it right. See, what you've got to do when the man starts to come, it'll be such a release for him that he'll be drained."

"But then he starts to thinking: hey, I been cheated here. I was supposed to get laid—and all I did was shoot my load? What gives?"

Ginger smiled slyly. "The trick in that case is to smooth the man up before he gets all steamed. Start giving him little kisses and caresses, telling him, yeah, what a great lover he is and all that bullshit."

"You'll have him around in no time."

* * * *

And that is exactly what Tonya did the next time Dr. Taylor assigned her to someone.

The guy's name was Mr. Walters. Kind of a German businessman type. Probably had a lot of money.

Before they went out, Dr. Taylor came around to Tonya's room once more.

"Now remember, Tonya, there is to be no funny business with Mr. Walters. He's a very valuable client."

Tonya just looked at her and smiled.

"Good, now we understand each other. Turn around. Very good, you look very presentable. Very sexy, if I do say so myself, my dear." Dr. Taylor started to get that dreamy look in her eye again as she hungrily eyed Tonya up and down.

Tonya just loudly cleared her throat and that snapped Dr. Taylor back to reality.

"By the way, where am I going to meet Mr. Walters?"

"Oh, don't worry about that, my dear. Sal will take care of that."

A little while later, Tonya was back in the car with Sal. One look from him quieted down any thoughts she may have had about taking flight.

They arrived at the restaurant and went through the same deal they had with the Japanese businessman. A lot of forced smiles and bullshit.

There was still no drinking allowed, so Tonya had to sit there and watch Mr. Walters down his gin martinis. (Maybe so many that he'll forget about sex?)

After a while, Sal got disinterested and left.

"So, Tonya, do you enjoy what you do?"

Tonya nearly gagged. What the hell do these people think? she thought.

"Oh, yes, Mr. Walters" she answered pleasantly. "It allows me to meet a lot of very nice gentlemen. And such interesting lives they lead!" Tonya was laying it on really thick, but couldn't think of anything else to say to this putz.

Eventually, the martinis got to Mr. Walters and he called for the check. Shortly thereafter they were in a car service heading for his hotel.

Tonya started to panic for a moment. Got to remember everything that Ginger told me, she thought.

They went upstairs to his hotel room as soon as they came in. Mr. Walters was starting to weave a little. Jesus, thought Tonya.

He went over to the sideboard and started to fix himself a drink. He stopped.

"Would you like some champagne, Tonya?"

Tonya couldn't think of a better suggestion. She was tempted to say, sure and make mine a double, but decided to stow the smart mouth.

"Yes, Mr. Walters that would be fine."

"Call me Lou."

"Alright, Lou."

He brought it over and sat down next to her. He raised the glass in a toast. "I'm so glad we got to spend time together and I got to meet you Tonya," he gushed. "You're every bit as pretty and sexy as Mr. Leone said you were."

Gee, thanks, Tonya thought. They talked for a little while, about nothing really, and at one point Mr. Walters leaned forward to kiss her.

She turned her head and Mr. Walters just got her cheek.

"Now, now, let's be a gentleman, shall we?" Tonya couldn't believe how strange that sounded.

As he got up to freshen their drinks, Tonya suddenly closed her eyes and thought: Condo, oh, Condo my love, WHERE ARE YOU?...

* * * * *

At that moment, Condo was talking with Tonya's assistant Mary at the little gift shop.

Mary appeared quite worried about Tonya's disappearance.

"I don't know what could have happened to her, Condo. It's not like Tonya to just... disappear. You know?"

"How have you been holding out?"

"Well, I've been running the place like I know she would want me to. But that's about it. Nothing much else to do."

Condo thought: There has to be clue of some kind that would lead a normal-thinking person to figure out where Tonya went to.

All of a sudden, he felt like he wanted to buy something for Tonya that would make him feel better. He thanked Mary for the conversation, said he would keep in touch and left the gift shop.

He headed for his truck and pointed it in the direction of Tierney's Lingerie shop.

If someone had witnessed this, they would have wondered just what the hell Condo was doing buying lingerie for Tonya when she was missing.

Yes, Condo admitted, it did seem kind of strange...

But it would make him feel good, he decided...

A short time later, he was standing in the shop thinking over what sort of favorite items Tonya liked to wear to drive him crazy with desire.

He was sort of torn between the purple G-string and the black G-string.

He had his back to the door when Dr. Taylor walked in...

He was examining some things on the rack as a salesgirl attempted to help Dr. Taylor with sizes.

"No, it's not for me," Dr. Taylor smiled. "It's for... a friend, yes that's right."

"Well, what does the friend look like?" asked the salesgirl, innocently enough.

"Oh, she is a medium-length blonde with very fine features. She's partial to leopard-skin prints."

Condo's head came up when he heard that. What the hell? Tonya was partial to leopard-skin prints. He edged over and listened closely, while pretending to be absorbed in what he was doing.

The salesgirl asked this person's sizes.

Dr. Taylor responded with Tonya's exact height, weight, dress size and bra size.

Could it just be coincidence? Condo thought.

He peeked over and saw some of the selection that Dr. Taylor bought.

Everything was EXACTLY what Tonya would have bought...

When Condo saw this, he knew that he had to follow whoever this person was. Things were just too coincidental and this was just too weird.

He left the stuff that he had right there on the stand. That could wait. This was important.

He loitered around his truck until he saw Dr. Taylor fire up her car and got going behind her. She drove straight down the highway and took the exit 10 miles down the road. Strange, thought Condo, I wonder where she's going. He decided to stake her out.

* * * * *

At the moment that this was going on with Condo, Mr. Walters was trying to remove the bra strap from Tonya's shoulder and not having too much luck. Mainly because she kept twisting away and slapping his hand back.

Finally, he just gave up. He sort of sat there and looked at Tonya with a look as if to say: what gives?

Tonya gave him a reassuring pat on the knee.

"Now, now, Mr. Walters, you don't want to go there. Let's be a gentleman."

Mr. Walters laughed and said, "But I **am** being a gentleman. Perhaps too much of a gentleman. Let's have some fun." He reached again and stumbled a little no doubt due to the alcohol.

Tonya remembered what Ginger said. Just try and take their minds off getting completely undressed. Cause once they were there—there might be no stopping them. And that was dangerous.

She decided that the only way to get this guy's mind off taking her bra off—was to distract him.

She gulped hard, fighting back the disgust and revulsion that this brought on—and started massaging the inside of his thigh.

Mr. Walters had a very strange reaction. He suddenly stopped fixating on Tonya's bra strap and began to concentrate on the pleasure that he was feeling that was creeping up his thigh.

"Ooohhh, yes, Mr. Walters, now don't you like this, hhhmmm?" said Tonya, practically gritting her teeth as she said the words.

Mr. Walters certainly was liking it...

Tonya's hand continued to rub until she was right around the base of his groin. She didn't exactly touch it, but instead concentrated on the area right around it.

Mr. Walters started to breathe heavy.

"Unzip my pants," he said, his voice panting now. He thrust himself up at her.

Tonya reached down gingerly, as if handling live dynamite. She undid his zipper.

That was all she had to do. Mr. Walters reached into the fly of his trousers and yanked out his manhood.

Tonya concentrated on not looking at it and continued to rub his thigh. Mr. Walters started stroking it, then suddenly stopped and said, "Hey, aren't you going to get undressed?"

She thought fast and said, "No, darling. Just the sight of you doing that, ooohhh, it makes me tingle. I want to watch you."

Mr. Walters blushed a little. "Well, I admit it *is* kind of a nice size, don't you think?"

"Oh, yes. Yes, it's perfect. Such a big man you are!"

She increased her efforts. He still had his trousers on part way, so she wasn't touching bare flesh. (Thank, God,) she thought.

Mr. Walters continued to breathe heavy.

"C'mon, that's a boy. Oohh, you're so sexy. You're so..."

Her hand felt his thigh shudder.

Mr. Walters gave out a little groan and then went limp.

"Stay right there, lover boy, I'll get you a warm washcloth."

Inside the bathroom, Tonya felt like she was going to throw up. What the hell was she doing? Witnessing this guy playing with himself, that's what she was doing.

Tonya thought fast. There had to be some way out of this. But she couldn't think of what. He would expect her back momentarily. Everything would be all right as long as he did not expect to perform again. How could she prevent that?

She decided that the way to do it was to rush Mr. Walters along, tell him that she had other people waiting for her time. Something along those lines; anything just to get his mind off of sex.

Tonya looked in the glass and breathed deeply. She would have had a hard time living with herself if he had touched her. But he had not managed to get his grimy hands or anything else for that matter into her.

Now, she just had to get out of this bathroom and play it cool.

When she came out, she had a washcloth in her hand and forced herself to use it on Mr. Walters. He was sitting there with a kind of dreamy look on his face.

Then, all of sudden, the look turned into a frown.

"What's the matter?" Tonya asked soothingly.

"We didn't do anything—I mean, nothing happened for you," Mr. Walters said with a puzzled tone.

Tonya grasped him by the shoulders.

"Are you kidding? I got aroused just by watching you!" she lied. "Don't ever say something like that again. Whoever told you that you had to have sexual intercourse to be satisfied was wrong!"

Mr. Walters looked a little dubious over that one, but said nothing.

Then Tonya pushed it into high gear. "Now then, we have got to get a move on here. I've got other people that I have appointments with." She started making abrupt movements that were designed to get him back into his clothes and out the door quickly.

He grabbed her by the wrist. "Well, when can I see you again, Tonya? I like you."

Oh, God, she thought. I was afraid of this.

She patted him on the hand. "There, there, Mr. Walters. I'm sure that we can arrange something. But the main thing for right now is just to get going. You don't want me to be late, do you? I mean, Sal gets mad when I'm late, and you don't want Sal to get mad, do you?"

At the mention of Sal's name, Mr. Walters manner changed. He snapped to quickly and put his clothes on.

So that was it, thought Tonya. He's afraid of Sal. Interesting...

Before they walked out, Tonya dialed Sal's beeper number. She felt rather like a pet dog, trying to get the attention of her keeper.

Above all, she had to concentrate on finding a way out of this. She had been lucky with Mr. Walters, but suppose she met a really hard customer. What then?

After they dropped Mr. Walters off at the lounge, she and Sal got going back to the hotel.

Once they were in the car, Sal started smirking. "So, how was it with that old guy?"

"None of your business, Sal," said Tonya somewhat defensively. God, she hated this creep.

"Yeah, I guess they got themselves a good one when they got you, huh?" he remarked. "I mean, you probably do anything they want, huh?" It sounded like he was beginning to breathe heavy.

She looked him square in the eye. "Yeah, and after I'm done, I dream about cutting it off."

The smirk came off his face like he had been hit. He cleared his throat and muttered, "Yeah, whatever."

* * * * *

When Tonya got back to her room, she sat down and tried to think rationally. OK, so she had gotten through the session with Walters. So what? Cause she knew there would be others.

The only question was how many more...?

The other, more terrifying question, was how much more of this could she take...?

If only there was a way to distract attention from herself long enough to plan some kind of escape. She needed a diversion, something, anything that would get her captor's mind off her for the few minutes she would need to escape. But what?

Tonya knew that they watched her all the time. All her meals were brought to her by Dr. Taylor all the time. In fact everything was brought to her by Dr. Taylor.

It hit Tonya like a brick. The key to this whole thing was *Dr. Taylor*!

Of course! It was perfect. Tonya thought back to the day when they had first met. Dr. Taylor had come in and right from the beginning had sort of fawned over her.

Tonya didn't know very much about who Dr. Taylor was, only one thing, and that was that, for whatever reason, she was attracted to Tonya.

She felt like she was going to throw up.

Then she controlled herself and thought: OK, there is a way that I can work that to my advantage. Yes, there is. If I know that she has the hots for me—I play into that. You don't actually have to *do* anything with Dr. Taylor (another shudder ran through her body). But just make her *think* that you were interested.

Now the next question was how could she capitalize on this?

She knew the routine enough to know when Dr. Taylor would be alone. That is when she could make her move.

The key to this would be to totally disarm Dr. Taylor of any weapons she had. Not that she would be carrying a .44 Magnum or anything. But she might be carrying a pair of big scissors or something.

If everything fell into place, it just might work...

Tonya took off her clothes and began to dress appropriately...

* * * * *

At just that moment, Condo was cursing his luck. He had tailed Dr. Taylor for miles—only to lose her. He pounded the steering wheel of his truck in frustration. What the hell was he going to do now?

He decided to drive around for awhile and see if he could catch a glimpse of her. Hell, he didn't have any other plans up his sleeve.

* * * * *

Tonya got ready. When you had to bait the trap, you had to use the right kind of bait. So she rummaged through her little closet and came up with a form-fitting negligee that showed off just the right amount of cleavage. She got some sheer stockings out of the drawer, put them on, and then got into her high heel pumps. She did her makeup over and looked in the mirror. She was ready. Tonya took a deep breath and waited for Dr. Taylor to make her appearance.

Sure enough, the good Doctor opened the door about 10 minutes later. In her hand she held Tonya's lunch. She took one look at Tonya sitting there coyly on the bed with her legs crossed seductively and gave a start.

"Tonya, what a surprise. I don't recall you having any other appointments this afternoon. Let me check." With that, she put the lunch down and took out her appointment book and started to leaf through it.

Tonya stood up and flounced over to Dr. Taylor. She felt ridiculous doing it, but knew that this was the only way out.

She reached out and took Dr. Taylor's book from her and placed it on the table next to her. She reached down and took Dr. Taylor's hands.

"No, I don't have any type of appointment Dr. Taylor. I was hoping that we could talk a little bit. Just the two of us." She cooed as she said this. She took a step closer and ran her finger down the side of Dr. Taylor's fact. "Why don't you close the door, hhmm?"

Dr. Taylor's face had gone from a frown to a look of joy. Without taking her eyes off Tonya, she backed up to the door, shut it and locked it. She hopped back quickly to where Tonya stood.

Tonya took hold of her shoulders and slowly slid her hands down her arms.

Dr. Taylor said in a hoarse whisper: "Tonya, I don't think this is appropriate." But she closed her eyes and a look of rapture came over her face.

Tonya thought: OK, you bitch. I've got you right where I want you!

"You look a little tense, Dr. Taylor. Perhaps a nice massage would help?"

Dr. Taylor opened her eyes. "Well, I guess that would be all right." She didn't look like she was objecting too much.

Tonya said: "Well, just turn around and let me get started on those shoulders."

Dr. Taylor turned around and made herself ready for Tonya's hands.

Tonya eyed the smock that she wore. Yes, she could see it clearly as she turned around. Dr. Taylor had a pair of scissors the size of long dagger in her pocket.

As she turned around the scissors were exposed...

Tonya took her time. She wanted Dr. Taylor nice and relaxed. She started kneading her hands into Dr. Taylor's shoulders.

Dr. Taylor's shoulders slumped in response to Tonya's touch and she became completely relaxed.

"There, there, Dr. Taylor. My you're so overworked what with watching me and all the other responsibilities you have with your girls. It's a wonder you're not more tense."

"Hhhhhhmmmmm," purred Dr. Taylor.

Just a few more seconds now, thought Tonya...

Dr. Taylor started to roll her head around as if in an effort to relax herself even more.

Tonya got ready...

Just as she felt Dr. Taylor slump again, Tonya suddenly tightened her arm around her throat with her left hand, and with her right hand snatched the scissors out of her pocket.

Tonya held the scissors up against Dr. Taylor's temple.

"Make one wrong move to scream or anything—and I will hurt you. Got it?"

Dr. Taylor nodded. She got it. Her eyes were wide with terror.

Tonya tried to think. There had been no time to pack anything. And she couldn't exactly ask Dr. Taylor to wait while she threw some things together.

But how was she going to get away in a negligee and high heels? She decided that Dr. Taylor's smock would have to do.

"Alright, lady, give me your smock. Now."

Tonya let go of her for a second and tugged at the smock hard to make her get it off faster.

"Let's go, let's go."

Dr. Taylor flashed her dark eyes at Tonya. "You know, you'll never get away with this, Tonya." She tried to resume the role of the patient Doctor. "Now, why don't you just stop this now and we'll forget all about this unpleasant little incident. Shall we?"

Tonya laughed. "Yeah, that's a hoot, Dr. You mean like I'm just going to stop this and stay your prisoner here awhile longer and everything will be fine. Right?"

"Yes, Tonya, that's right. We'll make like this never happened. With all the strain you're under..."

Tonya had by this time put the smock on. She put the tip of the dagger-like scissors up against Dr. Taylor's temple again. "Well, you can forget it, Doc."

She yanked her around and walked her to the doorway. The coast was clear. But Tonya couldn't take a chance on Dr. Taylor getting away. So she very cooly led her back inside the room and took her into the bathroom.

Dr. Taylor squirmed and said, "Now, Tonya, just what do you think you're doing?"

"It's easy, doc, I'm just going to tie you up. Now strip those clothes off and give 'em to me. Now!"

Fifteen minutes later, Tonya looked down and surveyed her handiwork. She had Dr. Taylor naked and hogtied in the bathtub. She had torn her shirt into strips to tie her hands with and stuff that loud mouth with, the mouth that she would use to yell for help.

She would take the rest of Dr. Taylor's clothes with her, including her shoes. (Unfortunately, they were not the same shoe size. Damn!) She closed the door on Dr. Taylor and surveyed the lobby. Good, no one was around.

Dressed in the doctor's smock and clutching her clothes (again, they were the wrong size!) she strode toward the door.

Outside, the sunlight hit her like a beacon. Tonya had no money on her and it looked like she was quite a ways from her apartment. Her options were to hoof it... and to hoof it... Shit. She would give anything to see Condo right about now.

A few immediate problems presented themselves. The first was lack of food.

...and the second was lack of money.

Then there was lack of clothes.

...and the third was lack of money.

Tonya could kick herself for not going with Dr. Taylor to force her to get more money. But she had wanted to get out so bad, that the thought didn't occur to her.

So now she was in kind of a spot. To compound matters, night would fall soon. And there she was. Looking like a hooker dressed in high heels, negligee and stockings. Well, at least she had the smock to keep covered up. But the smock wasn't very warm.

Tonya continued to walk for awhile until she couldn't walk any further. She was also hungry, so that would be another problem to deal with. All in all, things didn't look too promising right now.

* * * * *

Frank DeLuca walked back to where the other guys were assembled. He could tell they had questions in their minds by the way they looked hard at him.

Well, fuck 'em, he thought. If it was necessary to do to one of them what he had just done to Markos—so be it.

He thought about this as he approached them. The trick was to buy their complete silence. Not that they had to know anything about the caper that went down here tonight. No, as far as he was concerned they didn't have to know nothing.

He would just be cool about it and say that he and Markos had had a small disagreement which got out of hand. When you'd done time in as many places as these assholes had done time—he wasn't questioning how much they would grieve for Markos. Just shrug and go on.

Which is exactly what he did... And exactly what they did.

What it came down to was that they agreed not to say a word and DeLuca basically promised not to deport them. So both of them were on the same wavelength and everyone was happy.

The next order of business was to take the film to someone he knew he could trust. Someone who was reliable and wouldn't screw up the developing.

That wouldn't be a problem. He knew several guys who could do the job. He put the car in gear and got going.

A little while later, back at his favorite bar, DeLuca thought about how he would present the pictures to Atkinson. Hold the negatives, of course.

He didn't want some idiot like Atkinson gaining control of the whole scam. Atkinson had plenty of power and could make life pretty miserable for DeLuca if he wanted to.

The thing was that Atkinson was so convinced that Indians had to be behind *something* that he was almost forced to do this.

This would definitely take the heat off his "investigation." This way, he would have "proof" that something illegal was going on and that the Mob was getting kickbacks.

So this way, he stayed in good favor with Atkinson...

But more important, he stayed in good favor with the Mob...

Because if Atkinson could make life difficult for DeLuca, the mob could make him *dead*.

DeLuca knew though that Atkinson would not be stupid enough to publicize the pictures. I mean, that would be really dumb. C'mon. An attorney general going to the press with a bunch of pictures taken in the dead of night.

Yeah, well, kinda look like Indians, I guess, would go the common concensus.

No, Atkinson would not do something like that, without a lot more proof.

And all DeLuca had to do was to say he was searching for more clues, but gee, they just seemed so darned hard to find, you know, sir?

And if Atkinson pressed DeLuca on how he'd gotten the pictures, DeLuca could say, gee, they just came in the mail. Sort of like: thought you might be interested in these photos. Signed anonymous. And no one would be the wiser.

Which was not far from the truth. Private investigators got things like this all the time in the mail.

DeLuca never seriously thought about tailing this Condo character and pressing him for information. Shit, what was the point? Even if Condo had seen something like what he said he saw, how was he going to get any more hard evidence on the mob than that?

It was very difficult to nail the mob for anything unless you were dead to rights about so many things.

For instance, you could say, well, your honor on such and such a date I saw Vito Leone offer a bribe to Mr. X. Well, ok, that presented you with the question of asking, where was the evidence?

Just because you allegedly saw something, what hard proof do you have, Mr. Witness?

And it was at that point that many witnesses are usually struck deaf, dumb and blind.

Henceforth, many members of the mob tend to go free...

DeLuca got up and went home. He would take care of developing the film tomorrow.

He took the film to a reputable guy that he knew. It didn't cost that much and he was in and out in no time. The way he figured it, the pictures would buy him some time and that was what he wanted.

The next day he prepared for his meeting with Atkinson. The pictures that he had should be enough to put things to rest for awhile.

This guy was a fanatic for detail; that he knew. So the main thing was just to play along, give him the pictures and shut up.

He was ushered in to the Attorney General's office and took a seat.

Atkinson got right to the point:

"Well, have you got what I think you have?"
DeLuca cleared his throat. "Yeah, I think I have something interesting for you here." He slid the pictures across the desk.

Atkinson took his time studying the photos. He would pause from time to time and stare off into space for a moment. Finally he threw the pictures on the desk.

"So, what do you think? Is there evidence of criminal activity going on?"

DeLuca tried to be careful how he answered. He sort of shrugged, rolled his shoulders and said carefully. "Well, that's really more of your area, don't you think, sir?" Throwing the ball back into his court.

Atkinson said, "Well, it does appear as if there is criminal activity going on. I mean, after all they are unloading trucks with what appears to be contraband of some sort."

He paused and peered over his eyeglasses at DeLuca suspiciously. "Just how did you come to have these pictures in your possession, Mr. DeLuca?"

Take it nice and slow, DeLuca thought. "I know a lot of people in this line of work, sir. Someone slipped them to me in the mail, and that's really all there was to it," he said smoothly.

"Well, did you ask for payment of any kind?"

"No, sir."

"I see. Well, then what would they get out of giving them to you?"

DeLuca shrugged. "Who knows, sir. Blackmail, some shit, er, crap like that. There's a lot of weird people in the world today."

The Attorney General looked at him rather dubiously. The thought occurred to DeLuca that he probably didn't meet any of these type of people that DeLuca had just described. It made him chuckle.

The Attorney General leaned back in his chair. "So how do YOU think we should proceed with this, Mr. DeLuca?"

"I would be more than glad to keep tabs on this, sir, and see what develops."

"I see. Well, before you do that, do you know any more about the kind of involvement that Condo Cherokee ahs had with these people?"

DeLuca thought to himself: Be careful. You don't want to give this guy any ammunition.

"Well you can obviously see that the guys in this photograph are Indian, sir. But that doesn't necessarily implicate Condo Cherokee. I mean, the fact that he's Indian should have only a very minor bearing on all this."

Atkinson leaned forward, irritated. "You don't need to lecture me on that, Mr. DeLuca. I know full well what the charges are, or at least the allegations that Cherokee talks about in his newspaper articles."

"What I NEED to know is whether there is sufficient evidence to go after any of the mob members over this. These pictures are hardly what I would call absolutely conclusive evidence." His voice seemed to drip with contempt.

DeLuca grinned inwardly to himself. Things were going the way he had planned. If Atkinson was going to leap on the pictures as they stood, DeLuca would have been forced to go out and start rounding up people for the cops to haul them in for questioning.

But the fact that Atkinson believed there was room for doubt left the door wide open. Meaning that he would have to retain DeLuca to dig up more fresh dirt. Meaning that it would take time for the dirt to be found. And DeLuca could take his sweet time doing it.

What he was basically saying was: this could work out if he played his cards right.

One thing that DeLuca DID know was that he would have to give Atkinson something sooner or later. But he had plenty of time to figure that out. He could string it out for awhile.

* * * *

Tonya stretched out in the grass by the alcove in the side of the park. Earlier she had been forced to scrounge for food in a dumpster behind a restaurant. She had put a run in her stockings, but what the hell.

She got lucky and found a chicken that had been thrown out. Fully cooked and ready to go. Tonya had eaten it ravenously like an animal. She had to laugh. If only Condo could see her now!

She couldn't believe that things had turned out like this. Condo was nowhere to be found and there was no telling when or if she was going to see him.

Maybe it would help to sleep. She tried to drift off.

She woke up the next morning and lay there for a minute, dazed and not exactly knowing where she was. She had slept badly during the night and was groggy from lack of sleep. Also hungry. That chicken hadn't really been enough to stay with her.

All throughout the park, joggers, young moms and kids were all taking up space already.

Tonya looked down at herself. She was filthy and needed a bath desperately. Fat chance of that, she thought.

She got up and decided to walk. But it wasn't long until she decided that she had to get some food or collapse right there in the street.

Tonya found another dumpster and climbed into it. It was very degrading what she was doing, but her mother, Poca Daisy had taught her how to be tough and this was where the toughness was coming in handy.

She found some things to eat in there that were pretty fresh considering they had been inside a dumpster and was just climbing out when she heard the sound of a patrol car coming up the alleyway.

WWWWHHHRRRR... went the sound. And then she heard: "YOU THERE. MOVE AWAY FROM THE DUMPSTER WHERE WE CAN SEE YOU."

Tonya had no intention of being hauled in by the police. She took one look at them and started running...

Which was extremely difficult considering the type of shoes she was wearing...

She concentrated on running on the balls of her feet, which for some reason she was able to do considering she was wearing high heels.

Tonya went tear-assing out of the alleyway and bolted down the street with the cops in hot pursuit. Well, actually mild pursuit. They were taking their sweet time about it once they saw that she was unarmed and wearing a smock and high heels.

She had no idea where she was but just continued to run like the devil was after her.

She cut east down a wide sidestreet and looked back. Good, she thought, the cops haven't gotten here yet. She came to the intersection and stood there panting, looking wildly up and down the street for some type of help. Please help me, anybody, she thought! If only—

"T-O-N-Y-A!!!" came the cry from the only man she would ever love...

My God, she thought, it was *Condo...!*

Condo raced up to her in his truck. He started to put it into park. Tonya tore up to the side of the car, flung open the door and jumped in.

"Oh, honey, it's so good to see—"

"Never mind, Condo. Just get the hell outta here!!"

"Huh?"

"You heard me. The cops are looking for me and if they catch me, I'll be in trouble. So go, go!"

Condo didn't have to get the message twice. He got on the move and spun the truck around.

After they were on the road for a couple of minutes, Tonya could take it no longger and finally broke down in sobs. Great racking sounds came from her chest as she remembered what had happened to her.

Condo was bewildered. He just sat there grimly driving. Finally, he spoke.

"Honey, what happened? I've been looking for you for days. And all of a sudden I come over to this part of town and you're wandering the streets? And... why are you dressed like that? You look like—"

"CONDO, I WAS KIDNAPPED!! DON'T YOU UNDERSTAND," Tonya said with her voice trembling. "Those bastards took me out of my apartment, and—"

"Who took you out?"

"Carmine, that's who."

Condo screeched the truck to a halt. "WHAT!!!" he roared. He grabbed her by the shoulders. "Are you serious, Tonya?"

She nodded her head. "Yes, I am, Condo. Listen I'm too exhausted to talk right now. I need to go back home and sleep. Then we can talk, ok?"

Condo nodded, put the car in gear and went home.

* * * *

Chapter 17
FITTING JUSTICE

As soon as they got back to Tonya's apartment, he carried her in to the bedroom. She was a dead weight. He removed the ripped and torn stockings and garter belt from her, again wondering at why she was wearing it.

He put her in the shower and made her soap herself good and get clean. He helped her dry her hair and then put her into bed.

Tonya fell into an instant sleep.

Condo went into the living room to think...

He couldn't sit still so as was his custom, he began to pace. He couldn't figure out for the life of him why Carmine would do this. Why? he asked himself.

Condo searched his memory. As far as he knew there was no reason for Carmine to snatch Tonya. Condo didn't owe him any money or any favors. As far as Vito was concerned, he knew, at bottom, that Vito probably just tolerated him and the only reason he was still at the casino was because Condo was very popular.

So it didn't add up... None of it...

So what was he going to do if it turned out to be true what Tonya had said? And why wasn't Vito involved in any of this? Strange, Condo thought, Tonya had just mentioned Carmine. Nothing about Vito. But Condo couldn't believe that Vito wasn't involved somehow.

That was tough. Condo's mind boiled with rage when he thought about it, but he also knew that he was outmanned. I mean, he couldn't very well just stroll over to Carmine's office and start beating the shit out of him.

There had to be another way to get at Carmine...

Whatever that way was, Condo knew he could sure use it now...

A few hours later, he heard Tonya stir in the bedroom. He waited for her, and pretty soon she came out of the room in a bathrobe and slippers.

She came out scrubbed and clean, devoid of makeup of any kind. She came over and sat across from him and eyed him dully.

Condo said, "So, honey, tell me how it happened." He leaned forward in the chair.

Tonya let out her cheeks with a long sigh. Unbeknowst to Condo she had woken up an hour earlier—but had just laid there, thinking.

What in the name of God was she supposed to tell the man? I mean, one just didn't casually start in on what had happened to her. But the more she thought about it, the more she realized she had no choice.

"It's a long story, Condo. Basically, they kidnapped me and forced me to work as a prostitute."

Condo sat there speechless.

Tonya held up her hand. "Now, before you go off on me, honey, I just want to tell you that NOTHING happened. OK? Now, you've got to believe me."

"Start at the beginning, please Tonya."

"OK. Vito made me an offer to appear in one of the movies that he was going to make."

"Huh? I never knew Vito was making any movies."

"Neither did I. Listen, right now it's just a pipe dream for him, I guess. But he claims to have big plans, I don't know. Anyway, one thing led to another and pretty soon I found myself in the weird position of actually having to *listen* to him about this.

So, to make a long story short, he wanted me to appear nude in the movie. And I said, no way.

Condo got up and paced. He could not understand what had happened to Tonya from the time they took her till when he just found her. He said as much to her and asked her to explain it to him. He tried not to yell, but he was anxious as hell.

Tonya looked hesitant.

"What is it, honey?"

"Nothing, Condo, it's just that... well it's kind of difficult to explain what happened day to day, you know?"

"Well start from the beginning."

"Well, after they grabbed me, I was confined to a hotel room. And I really didn't have much to do—"

Condo broke in. "Did they hurt you?"

"No, no, nothing like that. They didn't lay a hand on me. Although, come to think of it, Carmine was a little rough when he snatched me up."

Condo silently remembered to pay Carmine back...

"Anyway, there was this Doctor Taylor who was kind of weird. She was assigned to monitor me."

"Monitor you?"

"Yes, she helped me pick out the clothes that I would... wear, when I, um, was sent out." Her voice trailed off in a small whisper.

Condo got up and stood there with his fists clenched.

"It's ok, honey," Tonya reassured him. She continued. "I guess Carmine was into providing rich businessmen some entertainment. So he included me and a bunch of other girls as sort of... escorts, you know?"

Condo was listening to Tonya but was having a hard time grasping all this. It was like she was saying all this but he was having a hard time comprehending. What the hell had happened to her for all this time?

He got up and walked over to where Tonya was sitting. Poor little thing, she looked so worn out from her ordeal. Condo half wondered if maybe she should see a therapist. And that's exactly what he said to her.

"Tonya, do you think after all this stuff that you've been through that, well, maybe you ought to see a counselor or something?" The truth was that Condo was sort of vacillating between rage at wanting to tear Carmine's guts out, and bewilderment at knowing exactly what to do.

Tonya looked up at Condo a little wearily. Poor guy, she thought. He doesn't have a clue as to what I went through. I mean, how do you explain to somebody that you were lucky to get out of there alive?

"Condo, honey, I know you mean well, but I just have to try and put this behind me."

"Yeah, I know that, honey, but my question is: How are you going to manage to do that? And I guess it seems to me like you could use help. You know? I mean, I'm not trained for any of this."

"I know you're not, Condo. Maybe the best thing you could do right now is just to be there for me and listen to me."

But Condo knew that he had to hear more of the ordeal that she went through. So he took a deep breath and plunged on.

"Babe, now you told me that nothing happened. OK, I believe you. But what exactly happened when you were alone with these men. I mean, they weren't exactly there to play cards with you, were they?"

Tonya knew she would have a hard time making Condo believe that nothing had happened. Hell, sometimes she thought that even she had a hard time with I.

She wondered if maybe she was blocking something out. Like maybe something HAD happened with one of those men but she had just dismissed it from her mind. She searched her mind. No, what was she thinking? What had happened was that she had gotten damn lucky that the stuff she went through was left at that.

One of the things that Tonya hadn't had time to think about yet though was revenge for any of this. She basically had two choices as far as she could tell:

One, was to forget about it and put her life back in order.

Two, was to make Carmine pay for what he had done to her.

The second choice was satisfying, but Tonya knew that it was going to be impossible. How was she supposed to go about doing that? And there was another thing: She was somehow convinced that Vito Leone was behind some of this. Vito Leone was a very powerful man and Tonya had no wish to involve Condo in any more of this than she had to.

She knew what Condo must be thinking. His first instinct, even though he was not a violent man, would be to

Confront Carmine. She thought that now would be a good time to voice her concern.

"Condo, you're not thinking of going after Carmine for this, are you?"

Condo had sat back down and looked at Tonya as she spoke. He had not anticipated the question from her and was a little surprised. Although, not that much. Tonya was a smart girl and she knew him.

He knew this would not go away. That it would fester in his mind for a long time. He could he in good conscience go back to work in the casino again? This was another problem. Because he knew that the minute he faced Vito, there would be bloodshed.

So now he was faced with ways of getting new employment. And he said as much to Tonya.

"Honey, I don't know what I'm going to do for work now. How can I go back to the casino?"

Tonya shook her head. "Don't worry about that, Condo. Remember the stock that my mother got from Bill Gates? We can simply trade some of it in. That won't be a problem."

Condo wasn't too thrilled with that prospect, though. "Well, maybe we can talk about it." His voice trailed off.

He sat up again, and said, "Wait a minute now. We haven't talked about what happened exactly when you were alone with these men."

"It was only a couple of times, Condo, I swear. And it was sort of like I was more caught up in a situation more than anything else."

"OK, so you're forced to go out with these guys. What were they like?"

"One was sort of a fat German. His name was Mr. Walters. The other guy was a Chinese guy, named Mr. Wang."

"Did they kiss you?"

"No."

"Did they like touch any private parts on you?"

"No."

"Well, what happened then?"

Tonya thought it best not to mention the part about the guy who had actually unzipped his pants and was in sort of a state of erection. How could she put it so she would not offend Condo?

"Well, this one guy did have sort of... uh, well, he was sort of aroused."

Condo just sat there with his face like stone.

Tonya hurried forward with the story. "And, uh, I just made sure that I stayed as far away from him as I could. I had no interest in touching any part of him."

Condo broke in. "So what did this jerk do? Just sit there. I mean, I can't believe that he didn't try to get you to have sex with him."

Tonya went up and put her hands on his arms. "Yes, I'm sure he did, Condo. But in a situation like that, a woman can have complete control. And believe me, if I say nothing went on—it didn't."

Condo sighed deeply. "OK, that's one. What about the other guy?"

"The other guy I just... well, I just kind of blew him off and went back to the hotel. This Doctor Taylor wasn't too happy about that. But I thought, to hell with her. She's the one that's holding me against her will. She can't force me to do something I don't want."

Then suddenly, inexplicably, there was silence between them.

Both of them just sat there and thought about things, each one lost in his thoughts...

Condo wondered again how things were going to play out. He believed Tonya, or so he thought. But he wondered if it would change the way he looked at her. He knew that was crazy; he loved Tonya with all his heart, but he couldn't help but wonder about it.

And there was another thing. Had this somehow changed her? Would she feel the same way about him again?

Condo had heard about things like this. Meaning, a woman who has been through this sort of thing was never quite the same. Something not quite right after that.

Because he fully expected that they would get married some day. And after they got married, who was to say that she would not turn away from him in bed? Resist his physical advances?

Condo had not made love with Tonya, of course, and therefore he had no way of knowing what she would be like.

But still he couldn't help but be concerned about this. There was only one way to find out and unfortunately that way would have to wait until they were married.

Tonya had been thinking along the same lines as Condo. She didn't want to believe that anything had happened with the awful experience she had been through that would taint her love for Condo in any way. Still, she couldn't be sure.

Only time would take care of that.

Both of them, having collectively thought their thoughts, suddenly turned to look at each other once again.

Condo was up out of the chair first. He rushed over to her and took her gently in his arms.

She flinched, and backed away as if snakebit...

Condo took a deep breath and stood there dumbfounded. "Honey, I, I..."

Tonya impatiently cut him off. "No, no, forget it, Condo. It's not you. It's me. I... I need time. I have to remember how to be a woman again. It's tough, you know? I mean, when you've been someone's slave, it's just so frightening."

Condo just stood there, mutely. Suddenly there was nothing to say. And more suddenly than ever, he knew that he would have to get Tonya some real professional help. This was obviously a nightmare for her, one that wasn't going to go away anytime soon.

But where to start to look? Where to start to search help?

"Tonya, I know that it's really soon, but we really have to think about getting some help for you."

Tonya got up and went into the kitchen. She knew that what he was saying was true, yet felt irritable and mildly irritated at him for saying it.

She slammed some things around the kitchen.

He got up and went into the kitchen to check on her.

She left as soon as he crossed the threshold.

He stood there helpless, with his hands just dangling at his side.

She placed her hands on her hips and said, "Look, honey, for God's sake will you stop following me around? You're like a little puppy dog. I KNOW I need to think about getting help. But right now, all I want to do is sleep. I feel like I could sleep for a week."

Condo nodded. Perhaps that was the ticket. Just rest and put everything behind her. But Condo also knew that it was probably just a temporary fix, that was all.

Tonya went back into the bedroom, but paused by the entranceway. She looked at Condo imploringly.

"Honey, don't follow me in here. Just leave things alone for now. OK? Things will work themselves out."

Condo nodded and sat back down. He had never felt so helpless in all his life.

* * * * *

Dr. Taylor stood in front of Vito Leone's desk and fidgeted. She felt like a young girl who got called to the principal's office.

Vito sat there in his chair and leaned back. "So, doc, you want to tell me what happened again?"

Dr. Taylor tried to summon up some of her professional dignity. "Well, Mr. Leone, it's very simple. What happened was that Tonya simply overpowered me. When I went in the room to check on her, she... she tried to seduce me and I fell for it, and that's when she grabbed a pair of scissors I had and said she'd use them on me. Then she tied me up and fled."

"That's it? That's what happened? All of it?"

"Uh, yes, Mr. Leone?"

"Cause I got to tell you that sounds pretty unbelievable."

"Well, I know, sir, but for her size Tonya is a pretty strong girl."

Vito slammmed his hand down on the table. "I DON'T CARE HOW STRONG SHE IS!! ALL I CARE ABOUT IS THAT SHE GOT AWAY!"

Dr. Taylor thought it best to keep quiet.

Vito yelled for Sal to come in.

A minute later, when Sal came in, glowering and kind of hunch-shouldered, Vito sat back and folded his hands across his stomach. "So, Sal, now do you want to tell me what went on?"

Sal fidgeted the same as Dr. Taylor. Man, no one liked getting called into Vito's office. It was like hell in there. He sighed and thought about what he could say.

"Well, boss, when I came up the room, the doc here was tied up in the bathroom, and I figured, well, something must have gone down, you know? So I kind of figured that Tonya had like, escaped. But I don't know how she did it."

"You don't know?"

"No."

"Well, you stupid ass, she got ahold of a pair of scissors that Dr. Taylor had and threatened her with them. What do you think about that?"

A slow grin started to inch its way around Sal's face. "Hey, that's something—I mean, shit, no I can't believe that." He coughed nervously and replaced the grin with a frown.

Dr. Taylor just stood there looking somewhere between indignant and pissed off. She thought about what she'd do to Tonya if their paths ever crossed again.

Sal just looked as if he wished he could get out of there.

Vito seemed to make up his mind. "OK, here's what we're going to do, folks. Since you guys lost her, you're going to find her. Now, we've already wasted enough time. Let's hotfoot it out of here and get going."

Sal spoke up. "But, boss, we don't even know where to look for this broad. She could be anywhere."

"That's right, Sal. She could. Now get going."

Both Sal and Dr. Taylor looked at each other with contempt and left.

* * * * *

Things did not work themselves out for Tonya and Condo. Instead of getting better and shrugging off her ordeal, Tonya seemed to get worse. Condo began to get really worried about her. She just seemed listless and wanted to lie around all day.

And at night, she would have terrible nightmares.

Condo did what he could to comfort her but it wasn't enough. He couldn't understand the ordeal that she had been through.

She lost interest in going back to the gift shop to work. Nothing seemed to be going right in her life. It was alarming because she now depended on Mary to virtually run the place. Mary would call to inquire about some problem that Tonya would have to straighten out and Tonya would say, "Oh, Mary, can't you handle it? I just don't have the energy for it."

And then she'd hang up, leaving poor Mary to fend for herself...

There were a lot of days like that.

Tonya seemed to be just content existing in her own little world and keeping everyone out.

Finally, Condo suggested that they go to seek out a therapist who could help her.

Tonya just shrugged her shoulders and said OK, whatever you say, Condo. Not putting much feeling into it.

A week later, both of them were sitting in the office of Dr. Dan Mitchell, who specialized in these types of trauma cases.

When everyone was seated, Dr. Mitchell asked them why they had come to seek him out.

Condo spoke first. "Well, Dr. Mitchell, it seems that my girlfriend, Tonya, has had a very personal problem that has happened to her in the last month and she doesn't seem to be getting any better."

"And what would that problem be, Mr., er, Cherokee?"

"Well, for starters, she was kidnapped, abducted, call it whatever you want to call it, and put to work as a prostitute."

Dr. Mitchell looked at Condo as if he'd gone mad. "Excuse me? Did you just say what I thought you said?"

Condo nodded.

"But surely you can prove this, right." Dr. Mitchell said, a little concerned by all this.

"Oh, sure, we can prove it. We just have to nail the bastard's feet to the floor who did it," said Condo, laughing bitterly.

"Well, surely this is a matter for the authorities. I mean, they'll want to find out who did this, so they can prosecute them."

Condo and Tonya both shook their heads. The doctor just didn't get it, apparently. He didn't understand that they suspected Vito, but could in no way prove anything.

* * * * *

Sgt. O'Brien walked into the bar where Michael Stipiconti had been abducted by Vito's two goons. He sat down at the bar and motioned to the bartender.

Pretty soon, one of them came lumbering over.

"What'll it be, pal?"

O'Brien flashed his badge. "A club soda, and some information, if you could."

The bartender swore underneath his breath. Someone was always coming in here lately busting chops.

Nevertheless, he stitched a pleasant smile on his mug.

"What sort of information would you like, Sergeant?" he asked as he set the glass of club soda on the bar in front of him.

O'Brien slid a $5 bill on top of a $20 bill under the drink. "The top one is for the drink and the bottom one is for you—if you've got the goods."

The bartender thought, well, now.

O'Brien waited...

"OK, what do you need?"

O'Brien leaned in. "Couple of weeks ago, you had a few young guys come in. Here's a picture." He held up a picture of Michael Stipiconti.

"What about the other one?"

"Never mind him. He was just a buddy that was along with him."

"So, what do you wanna know that's worth the $20 bucks?"

"What I wanna know is, there were two, count 'em two guys that came in here and basically escorted this kid Michael off his chair. That's what I want to know."

The bartender looked off...

He's stalling, thought O'Brien.

"Look, bartender, what's your name, Paulie? I don't want any trouble, Paulie. All I want to know is why was it so important that the kid leave. I mean, if you're kicking back with your buddy and two goons come in—isn't sort of natural to kind of wonder?"

"Well, I don't know," Paulie said slowly.

O'Brien sighed. And decided it was time to get tough. "OK, Paulie, I've tried the nice, easy way. And you still want to hang tough, don't you? Well, here is it, kid. Either you cooperate with me, or I'll haul your little ass down to the poh-leece station. You got it?"

Paulie grunted. "OK, ok. I think there might be some way that those guys worked for a certain, shall we say very powerful gentleman. But that's all I'm gonna say. And if you try to pin anything on me, I'll deny I said anything. OK?" He stood back from the bar and folded his arms across his chest.

Now we're getting somewhere, thought O'Brien. But he had to know more.

"OK, Paulie, I hear you. You don't want to get your nice pretty nose busted by this powerful gentleman. Am I right? I can respect that. But you're gonna have to give me a clue."

Paulie looked at O'Brien. Without saying a word, he took down a deck of cards and silently fanned them in O'Brien's face. "This particular gent might just happen to be in charge of, oh, a certain casino. But like I said, might, know what I mean?"

O'Brien lifted his glass. Paulie took the five off the top and rang it up in the register, giving O'Brien two dollars back. He then took two fingers and plucked the $20 bill off the bar. He folded it and tucked it into his shirt. "S'cuse me," he said. "Got other customers to attend to."

O'Brien was satisfied with his night's work.

O'Brien went back to the stationhouse and looked at the log. Good. Pete Connelly was expected in within a half-hour. He decided that if he had to go back to visit Vito, he wanted Connelly along with him. Pete had the kind of dead look that he'd need as backup.

And this time, he would take a search warrant. He'd start the process of the paperwork now and when Pete came on duty later, he would explain it to him.

What he was searching for at Vito's house he had no idea. I mean it was difficult to nail Vito on anything suspicious as it was. To look for physical evidence, that was just damn near impossible. That he knew.

That brought up an interesting point: physical evidence. It would have to be something the crime lab could dust down for fingerprints or any type of scratches or human skin deposited, stuff like that.

Let's see, what did he have? He had Glen who was scared shitless of Vito. And Glen's "proof" didn't amount to much. Same as Paulie, the bartender. For all he knew, the reason they were dragging the kid out of the bar was to settle a gambling debt.

He knew that Angela Leone had been raped. That much was positive. But the kid who might have been accused of raping her was now dead. And it would be very hard to tie Vito to this on the basis of his two goons dragging the kid out of the bar.

What O'Brien needed was *another* witness. Someone who had seen Mike Stipiconti *after* he left the bar. Meaning that if he was dragged out of the bar against his will, they might have settled the matter in the parking lot and then everyone went their own ways.

Might have...

O'Brien decided to head back to the bar as soon as Connelly came in.

When Connelly came in, he got a cup of coffee to go and followed out O'Brien in the car for the ride downtown. He listened to what he had to say and didn't say very much. What was there to say after all?

Connelly had complete faith in O'Brien's judgement. If he felt like he needed to find the witness—that was good enough for O'Brien. He'd just go along for the ride and provide needed backup, which O'Brien might need after all.

When they got back to the bar, O'Brien saw the same bartender again. He kind of winced when he saw him. O'Brien just gave him a hand salute and then eased his way up to the bar. Connelly followed him.

"Yes, sergeant, what can I get you?"

O'Brien waved his hand. "No, nothing. I was sort of interested though about whether you have some sort of valet parking. I'd like to talk to the person who was on duty the night that Michael Stipiconti got escorted out."

The bartender looked uneasy. "Look, I don't want to be getting anyone into trouble."

"And I'll tell you once again, that if you impede an official police investigation—there is going to be big trouble. Got me?"

The bartender nodded. He got it.

"All right then. Who was the person and where can we find them?"

"Um, that would be a guy named Lou Carmozi."

"What time is he due in?"

The bartender looked at his watch. "About an hour."

O'Brien planted himself on the barstool and motioned for Connelly to do the same. "In that case, barkeep, two coffees."

Lou Carmozi walked in holding his head. He had a small hangover, not much, but enough to just make him feel like shit. He went in the back and hung his jacket up. Man, I need some coffee, pronto, he thought.

He headed over to the bar and motioned for the bartender. As soon as he was in earshot, the bartender motioned for Carmodi to talk to him.

"Lou, am I glad to see you. We got two cops sitting here waiting to talk to you."

Carmodi got nervous. "About what? I ain't done nothing. I'm clean."

"Calm down, Lou. It's got nothing to do with you. It's about when you were on duty last week. Remember that kid got dragged out of the bar? Anyway, the cops want to ask you about that."

"OK, ok, listen, can I *please* have some coffee? My freaking head is ready to explode."

The bartender nodded and gestured towards the cops.

Carmodi moved down the bar.

At the sight of him, O'Brien got up off the barstool. "Are you Lou Carmodi?" he asked.

"Yeah, that's me," came the unenthusiastic reply.

"We just want to ask you some questions about a certain night that you were working, that's all."

"OK, go ahead."

"Now, Mr. Carmodi, or is it Lou? Anyway, Lou, we are very interested in what went down the night you were working. The bartender has already corroborated what we already know. That on last Tuesday night, there was a young kid here named Michael Stipiconti. He was here with his friend Glen Wallace.

Now sometime during the time they were here, two guys came in and had a talk with Stipiconti. That's where things get a little, shall we say, confusing?"

"How do you mean, confusing?"

O'Brien looked at Connelly. "What I mean is, these two guys took Stipiconti somewhere. Just lifted him off the barstool and out the door they went. And we want to know where."

"How would I know where?"

"No, you don't get it. We know that you have no idea where they took him. We just want to know what you saw when they came into the parking lot."

Carmodi screwed up his face as if in pain. It would be just his luck to run into these two cops when he came in today.

"C'mon, Lou, just tell us what you saw, and you can go back to whatever it is you're doing. OK? In fact, let's take a walk out to the parking lot. It may help jog your memory."

With that, all three men walked out the door.

They walked around the lot for a bit, O'Brien taking things in, Connelly and Lou Carmodi following him.

O'Brien suddenly stopped and gestured for Carmodi to stand next to him.

"OK, Lou, so from where you stood or sat, you could see these guys coming out with Michael Stipiconti, right?"

"Yeah, I could."

O'Brien walked a little closer. "How did they look?"

"What do you mean, how did they look? They looked like they meant business."

O'Brien edged into Carmodi's face. "Where were you sitting?"

"I was sitting right here," he said motioning to a chair by the side of the entranceway.

"Clear enough to see?"

"Yeah."

O'Brien leaned his arm against the wall. "So what did you see?"

"Nothing in particular."

O'Brien shook his head. "Try again."

"Nothing, I tell you."

O'Brien smoothed the lapels on Carmodi's jacket. "Try again."

"C'mon, I'm not screwing around with you. I didn't see anything."

O'Brien started to twist one of the lapels. "Lou, Lou, I can't hear you..."

Carmodi tried to twist away, but bumped into Connelly who was right behind him. Shit, he thought.

"Really, now, I'm telling you the—"

O'Brien twisted the other lapel until his hands were practically intertwined across Carmodi's neck.

Carmodi's eyes started to bug out. "Hey, you're going to choke me—"

O'Brien shook his head. "Naw, not so's you'd notice."

Connelly piped up: "Just tell the sergeant what he wants to know. Don't be a fool."

Finally, Carmodi could stand it no longer. "OK, OK, JESUS, STOP CHOKING ME!!!" He fell away, gasping for breath.

He staggered away, eyeing O'Brien warily.

Before Carmodi could get any of that swagger back, O'Brien pounced again.

"All right, Lou. Once and for all. Did you get a payoff from Vito Leone to look the other way, or what? Tell me, you little punk, or I swear I'll make you bleed."

Carmodi looked around nervously.

"They paid me off, yeah."

"Who?"

"Carmine, works for Vito. Vito didn't come out of the car."

O'Brien and Connelly both froze.

"You mean, you *saw* him in the car?" asked O'Brien.

Carmodi looked nervous, but nodded.

"What'd they say?" O'Brien pressed.

"Said basically to look the other way, that's all. Paid me $100 to keep quiet."

"Did they rough the kid up?"

Carmodi hesitated.

"C'mon, Lou, you've come this far. Did they beat the shit out of the kid or what?"

"Yeah, they put a little bit of a beating on him. Carmine hit him while the other guy held him."

O'Brien smiled. Gotcha, you bastard, he thought.

* * * *

O'Brien and Connelly went back to the office gleeful. They now had a witness that could testify that Michael Stipiconti had been beaten up, likely abducted and probably killed eventually.

And Vito had his hands all over it. . .

O'Brien sat down and looked across the desk at Connelly. "Now, we just have to figure out how to bring him in."

Connelly looked over at O'Brien. He knew what was going through his partner's head. That would be tough. Because Vito had already been down to the stationhouse once, and he wasn't going to relish going down there again.

How would they do it?

Connelly didn't see any way around it. They would have to bring in Vito by force. And he wouldn't come quietly. Unless he was accompanied by his lawyer. He said as much to O'Brien.

O'Brien nodded. They began to make plans to bring Vito Leone in for the suspected kidnapping and possible murder of Michael Stipiconti.

It was going to be tricky to prove, that O'Brien knew. Just because Carmodi had *seen* Vito in the car, didn't necessarily mean anything. For all he knew, Vito was giving the orders.

Or not...

That was what O'Brien was afraid of. It was one thing for Carmodi to see Carmine beating the shit out of Stipiconti. It was quite another for Vito Leone to be taking part in it.

So how did they prove it...?

* * * * *

As far as DeLuca was concerned, he could put this problem of finding evidence on Condo Cherokee on the back burner. Oh, he would dutifully report back to Atkinson once in awhile, but he wouldn't bust his butt getting all crazy about it.

DeLuca smiled and thought about the way he would spend the rest of his retainer, courtesy of the Attorney General of the state. Hey, he knew this great little Italian restaurant...

* * * * *

Tonya was having a hard time dealing with Condo's moods. Every time she thought that perhaps she was getting better and starting to forget about the awful thing that had happened to her, he would get into a rage about Vito. Tonya tried to explain to Condo that she had dealt primarily with Carmine – not Vito.

But that didn't seem to cut any ice with Condo...

She was afraid that he would just lose it one day and storm over there, totally out of control with anger and rage and thoughts of revenge swirling around his head.

It happened one Thursday afternoon...

Tonya had been resting quietly when Condo came home. He had been taking care of some errands, and he walked into the apartment and sat down in the chair.

He sat down on the couch and started to read the paper. Tonya could hear him rustling the pages. Suddenly, she heard dead silence, followed by the words, "Oh, My God." As soon as Tonya walked into the living room, she knew there would be trouble.

Condo strode up to Tonya and shook the newspaper in her face.

"Did you SEE this?" he asked.

"What is it, honey?"

"Oh nothing, just a little news item about a certain CALL GIRL RING, run by, or allegedly run by the Mob! Other than that, there's nothing to be concerned about!"

Tonya tried to calm him down but she could see he was pretty wound up.

"What are you going to do?" she asked him, hoping that his answer would be what she wanted to hear.

Condo looked around at Tonya. "What I'm going to do is to have it out with one Vito Leone, that's what. I've been waiting for this day too long! I'm convinced he was behind what happened to you and now he's going to pay for it!"
With that, he ran out the door and jumped into his truck and slammed the door. He took off at a high rate of speed.

* * * * *

Tonya was pushing the pedal of her blue Mazda as fast as she dared, without risking a ticket. Her only hope was to get to the club before Condo, but she knew he had a good 10 minute head start on her.

* * * * *

Hatchett pulled his truck into the alcove behind the casino and doused the lights. He reached into his pocket, brought out the .45 with the silencer on it, checked the chamber and racked the slide. This one had Vito Leone's name on it. He had taken the one good thing that had happened to Hatchett and destroyed it.

He crept silently out of the truck and made his way to the backdoor entrance, where he knew one of Vito's gorillas would be waiting.

* * * * *

Just as Hatchett disappeared through the doorway, Condo pulled into the lot. While Condo generally disapproved of guns and violence, there was a part of him that wished he were packing some firepower. What was he going to do, wave his finger sternly at Vito?

He would just confront him, man to man, and get the truth out of him about what has happened with Tonya. And God help him if he'd violated here in any way...

He didn't see the blue Mazda that came racing into the parking lot a few minutes later...

* * * * *

Hatchett crept along the wall, inching towards Vito's office. He needed to find a way to get Vito alone. Wait a minute. His eyes snapped towards the ceiling and the one lonely mini-chandelier with the one lonely 200 watt bulb shining in it. He slipped on a black glove and reached up to extinguish it. There - a couple of twists and the hall was plunged into semi-darkness.

There was, however, just enough light for Hatchett to see whoever came out. He reached over with his boot to the chair lying outside the office and tipped it over. With any luck, Sal would poke his fat head out the door to see what the sudden commotion was. Hatchett got ready.

Sure enough, a minute later, Sal opened the door cautiously, and took a few paced out into the hallway.

Hatchett came up behind him and clamped a hand over his mouth. With one swift motion, he dragged Sal deep out of sight back into the darkened hallway. Sal's eyes opened wide for a moment and muffled curses could be heard beneath Hatchett's hand.

Hatchett put his lips close to Sal's ear.

"Alright, you fucking fat calzone, listen up. We're going to have a little chat with Uncle Vito, OK? Just the three of us. When we go inside, you beep those other greaseheads wherever they are and tell 'em to stay there. Let's go." He gave Sal a jerk and pushed him back toward the office.

Hatchett never saw the form of Condo until he was right on top of both of them, and the three of them began wrestling for control of the gun.

At that moment, Tonya burst through the door and saw Condo on the floor in a fight for his life. Without a moment's hesitation, she threw herself on top of the three men and began wailing away with her tiny fists, hammering Hatchett, hammering Sal, screaming and fighting for her man.

Together, all of them toppled with a mighty crash through the door in front of an absolutely stunned Vito Leone, who just sat there motionless.

Before Vito could make a grab underneath is desk for his "equalizer," Hatchett tore himself loose and sprang up in on swift motion, sweeping the room with his gun.

Sal and Condo and Tonya came away from each other, gasping and all talking at once -

"Boss, these maniacs just tackled me in the hallway—"

"Tonya, what are you—?"

"Condo, oh sweetheart," are you—?"

"SHUT UP, ALL OF YOU!!" Hatchett screamed out. Four pairs of eyes suddenly snapped to attention at the muscular, wiry man who was training a gun on them.

Vito finally spoke up. "What the hell is going on here?"

Hatchett: "You've gotta answer for Val!"

Condo: "I'll kill you if you laid a hand on Tonya! But first I'll kill you for what you did to Tom Bighorn!"

Tonya: "I've got everything on tape, you prick!"

As Tonya waved the tape at Vito, he suddenly saw his whole world collapsing, all in this split second. So, that had been it: the bitch had taped him talking about all the phony mob businesses. She had ruined him!

It was then that they heard the bullhorn: "THIS IS THE POLICE. DROP THE WEAPONS AND COME OUT WITH YOUR HANDS UP."

You'll have to kill me first, Vito thought.

With a lightening quick motion for a burly man, Vito suddenly grabbed Hatchett, who had been distracted by the police, and wrestled the gun from his hand. Hatchett was so startled he stopped dead in his tracks and simply stared at Vito with an astonished expression on his mug.

But Vito wasn't doing any George Raft movie number now. With a look of pure hatred that spoke volumes, he raised the gun in the direction of Tonya and prepared to send a bullet down the long barrel, its trajectory poised to blast her to kingdom come.

Even as his arm began the upward arc and the finger started to squeeze off the rounds that would surely kill her, Condo launched himself at Vito from ten feet away, hoping and praying that his body would be able to shield Tonya.

Two immovable forces collided at once: a .38 caliber bullet and the right tip of Condo's shoulder.

Rrrriipp...!!! A split second later, the door frame buckled and split wide open as four uniformed officers came crashing through, their weapons drawn.

"LAY THE GUN DOWN AND STEP AWAY FROM IT!!! NOW, NOW, NOW, ASSHOLE!! ON THE GROUND, RIGHT NOW, RIGHT NOW, RIGHT NOW!! The voices collided with each other as four cops stood rigidly spread-eagle pointing their guns at Vito's skull.

He looked dully at all of them and as his hand lay there limply, a cop came up and snatched the piece away from him quickly, then handed it off to the other cop behind him and spun Vito around to handcuff him

Tonya had watched in horror as Condo had taken a bullet for her, her hand clenched against her mouth. Now she leaped to his fallen body and cradled it with her arms, sobbing and trying to wipe the blood from his shoulder.

"Oh, Condo, honey, are you in pain? Oh, God, God, someone call an ambulance. He's bleeding to death!!!" She half turned and beseeched the cops with a scream.

One of the officers knelt down and examined Condo's wound. "It's, ok, miss. It only looks like the bullet just grazed him. He's lucky."

The cop who had crashed through the door first, lowered his gun, walked over to Vito and said, "Vito Leone? We have a warrant for your arrest. You have the right to remain silent. You have the right to—"

Vito looked up and stared into Sergeant O'Brien's face. "Hey, knock that shit off, O'Brien. I know my rights."

O'Brien looked down at Vito, smiled, and continued.

Once he was done reading Vito his rights, the other cops led him, Sal and Hatchett out the door. All the fight was out of them and they just stared sullenly ahead.

* * * * *

Tonya kept her right hand wrapped tightly in Condo's left as the ambulance sped to the hospital. Everything would be all right now, she thought.

As if interrupting her thoughts, the big man on the gurney with the IV in his right arm, stirred and looked at Tonya.

"It's ok," Tonya said as she wiped the sweat from his brow.

Condo looked up at her and thought: I'll never find another woman like this. Why not make it always and forever?

He squeezed her hand and said, "Well, I can't get down on one knee... but, Tonya, would you marry me?" His eyes held hers.

Tonya gasped and looked down at him. "I can't think of anything better in the world than to be your wife. I love you." She knelt down beside him on the floor of the ambulance.

A soft rain scratched at the windows as the sirens wailed and screamed, the lovers inside waiting to heal—and start their own life together.

* * * * *

Chapter 18
CLOSURE

Three Years Later...

Tonya looked down at her daughter. She couldn't believe that she was a mother. All her dreams were coming true. Barely a year after she and Condo married, they were the proud parents of Shawna Marie, all 6 lbs. 2 ounces of her.

Tonya sat and reflected on the recent events of the year. Vito Leone had been tried and sent to prison. The tapes had been instrumental in getting the conviction. More importantly, the tribe had retained control of the casino once again.

It was at times like this that Tonya missed her mother, Poca Daisy most of all. But Tonya now had a daughter to raise and if she could do half the job that her mom had done with her, everything would be fine.

The sun started to set over the nearby mountains, and Tonya felt content. Family was everything in this world and Tonya and Condo's family was just beginning.

Tonya tried not to think about what had happened with Vito at the end. She didn't want to disturb the peace and equilibrium in her life.

The trial of Vito had been just that—a trial. In it, she had been forced to watch as Condo had to take the stand against Vito and testify, under oath, that there was all sorts of collusion and racketeering going on.

There were some awful things said up there. Things that Tonya never wanted to hear again as long as she lived.

She watched Condo bravely get through it every day, but it took its toll on him. He would come home at night and just be totally exhausted.

He couldn't figure out why he was being targeted. It was some sort of conspiracy, he felt. Like what did he have to say that was so great?

Tonya knew better...

"Condo," she would explain. "The reason that they wanted you to testify is because you have observed all of Vito's dirty tricks over the years. In a way, you sort of know where the bodies are buried. You know what I mean?"

Condo stared at her a little dubiously.

"OK, I guess I can accept some of what you say. But how come they didn't ask a whole bunch of other people to testify?"

Tonya had no answer for that. So she just let it go.

Vito had been sent up the river on two counts of racketeering. There had been other charges, but his attorney had plea-bargained them down to nothing.

Tonya had about screamed bloody murder when she heard that. It was insane! Here he was, a mobster, and all the prosecution could get him on was some kind of flimsy racketeering charges?

Tonya couldn't believe it.

But there was something else that was unsettling about the conviction of Vito Leone. Something that caused her to have nightmares sometimes at night when she contemplated the terror of it...

Vito Leone was eligible for parole this year...

The more she thought about it, the more she got goose bumps. When it had come time to hand down the sentencing, the judge had done an incredible flip-flop. She had given the bastard 10 years, with an option for parole after three if he behaved himself and was a good boy.

It kept Tonya awake more than one night, that was for sure....

When she thought about it, Tonya just knew that this man had put her through an incredible amount of stuff. So many of the bad things that had happened to her had been the direct result of one Vito Leone.

She also knew that nothing could ever pay him back for all the stuff that had happened.

Tonya supposed that prison time was punishment enough. But the length of time absolutely floored her. It meant that her family was never quite safe to look over their shoulder again.

Oh, she had heard through a reliable source that Condo knew that Vito was being a model prisoner. Oh, yes. He had caused no problems behind bars, and he had not conducted any Mob business behind there.

Just the type of prisoner that would take a shiny apple and present it to the warden!

Yeah, right, Tonya thought.

Tonya did not for a minute believe that Vito Leone had changed one iota. No way. The man was stone-cold Mob and everyone knew it. If they wanted proof, all they had to do was look into his eyes and see the fury that he had displayed during the final shootout.

That was proof enough as far as Tonya was concerned.

Yet there was no way that she could say anything during the trial. That was not considered relevant. So she sort of had to sit there on her hands and not say anything. That was difficult. She had wanted so many times to just burst out and tell the judge every terrible thing that had happened.

If she did that, the bailiffs would have just hauled her off.

So, basically, she and Condo sat there and just looked at each other. It was all so madly frustrating.

Tonya got up and looked at the calendar. Let's see, according to this, Vito was scheduled to get out of jail very very soon. And that was not good at all.

Tonya couldn't put her finger on exactly why she had this premonition of dread. She knew it was irrational; Vito was certainly not crazy enough to start anything that would violate his parole. Tonya and Condo were assured of at least a couple of things:

Vito Leone could not leave the state.

Vito Leone could not carry any firearms.

Vito Leone couldn't get so much as a parking ticket.

So with all of that, why did she feel so concerned? Why did she feel like she didn't trust any of those things?

Tonya knew that she couldn't go to Condo with any of this. He would just think she was overreacting. Even though she knew that he knew the implicit danger of everything. After all, he had tangled with Vito more than once and knew the man's power.

She went over and adjusted Shawna Marie's top. The child was such a joy and Tonya could not imagine how she had lived without her. She and Condo were such devoted parents. It was wonderful the way that Condo doted on her.

He had taken to fatherhood like a duck to water. He had went out and bought the child lots of toys and little gifts that she could play with.

One of her shining moments was to come home each day and see Condo playing with the child. It brought her near to tears.

The three of them were able to live modestly. It turned out that the expected windfall to Tonya from the money that had been left to Poca Daisy had some strings attached to it.

Meaning that she was not free to liquidate some of the stock until she herself was old and gray. Only a portion could be liquidated now.

So, as a result both she and Condo had to work. When Shawna was old enough she got a babysitter for her, and went back to the gift shop. And Condo, of course, was able to continue at the casino now that the threat from the Mob was over.

Tonya found that even though she loved being a mother, she actually liked working part-time at the gift shop. It was nice to get out and she found that she was much more stimulating conversation for Condo when he got home.

So the three of them had carved out a life such as it was. They were not really able to go on vacations very much since the baby was so young, but Tonya knew that would change at some point.

As far as having more babies, Tonya was certainly looking forward to that. She was young and she wanted to be able to give Condo as many children as he wanted.

Then just as abruptly as they came, those thoughts were gone out of her head and she returned to thoughts of Vito...

But even before *that* could happen, she was interrupted by Condo putting his arms around her.

He reached over to squeeze the baby's arm and give it a hug. He looked at Tonya's face and saw the worry and concern about Vito on it.

"What's wrong, hon?" he asked.

"Oh, nothing," she replied.

Condo was silent for a minute. He knew his Tonya, and he could always tell when something was up. So he pressed her again.

"C'mon, babe, you can't fool me, (It was true, she thought) why the long face?"

Damn, Tonya thought. I thought I was hiding it better than that. She knew she had to come up with something in a hurry but couldn't think of anything.

"Oh, I was just thinking about the trial," she said, knowing that now he would begin to give her the third degree about what exactly she was thinking.

She wasn't in the mood for that.

He surprised her, though.

"Well, the trial was a long time ago, honey," Condo said soothingly. "It's kind of odd for you to be thinking about it now, don't you think?"

"No, not really. I mean, it was a very important part of our lives. So it's not unnatural that I would think about it every now and then." She fiddled with the drapery at the side of the curtain.

"Well, what exactly *are* you thinking of?"

"Just that we did everything we could to bring Vito to justice and still, after all that, he walks away with a light sentence."

"I wouldn't call 10 years exactly a slap on the wrist."

Tonya looked at him as if he had lost his mind.

"Condo, for God's sake, you know that he is eligible for parole very soon, don't you?"

Condo sat there and fidgeted. The look on his face told her that she hadn't been thinking about it really.

"Yeah, I know he comes up soon. I mean, I have a vague idea of when he gets out."

Tonya got up and marched him to the calendar. She pointed at a date a month from now. "In case you're wondering at when the guy you helped send to prison gets out, take a look. That's the date."

She went back inside and sat down in the living room next to her daughter.

Condo followed her back in and sat down with her. He began to rub her neck the way she liked. "Look, hon, I know that he is scheduled to get out soon, but really it's not going to be any big deal."

Tonya looked up at him. For his sake, she hoped so.

* * * * *

Vito Leone walked over to the bank of phones that were set up for prisoners to talk to the people who came to see them.

Prison had not done terrible things to Vito. Probably because of the reputation that he carried into the joint with him. Everyone inside was so terrified of him that they gave him a wide berth.

Vito didn't even have to have anyone protect him, as would have been the custom in prison. No, no one wanted to mess around with Vito Leone.

He had seen the effect that his reputation had on the third day of prison. He had been standing in the chow line and had inadvertently cut in front of another prisoner. It was one of those quick things that you couldn't see coming. But the guy that it happened to got very pissed off and started to go for Vito.

Suddenly, it was as if there were these three huge arms planted around the kid. He didn't know what happened. His tray clattered to the floor and he was lifted bodily out of the line and carried away and planted somewhere else.

No one messed with Vito after that...

Today, Vito felt bad because his long-suffering wife Sophia was here and was waiting to talk to him. Vito hoped that she didn't have bad news. There was nothing worse in prison than having your wife come to you with bad news. That was difficult to take.

He reached over for the phone.

"Oh, Vito, honey, how are you?"

Vito looked through the mirror at the woman he had known and been married to for all these years.

"Good, Sophia, I'm ok. They're treating me alright. I can't complain. They're guys in here that got it a hell of a lot worse than I do.

Guys that are in the hole. That's solitary confinement. Compared to that, I'm great."

Vito leaned forward in his seat, his hand gripped on the phone and looked through the plexiglass into his wife's eyes. "So, Sophia, you don't have any bad news for me, do you?"

Sophia shook her head. "No, no, nothing like that. I just needed to come and see you. It's been so lonely without you... I just wonder when our life is going to be back together again." She sighed through the phone.

Vito didn't know what to tell her. He knew how rough it was on her. And on Angela. But, hey, he was the one doing the hard time. Not anyone else. Not that he would ever want his wife or daughter to have to endure anything like he went through.

"Well, that's good. It's a little hard to get bad news in prison if you know what I mean."

Sophia put her hand on the glass and squeezed the glass as if squeezing the hand of her husband.

"Now don't do anything foolish to jeopardize your parole, ok? I don't want to have to start waiting all over again."

Vito grinned a mirthless grin. "No way, baby."

Vito was led back to his cell after blowing his wife a kiss goodbye. It was so nice to see her, he thought.

He had to admit the one thing that he missed the most was regular sex. It was hard to think of his mistress Carmen, especially after his wife had just come to visit him, but he did. Vito thought of the things that he and Carmen used to do in bed. Or rather the things that she used to do to him. God, he thought, that seems like such a long time ago.

Vito had to admit that as far as sex went, sexual relations with Sophia were pedestrian at best. She was a great wife and a fantastic mother, but as a lover... well, she left things to be desired. That was where Carmen had come in.

He knew that he would never divorce Sophia. That was just a thought that would never enter his mind. She had been too good to him and besides Vito loved her, even though he cheated on her.

One thing that he did regret though was the fact that Carmen hadn't come to see him more often. She had come a total of twice in all this time. Each time she would come in all breathless and full of excuses why she didn't get there more often.

Vito would just listen and nod. He sort of guessed he understood, but wondered if she wasn't screwing around on him. There was no way to tell unless he assigned one of his boys to look after her, and he wasn't going to do that.

No, Carmen was on the honor system...

He sat back down in his cell and looked at the wall. He had been given a cell of his own after a few weeks in prison. Some strings had been pulled and he had finally gotten one. The warden didn't ask any questions, which Vito appreciated. He'd make sure that there was a little something for the warden.

Vito recalled the meeting that he and the warden had. He was kind of a mild-mannered man for someone who was supposed to run herd over about 1,000 inmates.

He had welcomed Vito into the office and sat him down. Vito was there with his attorney and one other guy. He ran through the numbers fairly quickly, telling him what the institution expected from him while he was there.

Blah, blah, blah...

Vito waited until his attorney and the other guy left and turned his focus on the warden who was still going on about correct behavior and what type of stuff would be allowed and what wouldn't be allowed.

"Hey, shit-brain."

The warden stopped. "Excuse me, Mr. Leone."

"You heard me. Hey, shit-brain. I heard you enough already. You told me everything, now I'm going to tell you something. I got a list of demands here that I want met while I'm here. You got me?"

The warden sat down, cringing a little. "Well, now, see here, Mr. Leone, you can't talk to me like that. I am, after all, the warden, and I have the power to—"

"Hey, you ain't got the power over me unless I say you do. Understand? Now here's what I want. I want my food prepared specially in the kitchen, I'm not eating the crap you serve here. I want you to make sure that I get my favorite cigar, Macanudos, in here. So I can enjoy one after dinner. And I want—"

The warden piped up, "There is to be no smoking in this prison, inmate."

Vito waved his hand as if swatting a fly. "Oh, shut up."

He continued. "And I also want to make sure that I don't stay too horny, you know? Cause I don't want to be eyeing some of these losers in here, you get my meaning."

"Well, what can I do about that?" the warden squeaked.

Vito eyeballed him. "What you can do is find me a nice young piece of ass who knows how to use her mouth, you get me? And she better be clean and fresh. No skanks."

He got up and walked towards the door. "Nice talking with you warden. I'm glad we understand each other."

Two weeks later, Vito had everything he asked for. He had gotten moved out of his cell, the cook was making him a specially prepared meal, his cigars were there and as far as the girl went, the warden had come through big time for him.

The girl's name was Violet and once a week she came in to the jail and was led to the basement where Vito was waiting.

All he had to do was unzip his pants and she took over from there. Actually, it was better than that. Violet unzipped his pants for him and the only thing Vito saw after that was the back of her head moving slowly and easily back and forth until he climaxed with a shudder. After that, Violet carefully cleaned up, zipped up Vito's fly again and smiled a luscious smile at him, and left.

Yes, Vito had to admit, she sure knew how to use her mouth...

Vito had many visitors there from among the inmate population. They were a little awestruck at having such an important and powerful man there and accorded him all the respect he was entitled to.

The only problem was that they were getting a little *too* chummy sometimes.

The way Vito figured it, he was always going to be *capo*. It's just that being in prison had made it very difficult for him to be *capo* inside. Outside was a different story.

Like this one guy, Johnny Rodriguez. Rodriguez was always coming to him with some cockamamie story about some big heist he was planning.

Vito listened patiently enough until one day he had to set Rodriguez straight.

"Listen, kid, I can appreciate what you're trying to do. When I was your age, man, I wanted to knock over every store there was. But times change, and I went on to bigger and better things."

Rodriguez looked at him a little confused. "Well, uh, I hear what you say, Mr. Leone, but uh what does this have to do with me?"

Vito sighed. He was going to have to lay it out for the kid.

"First of all, you got to realize something. Outside when I had my own crew, I had all the power I wanted. You know? I mean, it wasn't that hard to get the things I wanted.

But in here, it's different. The screws, they got eyes and ears everywhere." Vito lowered his voice. "What I'm saying, kid, is that outside if I could give you help that's a different story. Then you'd owe me one. But in here..." Vito spread his hands.

Rodriguez looked a little crestfallen.

"So, there's no way that I can like get anything while I'm in here."

Vito thought: Man, this kid is dense. "Like how, kid? How am I going to do that? What do you think I can just snap my fingers and all my boys'll come running? What are you dreaming! What I can do, I can send a word out with someone who comes in here."

"But let me tell you something kid." Vito leaned in close so Rodriguez got the message. "If you do anything to fuck up my parole, I'm not gonna be very happy. Do we understand each other?"

Rodriguez nodded. They understood each other.

The day finally came when Vito was released. He got up early, showered and shaved close and put on the suit that he had worn into this joint. Vito was pleased to see that it still fit him well. He had tried to watch what he ate in the place and not become a fat pig.

He went down to the warden's office and the guard knocked on the door. Then he went inside and sat down to wait.

The warden kept him waiting 15 minutes, designed to show him that he didn't care much for Vito. When he came out, he immediately squared his shoulders and tried to act very dignified with Vito.

"Well, inmate, I hope that you've learned your lesson well in here. I certainly don't want to see you come to any harm outside and I hope you do well. Do you have all your belongings?"

"Yeah, warden, I got them. No problem."

The warden set his mouth. "Well, you haven't been a discipline problem in here and for that I'm glad." He held out his hand. "Best of luck to you then."

Vito got up, looked down at the warden's hand and laughed. He turned on his heel and strode toward the door.

When he got to the door, he turned around and said, "Hey, Warden, I heard you got yourself a piece of Violet. That broad's got some mouth, don't she?"

The Warden turned beet red, and Vito strode out of the room, laughing as he went.

He got into the long black limousine that was sitting there idling at the curb. Carmine held the door for him.

"Hey, boss, it's good to see you back. They treat you all right in there?"

Vito settled his legs into the luxurious upholstery. Yeah, it felt good to be riding in the seat of power again. He glanced at Carmine who was sitting there waiting for Vito to tell him what prison had been like.

There's no way you could ever describe it, Vito thought...

"Where to first, boss?" asked Jackie, his driver.

Vito thought a moment. "Take me to The Luna. I want to have the biggest Italian meal I can eat. That's the one thing I missed in the joint. That cook don't know how to make a good lasagna for shit."

He settled back and said to Carmine, "So, you got those reports like I asked you?"

Carmine held up his hand. In it were details of how the business had been going since they had locked Vito up.

Vito took the reports, switched on the overhead light in the limo and began to read. That was the signal for everyone else to stay quiet.

Once inside The Luna, Vito was welcomed warmly as if he had never been away. The owner came up and gave him a big hug. Vito responded warmly back in kind.

He settled into a big meal of fettucine alfredo done just the way he liked it. Ah, it was good to be back, he thought.

Afterward he sat and held court a bit. Some of the diners came up and paid respects to him. It was gratifying to know that he hadn't been forgotten, Vito thought.

He then got up and walked through the streets a little bit, pausing to say hello to some of the shop and store owners. He even kissed an old lady or two.

Pretty soon, though, he got a bit tired and headed back to the limo. He climbed in, loosened his belt and said, "Let's get out of here, Sal."

Sal nodded and gunned the car

* * * * *

Vito got home, kissed his wife and settled into his chair. He had had a lot of time to think about certain things in jail. A LOT of time. And among the things that he thought about was revenge for what had been done to him.

Vito never seriously considered the notion that he should have served any jail time at all. He was a respected head of the Mob and he had to sit in some jail cell all because some broad had double-crossed him?

He was sure of one thing. He would take his time to slowly and carefully plot his revenge. This was not going to be just some incident that had happened and was going to be conveniently glossed over. Oh, no. The parties responsible for his incarceration were going to pay for this. Oh yes sir, they would.

But what would the proper punishment be? Vito knew that he wanted to have something that would make a definite impression. But what to use? He could very easily take out Condo or Tonya. That was no problem. But if he did that he wouldn't really have exacted revenge.

And revenge was what he wanted.

No, he wanted to find out what was most important to them. And the answer came in a flash: Their daughter.

Of course, Vito thought. If he had their little girl in his possession, he'd be in a much better position to dictate terms. Yes, that was it.

Naturally, he couldn't let his wife know or anyone close to him that wouldn't understand. They would not take kindly to that. They understood a great many things that Vito Leone did—but kidnapping (with the literal use of the word, kid) was not among them.

That sort of made Vito chuckle in a way. Here were all these real hard-ass guys and they could do the most unimaginable things, but yet they got all squeamish over a little kid.

He decided to run the subject by Carmine. He rang him on the cell phone and told him to get up here.

Carmine knocked on the door ten minutes later and came in. He was surprised that Vito would call him so late. He kind of thought that Vito was in for the night. Oh well, Carmine thought. You could never quite tell with Vito.

He settled in comfortably in one of the chairs opposite Vito.

"What's up, Boss?" he asked.

"Oh, nothing," said Vito casually. I just kind of wanted to know what you thought about something."

"Yeah, like what?"

"Like kidnapping, that's what."

Carmine paused. "Well, boss, that's all well and good, but you don't really want to do anything that's going to jeopardize your parole, do you?"

Now it was Vito's turn to pause. He hadn't really thought about that.

It seems that under the strict terms of his parole, Vito couldn't get so much as a hangnail that was illegal. Now that Carmine mentioned it, it did present some difficulties.

Nevertheless, he decided to tell Carmine about his thoughts.

"I was just thinking out loud, and I thought about the main reason I was sent up the river. And that reason has to do with a certain Indian and his wife. Know what I mean?"

Carmine did know but he was did not want to say anything that would get Vito mad. He couldn't figure out what was on his boss's mind. Did Vito just think he could do a snatching just like that? That no one would object? And anyway, who was he thinking about?

He looked at Vito now and said exactly that. "Uh, boss, who were you thinking about kidnapping?" Hoping that it would be no one he knew.

Vito looked up at the ceiling and then back down. His hands came to rest on his midsection.

"I was thinking about that rat bastard Condo Cherokee's kid. I got plenty to pay back him and that bitch of a wife he's got."

Carmine was afraid of that. He had thought about that from time to time while Vito was in jail. Wondering about the day when Vito got out. And today was the day that it happened.

He shifted uncomfortably in his seat.

"So, boss, just how do you propose that we snatch the kid?"

Vito looked at Carmine and said casually. "Well, I haven't quite worked that out yet. But when the time comes, you'll know it. Believe me, you'll know it."

Carmine persisted. "So, like, we're just going to hold this kid for ransom is that it?"

"Yeah, something like that."

"OK, boss, anything you say."

Vito looked at him and smiled. Carmine was on his wavelength. Just the way he liked it.

* * * *

In time, Tonya soon forgot about the threat from Vito. After all, she reasoned, she wasn't even sure if Vito was even around, much less a threat. Still, she couldn't help but wonder if Condo was a little worn out from all of this. Which would explain why he didn't have the same fear that she had had.

Each of them had their own ways, Tonya supposed. . .

She concentrated on building a life with her family. She knew that in time she and Condo would have another child, then another, and pretty soon, all ugly traces of her past life would be gone. She was wonderfully happy. . .

* * * *

The same could not be said, however, for one Donald T. Hatchett. . .

Right after Vito's trial, his came up. Considering his prior criminal record and considering that he was attempting to murder another human being at the time of his apprehension, it didn't take the jury long at all to find Hatchett guilty of criminal possession of a firearm and attempted murder.

No, the time it took them to deliberate – you could have ordered lunch in. . .

When they read the verdict to him, Hatchett grimaced a little but that was about it. Inwardly, Hatchett was resigned to being a three-time loser.

Seven to ten years, with a possibility of parole.

The sheriff lead him away in handcuffs.

In the three years that passed, Hatchett had tried to do his time straight up – that is, without complaining. But man, it was hard. He remembered all too well his earlier incarceration years ago. Remembered the fortitude that he had to have in order to make it through.

Christ, he thought, it was enough to have to keep the black guys away from him – much less everyone else.

Hatchett had survived the three years so far by focusing on what he would do when he got out. He had some skills as an auto mechanic that he knew had gone to waste – but he could still get them back. Hatchett was pretty confident he could fix any car known to man.

His emotional life, well, that was another story.

He remembered looking around the courtroom to see if he might catch a glimpse of Val there. She was nowhere to be found. He remembered that he had not been too surprised, but still, it would have been nice for her to show up for his goddamn trial.

He thought about her less and less these days...

The way he figured it was, that part of his life was over. He knew that, somehow, she had been corrupted by Vito Leone. So it wasn't entirely her fault.

But after a time in prison, you just cease to care about anything except getting out.

No, man, you just want out, big time.

Which is sort of where Hatchett's head was today.

He knew that he wouldn't last the next three or four years in here. No way. Either he'd wind up dead or kill someone else that was trying to mess with him in the process. So he had to figure out a way to get out.

Hatchett had been assigned to road "reclamation" duty. That was tough duty, yessir, laying tar and asphalt in the blazing hot sun. The first two years, Hatchett had lived with a shovel and rake in his hand as he waited for the spreader to dump his load of the hot, gooey mixture on to the road, where Hatchett and a bunch of other losers spread it all around.

He had watched as guys passed out from the heat and had to be hoisted back up into the truck and sent back to the main prison compound. Hatchett could never decide if they were goldbricking or not. They sure as hell looked sick to him.

Whatever happened to that old prison axiom about making license plates, Hatchett wondered? This was sure a hell of a lot different from making license plates. When you did that all you had to worry about was spelling the letters and numbers right. Hell, you didn't even have to worry about that. The machine did it for you.

It was a good thing that he was in decent shape, otherwise he would have suffered the same fate as those poor bastards being thrown into the truck.

Ten hours a day, one 45-minute chow break. That had been his existence.

And then one day, the regular inmate driver for the cookwagon got sick. (Probably from the shit they gave you to eat).

And that was the day that Donald T. Hatchett's lucky number came up.

One of the guards came up to him and said, "Hey, Hatchett, do you drive?"

Hatchett turned toward the man real slow so as to not betray his excitement. "Sure, I drive. 'Course I don't have my license with me right now, ya understand."

The guard didn't smile.

"So, where is it you want me to drive to?" asked Hatchett, his voice bored again.

"Just over to the prison cafeteria, pick up the buckets of food, bring them back here, that's it. Think you can handle that?" said the guard with a sneer to his voice.

Hatchett fought the urge to bust the guard right in the chops. No, he knew, I've gotta stay cool – at least for now.

"Yeah, I could handle it."

The guard motioned to one of his subordinates. "Hey, Pete, take Hatchett here over to the cafeteria to pick up the grub. And don't take your time – I'm getting' hungry."

Pete nodded and motioned to Hatchett. "He drive ok? I don't want to get myself killed with some convict."

The other guard looked Hatchett up and down. He strode up to Hatchett and smacked him hard on the shoulder with the flat of his palm. "Who, Hatchett? Aw, Pete, he's allright, ain't you, boy? Just as long as you know who's boss around here."

Hatchett wouldn't give him the satisfaction of knowing that the smack hurt. Bastard, he thought.

Then he shifted his thoughts to something else real quick. He needed a minute or two to think about what he was going to do. His mind racing, he said to the guard, "Yeah, but first I gotta pee, you know? Or is that ok?"

The guard looked at him and rolled his eyes. "Whatever. Go use the outhouse and make it quick."

Hatchett walked over some 20 yards away to the Port-A-John. The minute he got inside the stench was overpowering. But Hatchett ignored it. His mind was on other things.

He knew he was being handed a golden opportunity here. He had no way of knowing how long the cookwagon driver would be out sick.

And Hatchett had damn sure had enough of this prison life to last him a lifetime.

In his mind's eye, he could see his hands wrapped around the throat of that guard. . .

But this wasn't the time for revenge, this was the time for cool-headed thinking.

OK, so all he had to do was distract the guard long enough. Get him comfortable, loose and relaxed that was the ticket. Man who's loose and relaxed lets his guard down.

And that would be all the opening Hatchett needed.

He opened the door of the outhouse and walked back to the guards. "OK, I'm ready," he announced.

Pete motioned with his rifle. "All right, let's go." They started over to the cookwagon truck.

Pete went to the driver's side and opened the door for Hatchett. "Easy does it, convict," he said. "I don't want no trouble here. We're gonna take a short ride over, get the stuff and come right back." He put his gun up, and marched around to the other side, all the while keeping it trained on Hatchett.

He got in the other side, reached into his vest pocket and took out the keys. He leaned over, inserted the keys into the ignition and started the truck.

"OK, drive," he said to Hatchett.

Hatchett held up his manacled hands and shook them.

"Don't worry, it ain't a gear shift. Git going."

Hatchett put the truck in gear and pulled onto the highway.

A mile down the road, Hatchett said, "Hey, you driving around, you ever pick up a chick hitchiker, give her a ride?"

Pete just stared straight ahead and said, "Shutup."

Hatchett looked straight ahead. "OK." Then said, "I just was trying to make conversation. No, really, you ever pick one up?"

Pete grunted this time. "Yeah, once. She was a nice thing. About 22."

"Great body, huh?" said Hatchett, trying to lull Pete into the mood.

"Yeah, I gotta say that. She had one on her wouldn't quit."

"She probably liked a guy in uniform, huh?"

Pete chuckled, remembering the time.

Hatchett sped up the truck a little faster. . .

"Yeah, I've heard tell a lot of chicks go for corrections officers. No kidding, they really like a macho guy."

Pete's eyes narrowed, thinking of the young girl's thighs beneath those tight shorts. . .

Hatchett picked up the speed still more. . .

Suddenly, he snapped to attention. "Hey, Hatchett, slow this goddamn truck down, man!"

Hatchett looked straight over at Pete. He stepped on the gas a little more. "Oh, sorry, man. I guess I just got caught up in the story."

He gripped the steering wheel tightly, locking his arms, but in a way so that Pete wouldn't notice. He then ever so slightly arched his back, bracing for the stop that was coming.

He let his food off the gas slightly. . .

He looked over at Pete. Good, nice body posture, relaxed and not ready at all.

"Are you gonna slow this truck down or not?" Pete now yelled at Hatchett.

Hatchett gave Pete a slow, wide grin with a mouthful of teeth. "Why sure, captain."

Then, suddenly, tromped on the brakes full blast and just barely grazed the steering wheel with his chin.

The impact sent Pete's head smashing into the windshield where it hit once, crashed the whole passenger side and then sent his body jackhammering back into the seat as if thrown there. His forehead and face were soon covered in blood and the rifle went flying from his hands.

Hatchett snatched the piece up right away.

He reached across Pete's moaning body and opened the door handle. He then pivoted around, took both his feet and sent Pete flying with a kick out the door.

"See ya, chump," Hatchett chortled, as he slammed the door and got going.

* * * *

Hatchett drove like a man possessed. He wished he could have gotten the damn handcuffs off, but there was nothing that could be done about that now. He also realized that he was hungry, it being lunchtime and all when he decided to steal the truck and kick Pete the guard out.

That, and a little semi-exhausted. But he pressed on.

After driving for about several hours, he pulled the truck over to the side of the road. He just needed to nod off for a few minutes. Get his shit back together. . . his eyes felt heavy. Christ, man, he was nodding. . . nodding

. . . out.

When he awoke, it was nearing twilight. He sat up and looked down the road. The evening's colors would soon be painting the landscape around him. It was a time of the day that Hatchett had always liked. He looked at his gas gauge. Man, he was getting low on fuel.

It was then that he noticed a dim, sort of reddish light that was bouncing off the small tree range up ahead, about a couple of miles down the road. Hatchett started the car and crept along the shoulder of the road for a little bit.

The reddish lights grew in intensity...

Then he saw what was causing it. Two police cruisers were up ahead with their lights flashing.

Hatchett got out of the car and walked along the side of the road near the tree line, near the shadows. When he got up ahead another 100 yards he saw it. Two cops sitting there on the sides of their cars.

And two orange cones sitting between the space of the cars.

Hatchett sneered. Are you kidding me, he thought? That's the best you assholes can throw at me? He ran back to the car. This was going to be a piece of cake, he thought. I'll ram those cones and by the time those dickheads rev up their engines I'll be pulled into the nearest side road with my lights out and the engine off. And they'll keep going.

He jumped in the car and the started the engine which roared to life.

Hatchett pressed the accelerator to the floor. 40, 50, 60, 80, 100 m.p.h. He stared straight ahead and clasped his manacled hands on the steering wheel. Out of the way, suckers!!!!

The two officers, who were sipping coffee, looked up as they saw a truck bearing down on them – fast. The cups went flying in the air as they dove for the safety of their police cars.

A moment later, they saw that was foolish, and hightailed it for the sides of the road.

Hatchett broke through the cones like a jet fighter breaking the speed of sound.

TTHHWWUUMMPPP!!!!!!! came the sound of the soft, rubberized cones as they were smashed aside like tiny rag dolls.

Hatchett slowed briefly on impact, then turned his head around for a good long second and let out a bark of a laugh at the two stupid cops.

"HA-HA-HA-HA-HA, YOU MORONS, OH, YEAH, MAN, THAT WAS GREAT!!!!!!!"

He brought his head up and, still chortling, stared straight ahead...

... and saw a wall of state troopers with their lights flashing...

... and saw the biggest roadblock he had ever seen.

Hatchett managed to slow his car to 75 m.p.h. before he started to swerve.

The car swerved, then buckled, then pitched and finally started to roll. Once over, twice over, three times over, with Hatchett inside bouncing around like a monkey in a cage. When the car finally came to a crashing halt, it came to rest on its side with a ear-splitting crunch of twisted metal and human bone.

When the cops finally managed to pull him out from the wreckage, his cheekbone had been pushed into the side of his bloodied face, making him look like a particularly grotesque doll.

There was no need to feel for a pulse. . . Donald T. Hatchett was quite dead. . .

* * * * *

Tonya coaxed Shawna Marie away from the swing set in the park with a cookie. She loved watching her daughter play. It was like therapy for the soul. She tried to imagine her daughter as a grown-up, with children of her own, then stopped. Tonya laughed to herself thinking that she didn't want to admit to being that old yet!

Mother and daughter walked hand in hand away from the playground. If Tonya had been thinking of other things, she might have been aware that the playground seemed quieter than normal. She might have been aware that the day seemed to take on an eerie calm with the leaves barely blowing, like something threatening was in the air.

She might have been aware of the long black limo that sat on the opposite side of the park – watching her.

And watching Shawna Marie Cheroke. . .

* * * * *

Tonya was in a rush to get out the door. She was meeting Condo at the Civic Auditorium downtown. They had finally gotten tickets to a concert that both of them had wanted to see. James Taylor. Tonya, couldn't wait to see him sing his beautiful songs. Even though he was from another generation, Tonya and Condo both liked his songs a lot.

She wanted to make sure that the babysitter had her final instructions. She walked into Shawna's room and glanced down at her fast asleep. Such a pretty little girl. Tonya bent down and kissed her.

She then walked into the living room and said to Carla, the sitter, "Don't worry, she's fast asleep. Now you know where her bottle is, and her food and diapers, right? OK, then we shouldn't be too long at the concert."

Carla nodded. She would take care of everything.

Tonya had confidence in Carla. They had used her before many times and Shawna really liked her. That was important.

Tonya went out and locked the door.

Carla had just went to the refrigerator to get something to drink when she heard the sound. It sounded like. . . no, that couldn't be possible. How was anyone going to open the door? It was locked. She squatted down and looked inside the refrigerator for something yummy to eat.

She felt rather than saw the arm that suddenly snaked around her.

What the. . . she thought as she was jerked upright.

Suddenly she heard a voice, harsh, raspy, male, against her ear. "You're just gonna have a little nappy now, sister." It was a whispery voice.

That was when she first smelled the smell. God, she thought, that's horrible! But all of a sudden she was getting sleepy. . . couldn't keep her eyes open. Then she slumped down to the ground

Carmine removed the handkerchief with the chloroform away from her mouth. There, he thought, that ought to keep her out for awhile. . . He headed upstairs towards Shawna's room.

* * * * *

Inside the concert hall, Tonya and Condo were listening to J.T. sing "Carolina On My Mind." When the song ended, the lights came up for intermission. Everyone in the audience groaned, but they were all happy because J.T. would be coming back for another set of songs.

"I'm going to call Carla, honey, just to check on her," Tonya said as she got up and stretched.

"OK," said Condo, giving her a kiss.

Downstairs, Tonya had to wait a few minutes for the pay phones to clear. She dialed the number and waited. And waited. Finally, her answering machine came on.

Hhmmmm. . . thought Tonya. That's strange. Carla must have fallen asleep.

She returned to her seat and got ready for the second half of the concert. She wasn't sure if she should tell Condo or not.

"Did you get ahold of Carla?" he asked, rolling the program around in his hands.

Tonya hesitated. "Uumm, no, I guess she was already conked out." Her words trailed off.

Both of them looked at each other and started for the exit at the same time.

The loudest scream Condo had ever heard came from his wife as she ran out of Shawna's empty bedroom...

Ten minutes later, both of them listened as the phone rang. It was just as Tonya had suspected.

"Hello," said Condo.

"Put that bitch on," came the voice of Carmine.

Condo didn't fool around. He handed the phone directly over to Tonya.

Tonya put the phone next to her ear and listened.

"If you want to see your daughter alive again – meet me at Pier 22 tomorrow night at midnight. Bring $100,000 in cash. And come alone."

The phone went dead...

Tonya and Condo looked at each other with grim determination.

The following day was spent negotiating with the kind benefactors from Microsoft who had so generously given Poca Daisy all those shares of stock.

Right now, Tonya needed those shares liquidated as fast as possible. Because right now, she was fighting for the life of her daughter. She explained all this in a private phone conversation to Bill Carlton.

At the end of the conversation there was silence. Then Bill Carlton said quietly: "We'll have a cashier's check ready for you at 4:00 today."

Tonya reacted. "NO, NO, Mr. Carlton. It must be cash. These are kidnappers, don't you understand?"

Carlton cleared his throat. "Very well, it will be cash. But Tonya I do think this is a matter for the police."

Tonya said with firm resolve: "Believe me, Mr. Carlton, there is nothing the police can do."

She hung up.

* * * *

Promptly at 12:00 Tonya approached the pier. As instructed she had come alone.

There was no need to advertise Condo's presence and so she did not...

For all they knew, she walked out by herself with the bag of money. No one would ever see Condo who had slipped under the bridge and waited silently.

Tonya first saw Shawna and forced herself to keep quiet. A small cry went up in her throat but she composed herself. First, she had to get through this.

She came and stood 10 feet away from Carmine who had one hand clasped on her little girl's shoulder. Suddenly, from the gloom and the shadows, stepped Vito Leone.

"So, you brought the money, bitch?" Vito said with a sneer. "Yeah, of course you did, you don't want to see any harm come to your little girl."

Tonya just gestured with the bag and nodded.

Vito walked up to her and slapped her across the face.

"All those years I spent rotting away because of you. Well, your money's going to come in very handy especially where I'm going for awhile." He smirked and reached forward and to grab the bag.

As he got one hand around the handle, Tonya let out a yelp. Suddenly, Condo had materialized as if by magic, silently and swiftly disabling Carmine with one blow across his face. His hand let go of Shawna's hand and she scrambled to safety.

* * * *

Sergeant O'Brien snapped his book shut and banged on the ambulance door. The ambulance took off for the hospital, carrying the remains of one Vito Leone.

"Well, I've got more questions for you folks. But it looks as if you're in the clear. Vito Leone kidnapped your daughter. You brought the ransom money, you struggled and you defended your life. A clear case of self-defense. I'll call you tomorrow to wrap things up. Right now, I have to deliver a prisoner." He looked over at Carmine who glowered.

Tonya, Condo and Shawna Marie watched the police take Carmine away. Their long nightmare was over. The money had been retrieved and they would take that home. But money really had nothing to do with it, Tonya thought as they walked off the pier arms around each other.

Because they were a family, first, last and always...

EPILOGUE
ONE YEAR LATER...

Tonya looked over at Condo and smiled. Then she looked down at the baby in her arms and smiled even more. She had given birth to a second child and they had named it Alexandra. Finally, she thought, a sister for Shawna Marie to play with.

Tonya tried not to think about that awful day which had very nearly threatened to tear the thread of their family life apart a year ago. But, she thought, the Lord works in mysterious ways and He saw fit to save all of our lives.

She only wished that Poca Daisy could be here to share in their joy. Sometimes she regretted that her kids would grow up and not get to know their grandmother.

Things had improved somewhat for their fortunes. After a long time of pull and push back and forth she and Condo had been able to get some more of the shares that Tom Crawford had given her liquidated. That made things a little easier.

But the first thing that Condo had done when they got the money was to donate some of it towards one of the Indian schools. Tonya thought that was quite a noble thing to do.

Condo also talked a lot about wanting to help as many children as he could grow up to be proud of their heritage and not to shun it.

He had always been concerned with that, ever since Tonya could remember. And now that they had a little bit of money and some breathing room - he could act on his beliefs and spend as much time as he wanted doing what his heart told him to do, without having to worry about going to work at the casino. Condo asked if he could hold the baby.

"Yes, honey, of course you can," Tonya replied. "Just remember to be gentle, she's only a little thing, and you have such big, rough hands."

"I will," he promised.

Tonya slid the baby into Condo's arms and he smiled with joy. It always made him happy to be holding his child.

Just then, Shawna Marie walked in and started tugging at Tonya's sleeve.

"Mom, m-o-m," she pleaded.

"What honey?"

"How long before Alexandra can come play soccer with me?"

Both Condo and Tonya just looked at each other.

"Well, Alexandra, I think she should learn to walk before she plays goalie."

Shawna Marie looked at them and rolled her eyes.

Condo and Tonya burst out laughing and the sounds of their laughter filled the living room as the streams of sunlight bathed the room in a rich glow.

* * * *